AMENDMENT OF LIFE

A Novel
By
Elizabeth Sutherland

Published in 2010 by 'For The Right Reasons' Community Print
60 Grant St Inverness IV3 8BS

Email: burkitt@supanet.com
Tel 07717457247

ISBN 978-190-578-750-0

Cover: *The Old Man of Hoy, Orkney.* Acrylic painting by Jay Muirhead. Copyright Jay Muirhead 2010

Acknowledgements: the author gratefully acknowledges the support and advice of Rev'd R.F.Burkitt, Kevin Swanson, Jay Muirhead, Gill McWhirter, Jack Hermiston, Murdo Grant, Ramsay McGhee, John Waters and Marigold Atkey of David Higham Literary, Film and TV Agents.

Also by Elizabeth Sutherland
The Black Isle, (nf) 1972, *Lent Term* (f); *The Seer of Kintail*, (f) 1974, *Hannah Hereafter*, (f) 1976), *The Eye of God*, (f) 1977, *The Prophecies of the Brahan Seer* (edit) (nf) 1977, *The Weeping Tree*, (f) 1980, *Ravens and Black Rain*, (nf) 1985, *The Gold Key and the Green Life* (edit) (nf) 1986; *In search of the Picts*, (nf) 18994; *The Pictish Trail*, (nf) 1996; The *Five Euphemias*, (nf) 1997; *Lydia, Wife of Hugh Miller of Cromarty*, (b) 2002, *The Bird of Truth*, (f) 2006, *Boniface, Bishops and Bonfires*, (nf) 2010

Dedication: this book and the proceeds from its sale are gifted in gratitude and admiration to all those connected to the work in Inverness of 'For the Right Reasons'.

Amendment of Life

Voices

Part One: Coolwater Bay

Sunday, May 25 1972
The Revd Francis Freel, 42, Rector of St Ambrose Episcopal
Church
Jane (Jenny) Freel, 15, his eldest daughter
Richard (Dicky) Freel,14, his son
Rosamund (Ro) Freel, 38, his wife
Marjorie (Minnie) Freel, 10, his youngest daughter
Mrs Doris Croft, 79, verger and baby-sitter
George Fenton, 67, retired engineer, St Ambrose Church
treasurer
Vera Shotton, 40, chemist assistant
The Revd Sam Gardner, 30, assistant priest at St Ambrose
Monday, May 26 1972
Ro Freel
Minnie Freel
The Right Revd Paul Arnot, 69, Bishop of Strathclyde
D.I. Ian Ross, 44, Coolwater Bay Police Force
Dicky Freel
Jenny Freel
Revd Sam Gardner
Doris Croft
George Fenton
Vera Shotton
The Revd Francis Freel

Part Two: St Magnus Isle, Orkney

Wednesday, May 1 1946
Aidan Francis Melvick, 14, youngest son of Major Magnus
Melvick, the Castle
Nanny Melvick, 72, retired family nurse.

4

Alastair Melvick (Ali), 20, second son of Major Melvick
Major Magnus Melvick, 50, laird of St Magnus Isle
Kristin, (Kristy) Ugo, 40, cook and housekeeper at the Castle
Jennet Flett, 16,youngest daughter of Jimmy and Mari Flett,
the Mains Farm
Ingrid Grant, 65, nee Melvick, the Dower, St Magnus Isle
John and Meg Shearer, retired landowners from the Mainland,
Orkney

Part Three: Coolwater Bay

Sunday, May 24 1987
Marjorie Freel, 25, ornithologist
The Revd Sam Gardner, 45, Rector St Ambrose Episcopal
Church, Coolwater Bay
Doris Croft, 94, resident Coolwater Bay Residential Care
Home.
Vera Shotton, 55, chemist assistant
George Fenton, 82, member of St Ambrose Church
congregation
Ian Ross, 59, retired Detective Inspector, Coolwater Bay
Police Force

Monday, May 25 1987
Marjorie Freel
The Revd Sam Gardner
Jane Anderson, 30, nee Freel, married with two daughters in
Kent
Richard Freel, 29, PE teacher in Maidstone, Kent
Rosamund Freel, 53, primary teacher in Kent.

Part Four: St Magnus Isle, Orkney

Monday, June 2 1972
Aidan Francis Melvick, 42, only surviving son of Major
Magnus Melvick
Kristin Ugo, 71, cook housekeeper at the Castle

Major Magnus Melvick, 81, the Castle
Evie Grant, 55, daughter of the late Ingrid Grant, goat farmer at the Dower
Dr Ewan Stout, 37, General Practitioner to the Islanders

Part Five: St Magnus Isle

Thursday, 28 May 1987
Minnie Freel, 25
Kristin Ugo, 86, the Castle
Evie Grant, 70, the Dower
Aidan Melvick, 57, lobster fisherman, Beelock's Bothy, St Magnus Isle
Erlend Linklater, 71, sheep crofter, St Magnus Isle
Rosamond Freel, 54
Jane Anderson, 30
Revd Sam Gardner, 45
Thursday, June 4 1987
Ro Freel
Erlend Linlater
Jane Anderson
Richard Freel
Kristin Ugo
The Revd Sam Gardner
Minnie Freel
Evie Grant

Postscript: St Magnus Isle

June 24 1997
Dr Ewan Stout, 52, General Practitioner, St Magnus Isle

PART ONE

Chapter One

Coolwater Bay: Sunday May 25 1972

Morning

The priest needed to reach the cave. Small waves snuffled incuriously around his feet as he strode along the tide line but he made no effort to avoid them. His Sunday shoes would be scalloped with salt stains but he did not care. He had not been so close to the sea since the children had turned the great conglomerate boulders strewn across the sand into dinosaurs, aliens or tanks depending upon their ages and interests. He did not much care for the sea.

Not a soul in sight. Sunday lunch-time was still sacred to the great god belly in Coolwater Bay. An hour from now and the beach would be alive with children and dogs and energetic couples determined to walk off the excesses of roast beef and rhubarb crumble. By that time he would be safe in the cave.

It began to rain, fine drops that drifted down from one of the big soft clouds that bustled across the sky. There was sun ahead and sun on the sea, but he moved in a mist of rain until he reached the cliffs. The rocks were slippery as he climbed the few metres to the sheltering fold of the cave. Automatically he peered into its depths but there was no sign of the crude cross carved into its interior wall. How was that? He must have dreamed it. Was he dreaming now? It was becoming harder and harder to disentangle the dream world from reality. He pulled the dank darkness over him like a blanket and crouched down on a stone blackened by picnic fires to recover his breath. He knew now that he was dreaming. After a while he began slowly to unbutton his cassock.

He looked up once. It was still raining but northwards across the sea he saw the rainbow. It had been there on and off for most of a watery week and he had been conscious of its presence but only now aware of its significance. A third of the arc rose out of the sea, its colours so intense that it looked solid. Far to the south he could see where it ended but the apex of the arch was invisible, if indeed it was there at all. The end of a favourite childhood tale stormed into his memory. Tangle and Mossy were in a rainbow. They knew they were going up to a country whence the shadows fall. Heaven? But

7

was it heaven he yearned for? Or that country...island... half remembered in his dreams? Where Ali was.

He stood up abruptly. 'I can't do this anymore,' he said aloud. He had to get home.

At three minutes to one Jane Freel reluctantly switched off her tape recorder. Her mother had called three times that lunch was ready so she supposed she had better go down. It was stupid really this insistence on having Sunday lunch in the dining room. Why couldn't she make herself a cheese butty and take it to her room like any other day of the week? What was so special about Sundays? Well of course she knew what was special about Sundays. It was Pa's day. 'God's day', he once rebuked her mildly, but as far as she was concerned it came to the same thing. It was Pa's voice and Pa's presence that dominated Pa's church. She had never seen God. As far as she was concerned, God was an invention to give men like her father an income and force everyone else including herself to behave. It seemed to her that if you couldn't behave without the threat of hell dangling over you like a rotten carrot then you were simply not adult. Like giving up sweets for Lent or sugar in your coffee. One lot, she couldn't remember which, didn't drink coffee at all, nor tea or wine. She might be more inclined to listen if they told you not to eat meat. But sweets! It was all so painfully childish. It was also acutely embarrassing to have a father who stood up in church and told you that God loved you and that God would be hurt and disappointed if you didn't love him back. Worse still you would go to hell - whatever that was - if you didn't give up sweets for Lent. Not that Pa had ever said that in so many words, but it was implied every time he opened his mouth. Sheer emotional blackmail. Well stick hell, stick God and stick Sunday lunch.

The smell of roast whatever-it-was sickened her as she clumped reluctantly downstairs. She hoped it wasn't warmed-up macaroni cheese left over from last night's supper for her but knew it would be. Ma was so thoughtless. She knew she had a weight problem. That was the worst of being vegetarian, all that carbohydrate. She sighed deeply. No one, least of all Ma, realised how hard it was sticking to your principles.

'Where's Pa?' she asked as she sat down opposite her brother and sister at the dining room table which had been carefully laid by Minnie with the good silver and the English cathedral table-mats.

'A good point,' said her mother. 'Where is your father?' she asked Minnie, the only one of the family who had been to church. 'He's not usually so late.'

'Mum, can you get on with it,' Dicky interrupted impatiently. 'I've got rugby this afternoon.'

'Jane, you've done nothing all morning. Would you go down to the church and remind your father that lunch is on the table.'

'I don't think he's there,' said Minnie measuring pineapple juice from a carton equally into five glasses 'Sam did the Communion.'

'Just go. Please,' said her mother impatiently.

'Okay, okay, I'm going,' she said with an exaggerated sigh.

In fact she didn't at all mind going down to the church. If Sam had done the service then Sam might still be in the vestry folding away his robes, and though she would have admitted it to no one, absolutely no one, she rather liked Sam. He had been her father's curate for about a year now and they all liked Sam. She knew that Dicky liked him too because he had played rugby for the county. As Dicky said, he was rugby literate. Minnie adored him because he teased her about her red hair. He had red hair too, very thick and very red. Jane liked him because he treated her like an adult.

It was raining, just a few thin drops from a sky that was more blue than grey as she ran down the sloping path between the aged apple trees, unlatched the wooden gate that led from the vicarage garden into the graveyard that surrounded the church, careful to avert her eyes from the sad grey tombstones that lined her path. She could never pass them without imagining what lay beneath. Even in day-time they were spooky.

The familiar shiver twitched her shoulders as she slowed her pace and forced herself to look calmly at the mossy indecipherable monuments that lined her path. Sam might be watching.

Sam was not in the vestry but Mr Fenton, the treasurer, was still there counting and bagging the collection into little cellophane envelopes, and ticking off the numbers in the freewill-offering register.

'Where's my father?' she asked coolly. She did not like Mr Fenton. He had piggy eyes.

George Fenton continued to count until he had finished the ledger. Then he lifted his head and gave her his inquisitive stare. 'And good-morning to you too, Miss Jenny.'

9

'Jane.' she told him shortly. Only her family was permitted to use the diminutive Pa had invented and call her Jenny Wren.

His eyes shifted from her face to her breasts, lingered on the level of her crotch and then flicked up again. 'I have not seen hide nor hair of your father all morning, except of course in the pulpit. He preached as usual in case your family was wondering.'

She knew this was a dig at the empty rectory pew and a dozen crushing retorts crowded into her mind but as she stood in the chancel looking down the length of St Ambrose they died out of her mind. The faint but familiar odour of extinguished candles and stale wine remembered from the days she had served her father at the altar assaulted her now with a nostalgia that both irritated and filled her with guilt; irritation because she believed herself grown out of her childhood beliefs, and guilt because the atmosphere in the empty church seemed like a reproach. The eyes of the stained-glass saints in their windows, the gilded angels on the columns that held up the carved wooden reredos were all watching her with the sad eyes of their God and she was no longer secure in her unbelief. St Ambrose always had this effect on her which was why she seldom went to church. It was not that she didn't believe in God, she protested in her heart as she turned to walk the length of the crimson-carpeted nave towards the west door. It was the way he was presented that was so childish. Those silly hymns, those long boring prayers. Congregations, she reckoned, had either prayed God to death or bored him out of existence. The druids had got it about right. Their God existed in sun and in dew, in mistletoe and twilight. An oak grove was a more fitting temple than any man-made building. She would have no objection to getting up at dawn on a May morning to visit an oak grove for morning prayer, dressed in white with a wreath of mistletoe in her newly-washed hair.

Sam was not in the porch but Mrs Croft was still there tidying away the hymn-books. 'He's just left,' she replied to Jenny's question and no she hadn't seen the vicar though she reckoned he had probably gone up to the residential home. 'I heard that one of the old folks was taken poorly in the night.'

'Oh, right,' said Jenny. 'Thanks Mrs Croft.' She liked the stout little verger with the frizzy greying hair who, when she had baby-sat for her parents, brought bags of liquorice allsorts or wine gums, her own particular weaknesses, which they all chewed while they watched Coronation Street or Crossroads curled up with her on the old leather sofa where Minnie inevitably fell asleep on her lap. Ten minutes before her parents were due to return she and Dicky staggered off to bed, sleepy, unwashed and sometimes not even properly undressed. Mrs Croft was the baby-sitter from heaven.

'How's Napoleon?' she asked helping her to stack hymn-books on the appropriate shelf.

Her eyes clouded. 'Come and see for yourself. Poor old puss, he's not good.'

Napoleon was deaf, crotchety and had a bladder problem but then he had always been like that for as long as Jenny could remember. 'I will, I will,' she promised full of good intentions, 'and if you see Pa, can you tell him lunch is getting cold.'

Outside the sun was shining again. The first thing she noticed was the rainbow.

Dicky Freel hacked off the rims of fat from the slices of roast pork and heaped them on the side of his plate. If asked he would probably have said he loathed roast pork but he was always so hungry he would have eaten roast rat if it had been put in front of him. He shovelled the food into his mouth washing it down with slurps of pineapple juice. If asked he would probably have said he hated pineapple juice but Dicky rarely noticed what he was eating or drinking these days. Apart from chips and sausages liberally doctored with tomato sauce he thought he hated most other food but as he was always ravenous he ate it just the same.

'Ma,' he said from a full mouth with his plate held out for more potatoes. 'Could you please, please give me a lift this afternoon?'

'Where on earth do you put it all,' said his mother, spooning three more roast potatoes on to his plate.

'Leave some for Pa,' said Minnie anxiously.

'What's wrong with your bike?' his mother asked with an exasperated sigh.

'Something. Can you, Ma?'

'Can't you ask one of your friends?'

What friends, he thought. The few he had lived miles away. 'I might get a lift back,' he said encouragingly.

'You know I like to put my feet up on Sunday afternoons.'

He grinned, aware that she had already given in.

'Why don't you ask your father for a change?'

Come off it Mother, he thought, on a Sunday? 'I would, I would,' he placated, 'but he's not here, is he? And I'm desperate.' He pushed back his chair. 'I'll get my things.'

'What about pudding? It's apple tart.'

'Keep some for me. ...please, Ma?'

'Wait a minute. You'd better see if the car's there. Your father may have it.'

'It was there five minutes ago when I was trying to mend my bike.'

She pushed back her chair. 'Minnie, tell Jenny her macaroni's still in the oven. And can you do the washing-up when you've finished your pudding.' It was an order not a question.

'Oh Mum, do I have to. Why can't Jane do it? I laid the table.'

'I don't give a toss who does it as long as it's done,' her mother snapped as she left the dining room, 'and put the pudding back in a low oven when you've taken some.'

Dicky leapt down the stairs three at a time making the flimsily-built newish vicarage shudder. 'I'll start the car,' he shouted. Only two more years and he could get his provisional license. No more begging for lifts. God, he couldn't wait, nor could he wait to be out of the house and on to the field. A guy who had played for Scotland was coming to coach them this afternoon. If he played well he might be selected to play for the county under-fifteens. Careful to see that the car was out of gear, he switched on the engine. Once when he had forgotten to check, the car had leapt forward and wrecked the garage door. The recriminations had droned on for months. He would never make that mistake again.

'Come on, Ma!' He put the car into reverse and inched up the clutch pedal. He was practising three-point turns on the rare occasions when his parents were both out. Last time he couldn't find the car keys and he suspected that Jenny had snitched on him. Some months ago Pa had taken him up to a private farm road and allowed him to drive. That had been great but it hadn't happened again. Pa was always too busy and when he wasn't out Ma had the car. Ideally he would like a motorbike. Nick's older brother had a motorbike that he wanted to sell but Pa had been dead against it for some reason or other.

'Move over,' said his mother in the middle of his three-point turn and dumped her bag on his lap.

'Ma, I'm thinking of saving up for a motor-bike.'

12

'The sooner the better as far as I'm concerned.'

He was astonished. 'You mean you wouldn't mind?'

'What would be the point?'

'You're supposed to mind. Pa does. He got cross when I mentioned it.'

She looked at him and sighed. 'Fortunately, knowing the state of your finances, I can't see it ever happening.'

They drove on in companionable silence. Just before they reached the playing fields she said, 'So who's going to bring you back?'

He looked at her and shrugged. 'Maybe I'll get a lift.'

'You're absolutely hopeless,' she told him. 'I'm making no promises.'

'Thanks.' He grinned. They both knew she would be there two and a half hours later.

'Don't mention it,' she told him dryly.

Afternoon

Ro watched her son amble off to join the ragged cluster of boys waiting to start their game. His floppy clumsiness was endearing, a little boy at heart not yet used to the size of his body. A flurry of rain spattered the wind-shield as she reversed the car.

Lord, she thought, he'll come home soaked and filthy, which reminded her that the washing machine was on the blink. She must remember to get hold of Benny tomorrow. He could usually put it right for a few quid. If not that meant another machine, but she'd rather not think about that. Her Barclay card was fast becoming water-logged. How on earth did other clergy families with teenagers manage and she was one of the lucky ones. She had a reasonable pay packet from the school and a class of seven year olds to escape to. Her problems as a teacher, stressful as they were, paled into insignificance in comparison to the problems of running a parish. She had never enjoyed parish life, being at the centre of a group of - for the most part - sniping, discontented old bats, male and female. How Francis stood it year after year she could not begin to understand. But then she had never really understood Francis.

In the staffroom Sylvia talked about her husbands - two in the past, one in the offing - 'I knew exactly what they were thinking, the silly saps, all the time, all day and particularly all night,' she would say with a half-contemptuous, part-indulgent laugh. Ro never knew what Francis was thinking, had never known, which had intrigued and attracted her in the early years but now it only irritated. He refused even to discuss his bad dreams that seemed lately to have been getting worse. It was all part of the general lack of communication between them. Why, for example, couldn't he have told her that he was going to be late for lunch? He was the one, after all, who expected a proper Sunday dinner and insisted that they sat down together as if it were some sacred feast, 'It's the only chance in the week I have of seeing you all together,' he once explained and she had agreed with him, ready to give the morning over to preparing a decent meal even though it would have been more convenient for her to do her school preparation work in the morning, leaving Sunday afternoons free to slump with the papers and some chocolate or even a walk like they used to do when the kids were small. When had they last walked together as a family? She couldn't remember. When had they last talked together properly, seriously, just the two of them? If she had to choose one word to describe their marriage it would have to be silence. A marriage of silence. She sighed. She knew it was largely her fault. A proper conversation usually turned into a catalogue of complaints from herself. Why don't you...? Why can't we...? She could hear her voice nagging him and hating herself for it, but hating him too for the blinds which blinkered his eyes whenever she attempted to say anything serious.

She sighed as she turned into Rectory Lane and promised herself that she would be more patient, less prickly both with him and with the children. He had a tough job, she knew that, but so had she and she had the added burden of running the household and looking after the children.

Remembering Dicky, she left the car outside the garage. Perhaps Francis would find time to pick him up before the evening service, but knew that he wouldn't. I will not make a fuss, she told herself severely. Perhaps I won't even ask him, she thought, and knew that she would, which would mean another argument but even that was better than silence.

'Isn't your father back?' she asked Minnie who was sitting at the far end of the dining room table with her scrap book, sorting out photographs of horses. Stupid question. She could see the knife fork and spoon still unused, neatly arranged around the tablemat laminated with Lincoln Cathedral.

'Ma,' said Minnie with the scissors in her hands as she snipped carefully round an image of a particularly glossy Cleveland Bay. 'I really don't see why I can't have a pony, not if I pay for it myself and look after it. There's plenty of room in the garden. He'd be no bother I absolutely promise you.'

She was about to snap back with the usual negative reply. They had been over the same ground so often. No to Dicky when he wanted to play about with the car, no to Jane when she wanted to go to a disco, no to Minnie who wanted above all to own a pony. Let Francis do it this time. She was sick of saying no, of watching disappointment continually dim the eyes of her children. Why should Minnie not have her pony? Let Francis make the decision and take the responsibility for it.

'Find out what Pa thinks, then,' she said mildly.

Minnie looked up at her astonished.

Seeing her expression, Ro was quick to add, 'Don't count on it, Minnie. Have you the remotest idea how much keeping a pony costs?'

A pony. The word which had for years glittered like a distant star on the horizon of her dreams zoomed close enough to become a reality in Minnie's head. The bright nebulous shape took on a thick chestnut coat, large long-lashed brown eyes and four sturdy legs with neat white fetlocks. Her brain teemed with practicalities. The garden shed was big enough to become a cosy little stable and there was more than enough grass in the huge overgrown rectory garden to keep him - or her - in fodder at least from May to September. In fact it would be doing Pa a service to have a pony to eat the grass. He - or rather Dicky - wouldn't have to spend hours mowing it. Perhaps she could charge the same amount that Pa paid Dicky and that would go towards buying in hay for the winter and help pay for other food, not to mention the farrier and vet bills. She knew from her bedtime - and all other spare time - reading, *Horse and Pony*, exactly how much it would cost to buy and keep. There was enough - just - in her savings account because Ma had been keeping her Christmas and birthday money now for at least two years. Come to think of it, she could charge for rides at the summer fete and hold back at least half of the profit for its upkeep. That was only fair. There were lots of ways to make a pony pay for itself.

She closed her scrap-book and turned to the adverts in *Horse and Pony*. The choice was mind-boggling. Old, middle-aged or young enough to be called a foal. How many hands should she go for? Skewbald, pinto or roan, mare or filly, stallion or gelding? Young, she decided would be best and female because then she might breed from her. She already knew that she would call her Kelpie. In her dreams she would place upon her the magic bridle and ride all the way to Tir nan Og, or maybe she would call her Pegasus, the flying horse. She would consult Pa on that as they were his bedtime stories remembered from her early childhood. Come to think of it, there had been no stories for a long time. He probably thought her too old and of course at ten she was, but she still liked to hear them. She would ask him to tell her about the Kelpie who pulled St Columba's boat all the way up Loch Ness through a storm safely to the king's castle at Inverness. Then she would ask him about having the pony. She was sure that if Ma agreed, he would say yes. Dear God, please let him say yes.

She closed the magazine and put away her paste pot and magazines. She wanted to please her mother. With that thought in mind, she might tidy her room but instead of going upstairs she slipped outside through the front door to have another look at the tool-shed. The rain had cleared and there were only a few ballooning clouds bumbling across a blue sky. She trotted through the long grass which badly needed to be cut - how could Pa refuse the help of a pony? - and tried to open the tool-shed door, but a clump of virulent nettles had grown across it and she could only budge it an inch or so. The clutter she glimpsed inside was daunting. Perhaps Sam would help to clear it and there was always Julie from school. Julie could be bribed with the promise of a ride.

She gave up trying to force open the door and lifting her trainers cantered in three time through dandelions, daisies and the leggy leaves of dead daffodils to where her swing lay abandoned over the winter months. The slightly skewed seat was damp and partially overgrown with a fine orange lichen. She wiped it with the edge of her jersey and sat down. The posts creaked alarmingly but the rope held as she pushed herself forwards and backwards imagining herself riding on the warm back of her new pony. Faster, faster she murmured and as she closed her eyes against the bright rays of the sun it seemed to her that she was her pony galloping up over mountains, down through valleys and her two frizzy bunches of

16

thick red hair as they lifted and fell on her shoulders felt like a mane.

The dream changed. She was at the Pony Club rally. She was about to be presented with a blue rosette. 'Well done, Marjorie. You and Kelpie are a credit to the Pony Club. Now just show us once again how you took that fence.' Mrs Forbes-Dobson, the District Commissioner's teeth gleamed with approval. Mrs F-D came to church, not every Sunday, but always during the sermon Minnie's eyes would search the congregation eagerly and if she was in her usual pew, Minnie would tear off her choir robes after the service and gallop round to the church door, hang about casually in the hopes that Mrs F-D would not be too busy talking to the grown-ups to notice her. One never-to-be-forgotten Saturday late last summer, Mrs F-D had invited her to tea to meet her grand-daughters who kept their own ponies in one of Mrs F-D's paddocks for a week or two during the summer holidays. Older than Minnie, they had answered her feverish questions laconically and eventually with an amusement that bordered on contempt, allowed her to touch and groom and finally mount in turn their placid beasts. 'I'm glad you enjoyed yourself, my dear,' Mrs F-D had said as she drove her home. 'What a pity the girls are going home next week. I had no idea you were so interested in riding. You must come again when they are here next summer.' By next summer, this summer in fact, she might have a pony of her own. In case Ma and Pa were worried she could get them to ask Mrs F-D to help with the choice.

In an ecstasy of excitement, still, so to speak, in the saddle, she swung the swing as high as it would go, then leapt off to land in a weedy patch of sand that Pa had put there some years ago when Dicky used to measure his jumps.

She trotted back to the house lifting her feet high - one two three, one two three - and found her mother lying on the sitting-room sofa doing the crossword in the Sunday Times. 'Is Pa back?' she asked, knowing he was not. The house always felt different, fuller somehow, when Pa was in his study. Just now it felt empty. Before Ro could answer the phone rang. 'That's probably him now.'

Minnie flew to answer but it was only someone from St Leonards, the residential care home, wanting her father.

'Where is he?' Minnie asked her mother.

'How the hell should I know?' Ro replied crossly. 'Have you tidied your room yet?'

Minnie shook her head miserably.

'Then I suggest you get on with it.' Her mother was in full teacher mode as she pulled on a jacket and picked up the car keys from the hall table. 'And you might just as well switch the oven off.' she called out, forcing herself to sound reasonable. There was no point in getting angry until she knew why Francis was so late. But anger is not so easily controlled nor was Minnie fooled.

Music from Pink Floyd thundered out of Jenny's room as Minnie opened the door. 'Dum dum dum dum-dum-dum-dum-dum,' Jenny was singing at the top of her voice. 'God, this is wonderful,' she shouted as she pirouetted, twisted and clapped her hands in time to the beat. 'Don't you think it's just' she groped for the right word and came up somewhat lamely with 'great'.

'I suppose.'

'What's up?' Jenny shouted still thumping about her room. She knew she was too plump and busty to dance but she was never self-conscious in front of Minnie.

'Pa's not back.'

'So?' said Jenny flopping down on her bean-bag and swivelling round to face her sister.

Minnie shrugged. 'Ma said I could ask him about a pony.'

'God, Min, do you never give up? Why do you give yourself such grief? Do you know what ponies cost? Don't you know what Pa earns?'

'Of course I do. I've got a hundred and three pounds saved up and it's my birthday next month. That'll be at least another fifty with any luck.'

'And ponies cost?' They both knew the answer to that. Not less than three hundred, more including the tackle.

Minnie's eyes filled with tears. 'You always spoil things.'

Jenny's heart ached suddenly for her sister. Why the bloody hell shouldn't she have a pony. It was all she wanted in life, all she had ever wanted.

'Hey, I'm on your side. I've got about fifteen quid stashed. You can have that if it helps.'

Somehow it didn't, but Minnie thanked her all the same 'I just wish Pa would come home.'

'Yeah' said Jen absently. She had put the tape back to the beginning of her favourite bit and was now sitting at her desk. She had an essay to finish before Monday.

18

Three choices: onwards, backwards or behind him into the deep black dripping cross-less well of this unfamiliar cave. He turned his head to peer into the darkness. A small insect crawled into a crack in the rock and disappeared. In his imagination he shrank to the size of that beetle and entered the gloom of Lethe. In the dank darkness there was immeasurable discomfort but no escape. Within the hard black carapace of the beetle he was still himself.

There was a fourth choice. Forwards. He turned to look at the sea, silver grey like a huge brimming chalice with no sign of the rainbow. In his mind he climbed down the boulder-strewn cliff and onwards into the cold clutch of the greedy water. He began to shiver as if he were already drowning and gasped at the thought of the jostling waves. He had been there before.

'Not that,' he protested aloud.

At the sound of his voice a fulmar rose silently from its roost in the cliff above, swooped past the open mouth of the cave and soared out over the water. As he watched its graceful flight, he knew that this was what he sought. Freedom to fly out of his life and alight on the Island. What Island? The Island that was always there on the tip of his mind. Heaven? Perhaps. Yet the Island that was, or was not heaven, was an irrelevancy. It was not the Island he wanted to reach but the self he wanted to lose, this self that had become an unbearable burden. How was it possible to escape not from his family - his mind shied off that image - nor his congregation - God help them - but only from himself, the one who awoke to hell every night when he fell asleep, the one whom he could not avoid by day. A beetle might crawl into the bowels of the earth, a fulmar climb into the upper thermals but where was there in heaven or earth a place where he could be as nothing? In death? He doubted it. In death he might even be more himself than in life. Eternally himself. Oh God, what a burden it was to be human. In accepting the gift of life, man did not realise the implications of immortality, never to be able to escape from his self. Sometimes at a baptism as he held the infant in his arms, he had thought this child, this God-created soul is here, as I am here, imprisoned in eternity. Give him grace to be at peace with his self and if that is not possible, let him remain ignorant of his immortality for at least as long as he remains on earth.

What then was he doing here? He had wanted to escape from the pressures of his parish certainly but what was so hard about his life? Why had it always been for him like a Victorian mourning card relentlessly etched in black. He did not know. Nor did he know how to cut the cord that bound him to eternity. Death certainly would release him from his body, that temporary expendable piece of clothing, but he was stuck with his self, his soul, for good. Even if he were to be reincarnated in another body he would still be the same miserable, unsettled, ungrateful, guilt-ridden sod. There had to be another way.

The path of sacrifice. Father George's words came unbidden into his mind. Lose your life that you may find it. How he missed Father George. How he missed his mantra *All will be well; and all will be well; and all manner of things will be well.* He tried the words aloud. He tried to believe them.

Doris Croft wiped a tear from her cheeks and blew her nose. She could actually see the growth in Napoleon's gut through his thinning coat and she knew that the time had come. She would have to take him to the vet tomorrow.

She had asked Rector if animals went to heaven but he had not given her a straight answer. He had told her a story about some preacher - George MacDonald was it? - who had lost his job because he had told his congregation that animals and the heathen had a place in God's kingdom, and he had quoted the words from the bible about sparrows. She had not quite liked to ask him outright what he thought, because she was afraid he might have given her the answer she didn't want to hear.

'Of course animals go to heaven,' her friend Jessie had told her dismissively outside the lunch club when she had brought the subject up. 'Why else would God bother to create them in the first place?'

But Jessie would say that. She subscribed to all the animal charities and was forever selling raffle tickets to save whales or tigers or making marmalade to raise money for the RSPCA. Most of her friends at the lunch club sent money to that one and Doris felt guilty because she didn't. It was as much as she could afford to put fifty pence a week into her free will offering envelope. Ten bob actually. It seemed more if you converted it into proper money. Nowhere near a tenth of her pension, she thought with shame.

Rector said when they first had free-will envelopes (and what a fuss there had been over that) it should be a tenth after you had deducted the necessities like rent and electricity but she always felt deep down that was cheating. She should be giving at least four pounds. Well, she couldn't afford that not with Napoleon to feed, not to mention the vet bills. If she won the Pools it would be different. Doris often fantasised about winning money. She had it all worked out. A million never seemed to be enough by the time she had decided who was to get what. But you had to be careful. Money spoiled people or so she had heard. Would it spoil her? She had a fleeting image of herself in a fur coat like Mrs Richmond at church, sailing on a waft of perfume down the aisle putting a five pound note - maybe a tenner - into the plate, and laughed aloud at such an improbability She could surely put the money to better use than that. She had long ago decided to send the Rectory family away on a holiday. Where to? The Holy Land was her first thought. All right for Rector but maybe not for the rest of them. Missis was not much of a church-goer and though it would be good for the children, that was not her objective. She wanted them to have fun. A cruise? One of those posh ones to the Caribbean maybe. They were always advertising them on the box. She imagined Rector in shorts and a flowery shirt. Definitely no. Winter sports then? Fine for Dicky but she couldn't see Jenny on skis, not until she had lost some of that puppy fat, poor lamb. Jessie's grandchildren had gone to Turkey last summer, discotheques, whatever they were, for the teenagers and beaches for the wee ones and you can visit Mary's house in Ephesus. 'Mary's house?' she had asked. -'Yes Mary, the Mother of God.' 'The Virgin Mary you mean,' Doris had replied reprovingly and Jessie had sniffed significantly. She was a chapel-goer. But Doris' mind was made up. Turkey it would be.

She had told Minnie, 'When I win the Pools I'll send you all on a lovely holiday to Turkey.'

'Don't you mean if,' said Minnie politely, 'but actually I'd rather have a pony.'

'So you shall, pet, so you shall. The best that money can buy.'

And Minnie had hugged her and asked about Napoleon.

She looked at the clock. Half past five. Time to have a boiled egg before Evening Prayer. She made up her mind to ask Rector to come and give Napoleon a blessing. She would not put him on the spot about heaven but she was sure he would not object to giving the poor creature a blessing. Better still, she could take Napoleon to church in his carrier basket. Surely no one would object if she left him in the porch? She liked the idea of him spending his last evening in church. It wasn't as if she was asking for Holy Unction, whatever that was. And it would save Rector the bother of having to come to her house at the end of a long Sunday. But what if he yowled, what if he needed to pee? Worse, what if she broke down in front of everyone? How embarrassing that would be. Tears started to her eyes at the thought. She didn't mind weeping in front of Rector at her own fireside. He must be used to tears by now, hers included. She remembered how he had consoled her when her Jim had died all of seven years ago, taken her hand and told her firmly, 'This isn't the end for Jim and it isn't the end for you,' and she had believed him. So why should it be the end for Napoleon, she thought briskly.

She stroked his head and he opened his hot dim eyes for a moment. It occurred to her that she might miss him even more than she missed Jim and as hastily dismissed the thought as she set the pan on the stove to boil her egg. After a moment she turned off the gas. She wasn't hungry.

Evening

George Fenton slung his raincoat over his arm. Though the weather looked settled it might be pouring again when he came out of Evensong. As it was barely six o'clock he decided to walk partly because he knew it was good for his heart but mostly because Pam's sisters were still visiting and he could not abide the cackle a moment longer. The three ugly sisters, he called them privately, for Pam herself was no Cinderella. They were all as alike as three rats in a litter, flat-chested, thin with stick-like legs and iron grey curly hair. It was Pam's hair that had attracted him to her in the first place, lushly curling, black and lustrous, that and her slim elegant figure which with age had become scrawny, while the voice she was always so proud of had deepened and become hoarse. Someone, not him, had once called it husky and equating that with sexy, she had cultivated a slow deep drawl unfortunately punctuated with a rasping smokers' cough. She still smoked in spite of the warnings and the price and so did her sisters. When they were all three together, as they were on this particular Sunday afternoon, the sitting room, with the gas fire glowing and each sister wreathed in smoke, resembled a furnace, the burning fiery furnace, he thought with a glimmer of humour but the three creatures it contained were no Shadrach, Meshach or Abednego, more like the three witches of Macbeth.

He popped his head round the sitting-room door, made a play at brushing away the smoke, and announced cheerfully, 'I'm off. Bye all,' and shut the door quickly before he could be given any instructions. Pam usually had some task for him to do when her sisters were there. It was a power thing he supposed. If it wasn't to remember to put out the bin when he got back from church or fill the kettle, it was to wash up the pans left to steep since dinner. He had already done them and the bin was out. She could bloody well fill her own kettle, the lazy bitch.

Outside the gate and safely on the street, he happily dropped the weird sisters from his mind. By the time he got home they would be gone and Pam absorbed in telly having left a round of cold meat sandwiches under a beaded net cover on a tray on the kitchen table ready for his supper. She would have had hers. He could safely escape to his den to get on with his books. He was treasurer of three organisations, the Bowlers, the Darts Team at the Legion and St Ambrose. Thinking about his responsibilities straightened his back and quickened his step as he wound through the surburban streets of Coolwater Bay towards the church. It was his ambition to leave each account in a healthier state than when he took it over and he would spend hours with project sheets, proposals for budgets and prognoses of future growth. AGMs were the highlights of his years and he took it as a compliment when the chairman of the Coolwater Bowlers had told him in a fit of frustration that he sat on the budget account like a mother goose. 'So long as the eggs are golden' he had replied cheerfully, but he did not always feel cheerful. The church income fluctuated fearsomely and as the outgoings always seemed to go up, he had his work cut out to keep the church account out of the red. He could retire at the next AGM if he wanted. His three years were up and though there were times when the idea was tempting, he could not tolerate the thought of handing over his neat ledgers to someone else. The fact was that although the responsibility sometimes seemed overwhelming he enjoyed holding the purse strings of St Ambrose. He comforted himself with the thought that there was no one else willing or able to take over. Who in the congregation would be prepared to give up evening after evening to balancing the church books? As for the Bowlers and the Darts Team, he could manage those accounts standing on his head and he positively enjoyed collecting the subscriptions. Got him out of the house especially in the winter when there was no garden to escape to. But the church was different. Somebody was always wanting something either for charity or for repairs or for expenses, not to mention the diocesan quota. The rector was no help at all. Touchy chap. Flew off the handle at the hint of an argument. He of all people ought to realise that money did not grow on trees. George had come to dread the meetings of the finance committee for it seemed that every time it convened there was a row over something or someone. Last month had been one of the worst. He had had a bone to pick with Mister High and Mighty Francis Freel over that contract for new heating in the vestry and had lost his rag completely. 'I may not be one of your soothie-moothed English toffs, I'm only a coal miner's son from Cowdenbeath but I bloody well know a bad deal when it sits up and begs,' he had shouted. Freel had thumped the table. 'Why is it that all treasurers end up behaving as if the cash came out of their personal bank accounts? The vestry is like an ice-box in winter and Anne is not prepared to conduct any more choir practices on a Thursday evening unless the place is properly heated,' he had shouted with clenched fists. George thought he was going to hit him. Pity he hadn't, come to think of it. That would have been a sacking matter. Instead he had thrust back his chair and stormed out of the meeting rigid with rage

'Time the bugger found a new job,' he had shouted to the hushed horror of the rest of the committee. He shouldn't have said that but it was bloody true.

Mrs Forbes Dobson had calmed them all down and told them she was prepared to lend a couple of convector heaters and when, next day, Freel had apologised, he had allowed himself to be partially mollified but it was an uneasy truce He had seriously considered leaving the church. See how they managed without him! But Pam would never have gone with him. She was wedded to St Ambrose where she happily served coffee in the hall after service with the other women, baked cakes for the summer fetes, organised whist drives and social evenings. Been her lifeline since Kyle had been taken from them, his too, if he were to be honest. No, if anyone was to leave it should be Freel. If he did his job properly there would be no need for arguments.

The warm sandstone walls of St Ambrose glowed in the early evening light. He opened the wicket gate, mentally saluted the war memorial to the congregation's dead in two world wars and looked at his watch. Six-ten. Just time to look at the tea urn in the hall which, according to Pam, had been playing up again. The MU was clamouring for a new one. Let them pay for it then, had been his immediate retort. They were the organisation which used it most. That seemed even to his own ears a little harsh considering that he too drank the coffee they served so he decided to have a look for himself. It probably needed no more than a new fuse. Women were so handless in that department.

He entered the porch, went through the side door into the passage that led to the new hall, as it was still called, though it had been built some twenty years earlier to commemorate St Ambrose's centenary. It still smelled faintly of the Sunday School children, that rubbery, chalky smell that reminded him of his own classroom in Fife. Images of scarred desks, a shabby blackboard and the teacher's strap which had stung his own fingers often, enough flooded back to him as he looked at the bright animal posters blue-tacked on to the wall, interspersed with children's drawings of Noah's Ark. Children had it good these days, he thought and as quickly thrust the thought from him. Some children. Glimpses of Kyle's face as white as the hospital pillow leaked through cracks in the shell of his conscious mind. …Kyle. After sixteen years he still found thinking about Kyle a painful process. Talking about him was impossible.

One of the posters had fallen on to the floor. He noted that the blue tack had removed a portion of plaster. No doubt the hall committee would be wanting the place painted again. Why couldn't the organisations that used the hall look after it properly? Was it too much to ask? He would have to speak to Freel about it. A cigarette stub had wedged itself under one of the stacked chairs. He dislodged it with his foot and carried it gingerly to the litter bin in the kitchen. He hoped it had been left by one of the coffee drinkers and not the Youth Club but feared the worst. He remembered how he had once looked in on a Youth Club evening and a wee fellow no more than ten, he reckoned, had come up and asked him for a light. He had looked down at the eager cheeky face and spluttered, 'I'll give you a light right enough, across your backside if I catch you smoking in here.' But the kid had merely laughed and dodged away from his threatening hand. And what had happened to the Nosmo King signs that usually adorned at least two of the walls? No sign of them. Freel ought to keep an eye on these things. Run a tighter ship altogether. It was hardly the treasurer's job.

The litter bin was brimming over with empty crisp-packets, coke cans and squashed tea-bags. That was what you got with no regular hall keeper. Each organisation was supposed to be responsible for its own rubbish, but unless you had a proper boss the Injuns weren't going to bother. Hadn't he said so at the last meeting of the hall committee? It gave him no pleasure to be proved right. He lifted the lid of the urn. A few inches of rusty discoloured water covered the flaky element. If only they'd empty it properly after every use. Funds would allow for a new one, just, but the MU would have to be told - officially - to look after the equipment, and the Youth Club organisers should see to it that there was absolutely no smoking. He supposed he had better put the bin out himself after the service, not to mention cart the urn back to his shed to have a proper look at it. He should have brought the car.

He looked at his watch again. Two minutes to the half hour. What had happened to the bells? Everything was going to pot. He'd see Freel after the service, tell him to pull his socks up. It was not the treasurer's job to see to everything.

As he heaved the urn into the porch, he noticed the cat basket underneath the tract table half-hidden by the bookcase. He bent down to have a closer look and saw a pathetic mangy creature curled up seemingly asleep. For a moment he was outraged. This was the last straw. How could Doris Croft bring her nasty animal into the sacred precincts of St Ambrose. What was she thinking? She would have to be told. It wasn't seemly.

George Fenton did not like cats. Every spring after he had planted out patriotic rows of red anchusas, white alyssum and blue lobelia grown with care from seed in his green house, the neighbourhood cats left their untidy humps and hillocks of shit in his front garden beds. Some of the brutes didn't even bother to cover up their disgusting leavings. For once, Pam agreed with him, though not for the same reasons. She liked birds. 'Cats!' she would shout to him from her vantage point at the kitchen sink and rattle the window. He didn't quite like to throw stones at them but there were times when he was sorely tempted. And now here was a bloody beast stinking out the church porch.

He pushed open the swing door that led into the church. Doris was on her knees in the back pew, the tears running unchecked down her cheeks. He hesitated. Suddenly Kyle lurched into his mind. Took him back to the white face on the hospital pillow, the eyes closed, Pam's harsh sobbing, his own hot tears. It still hurt like hell. Roughly he thrust himself out through the swing door, reached down and pulled out the cat basket from under the table. The creature inside did not so much as open its eyes. He lifted it, aware that it weighed next to nothing, and, backing into the church, put it carefully down on the pew beside Doris.

'If anyone objects, refer them to yours truly,' he said roughly and strode into his usual pew half way up the nave - sixth row on the left from the front to be precise - close to a pillar which kept away some of the draughts, and crouched forwards for a few seconds in what Pam called disparagingly the shampoo position. He had never been able to bring himself to kneel.

And suddenly he felt better, able to look round him as he waited for the service to begin. Eleven there. He nodded at Vera Shotton two rows in front of him in her usual seat. He liked Vera. A looker too with her big bust and curvy hips. An armful and a half. Funny how his taste in women had changed. He liked them with a bit of flesh these days, and young. Not that Vera was all that young, but she was a lot less than his sixty-seven years. Ashamed of the way his thoughts were lurching, he looked away from her. The brasses needed doing. He wondered whose turn it had been last week. Perhaps Freel should put a reminder in the monthly magazine. Now that was a good idea. No perhaps about it. He began to tick off in his mind the points he wanted to raise with the rector when the service was over. It amounted to five.

Vera Shotton's eyes were fixed on the vestry door. They were late. It was almost twenty minutes to seven and the evening organist, a music teacher from Coolwater Academy had begun yet another extemporisation on *Sheep May Safely Graze*. Vera was worried about Frank, her private name for the rector because his voice when he sang the services reminded her a little of Sinatra. His sermon this morning had seemed a little disjointed, poor pet, but as she had said to Doris after the service, you couldn't expect the same high standard every week, and they had agreed that he was probably sickening for something, there was a nasty bug about. Nor had he

27

been at the door to shake hands afterwards. He had such lovely hands, so clean, and his shoes what you could see of them under his robes when he was walking down the aisle after a service, polished to perfection. But he hadn't finished the service today. It had been Sam, which was not the same. You felt properly blessed when Frank raised his hand and made the sign of the Cross, and though she had hung about a bit afterwards, he hadn't turned up in the hall for coffee either.

The vestry door opened at last. Five adult choir members - the children were no longer expected to turn out for Evensong - dressed in their blue cassocks and white surplices processed in and took their places in the quire. Sam Gardner, the curate, followed them and took his usual desk behind the lectern. To Vera's searing disappointment, the Rector's stall remained empty.

Vera had been in love with Frank for eleven months, five days and four hours less twenty minutes. The exact date was written in her five-year diary surrounded by roses and hearts and crosses. Though she had not been a church-goer since her Sunday School days, she had known who he was since his arrival in Coolwater Bay, had served him occasionally when he had called into the chemist - oops! Sorry, pharmacy, as her boss preferred her to call it - for toothpaste or a prescription, liked what she saw but no more than that. It was not until he visited her in hospital after her gall bladder op that she had fallen in love with him. She had been dozing, relishing freedom from pain for the first time in months, not expecting visitors that afternoon when she had heard her name, 'Mrs Shotton?' opened her eyes and seen him there standing beside her bed looking down at her, his brow wrinkled in kindly concern. He explained who he was and she remembered she had called herself C of E. on her hospital admittance form. Her heart had turned over. She remembered every word of that conversation, trivial though it had been, and then just before he left he had laid his cool clean hand on her brow and prayed for her. She had once heard a talk on the radio about epiphanal moments and she had recognised those five minutes in the hospital as hers. It had changed her life.

In trepidation she had started to attend St Ambrose, at first on Sunday mornings, latterly for both services. That first Sunday she had been shaking with nervousness. She knew many of the congregation by sight and some by name for most of them had visited the shop and some were regular customers. A few smiled at her politely, others ignored her but good old Doris had made her feel welcome, invited her into her own pew at the back, shown her the pages in the prayer book and taken her into the new hall for coffee afterwards where Frank had come up to her with his beautiful hand outstretched and told her he hoped that she had recovered and how good it was to see her in church. The following Sunday it had been easier and within a month she had felt like an old hand, though she had not as yet dared to approach the altar for communion. She was not too sure what you did. After her third Sunday, Frank had asked for her address and visited her on her afternoon off. She had told him about Bob and the divorce and how lonely she had been, had cried a little and he had sat opposite her and held her two hands and told her it was all right to cry and how now that she had found her way to God and St Ambrose she need never feel lonely again. All she had wanted was for him to put his arms round her and hold her close but of course that didn't happen so she had wiped her eyes and made him a cup of tea instead.

When it became apparent that she had joined St Ambrose she found herself in demand for various jobs. Would she help with the coffee rota, put her name down for arranging flowers, cleaning the brasses? So she did. George Fenton suggested she take envelopes for the Free Will Offering. She did that too, but deep down she felt a bit of a sham. She was not doing any of it for God who seemed rather irrelevant. She was doing it all for Frank, which was why she could not quite bring herself to take communion. There was that problem over her divorce for one thing, nor had she ever been confirmed, but Doris had said Rector wouldn't mind, not like the previous incumbent who was one of the old school and anti-divorce. It was not as if she were the only divorced person in the church to take communion. There were at least three others that Doris could but wouldn't name. 'There's nothing to stop you getting confirmed apart from the divorce, is there?" Doris had asked her. 'Not really,' Vera had replied. 'Why don't you ask Rector then?' Vera replied she would think about it.

Thinking about it always started off in the same way in her sitting room in the semi-detached two-up two-down she had managed to buy with her divorce settlement. The fire would be blazing in the grate because it was always a stormy afternoon with the wind hurling rain drops against the window. He would come to the house chilled and wet. She would help him take off his jacket, hang it up in the airing cupboard to dry, sit him down on the settee and make him tea. She would pass the cup to him and somehow their fingers would touch. At that point, depending upon her mood and whether she was in church, or in the back shop having her coffee break, or in bed at night, the fantasy would change. In church he was God and she a worshipper at his feet, lost in the beauty of his voice and his presence. She was content to adore on her knees, to kiss his hands, to minister to him, be his Magdalene. In the back shop fantasy, he became her child, sick, shivering, in need of comfort. She delighted in fussing over him, nursing him, serving him. In the darkness of the night as she lay alone in her double bed, he became her lover, his kisses long and sweet and deep, his hands...but this fantasy was too bold for daylight. Blushing internally, she thrust it from her thoughts, but whether he was her God, her son or her lover, the daydream always started on the settee in her sitting room on a wet Thursday afternoon.

Today she had made up her mind to bring her fantasy a step nearer to reality. After Evensong she had been going to ask him how to set about getting confirmed. She knew that it involved classes. Doris said they were usually held in the vestry and that adults and children were taken separately. She might be the only adult. The thought was both sweet and terrifying. Only now he wasn't here to ask. She would have to wait another week, unless of course he came into the shop. She could take him aside behind the male toiletries, usually a quiet spot, and see what he said. It would be just her luck if the shop were full of people hanging about waiting for their prescriptions, all of them lugging in. Perhaps it would be better to phone him sometime but you never knew when he would be in and she didn't much relish the thought of speaking to his wife. She had nothing personal against Mrs Freel, Ro as they called her, (what a ridiculous name) but she could not approve of her. A wife should support her husband, especially a vicar's wife. Bob had only been an insurance agent but Vera had always supported him by providing nice meals and a comfortable home. It wasn't her fault that he had found other homes, several of them, cosier and the comforts offered preferable. It would serve Ro right if Frank found his comforts elsewhere. Ah, sweet, sweet thought ... She would have liked to discuss Ro with Doris but Doris refused to be critical. All Doris would say was that she was a very nice lady, and a very good teacher, which meant damn all, and Doris was always on about the vicarage kids. There again, Vera could not approve. Like their mother, they were never seen in church, except for the little one who sang in the choir. She had once said as much to Doris. 'They ought to support their father more.' She had merely laughed and said, 'They're teenagers!' as if that explained everything.

During the last verse of *The day thou gavest, Lord, has ended*, Sam left his stall and lifting the skirts of his robes ascended into the pulpit. Funny how she could take in every word Frank said but Sam was incomprehensible. She had once tried to say this to Doris but she had looked surprised. 'Sam's all right.' Vera studied his looks closely, if not his words. He was the antithesis of Frank, a big muscular young man more at home in the rugby field than in the pulpit whereas Frank was lean and spare and in Vera's opinion frail. Sam's hair was sunset red, thick and unkempt, where Frank's was black and sleek, beginning to streak with white and thinning at the temples. Sam's face was craggy, his eyes sky-blue and his skin a healthy pink whereas Frank's features were regular, his eyes an astonishing green, and his skin pallid. She thought about their ages. Sam was still in his late twenties, in his second curacy where he was responsible for the mission chapel near the caravan site on the other side of the town which was due to open for the summer in a week's time. He also assisted Frank and two others, one a retired cleric and the other a lay-reader, with two small parishes outside the town. Frank was forty-one, a year younger than Vera, and according to Doris, worked off his feet. He was part of the bishop's team to re-examine the way the diocese was administered, heavily involved in a project about Shared Ministry and another called Christian Outreach. Doris tried to explain how important these things were and how much time Frank gave to diocesan affairs. 'I reckon he's the bishop's right-hand man. He's tipped to be the next dean.' Vera asked her what that meant, but Doris wasn't too sure. 'More work that's for certain.' Vera tried to think of all the other things he did like going into the schools, visiting the hospital where he had come to see her and the two residential care homes; there were funerals and weddings to take, confirmation classes, parish meetings, a fistful of committees and a host of financial problems which George Fenton tried to explain to her when he brought round her envelopes. At home, he had his family and all their demands on his time. She hoped they took care of him in spite of not supporting him in

31

church. If only it were she waiting for him, his supper ready, candles lit on the dining room table, how she would cherish him.

By the time the congregation rose to sing the final hymn she was feeling thoroughly depressed. Frank was far too busy to think about her. On the other hand, perhaps he would be pleased to know he had her support. Yes, she would speak to him, she might even phone him this evening when he would be bound to be in to ask him about confirmation.

In the vestry Sam Gardner dismissed the choir and looked at his watch. He had a date with Tony this evening and in five minutes time he would be late. From the pulpit he had seen a tearful Doris at the back of the church with the cat basket on the pew beside her and his heart sank. What was she doing with Napoleon in church? He knew the cat was ailing. Did she really expect him to lay his hands on it? Obviously she did. Tony did not like him to be late. He supposed he could slip out by the vestry door but that seemed a bit mean. Tony would just have to wait. And where in hell's teeth was Francis? He hadn't seen him since before the morning service and there were things he wanted to resolve before he saw Tony. He needed to be sure he could have the weekend after next off to go to the match in Manchester and he wanted Tony to go with him. He supposed he would have to wait till the staff meeting on Tuesday morning. Meanwhile there was Doris to cope with. Pulling on his denim jacket that co-ordinated with his jeans he opened the door into the church and strode down the side aisle.

Most of the small congregation had gathered round the little old woman who was still sitting in her pew. Tears had left unsightly furrows on her cheeks and she was trembling. George broke away from the group to explain to him. 'Cat's died. She's upset.'

Sam nodded, sighing inwardly. This was not something that could be rushed.

'What happened, Doris?'

The story poured out with interjections from Vera Shotton, George and the others.

Sam took a deep breath. 'Do you know what I think,' he said heartily. 'Napoleon's a lucky old chap.'

'How's that, Sam?' George asked matching his tone.

'Think of it, mate. He was due to go to the - to be put to sleep tomorrow. Instead he died in his Maker's presence so to speak. I call that a bonus.'

With relief the gathering agreed, nodding their heads and murmuring words of encouragement. After a moment Doris looked up hopefully. 'I was going to have asked Rector but would you give him a wee blessing?' she asked timidly.

Sam, moved with pity, put his hand on her shoulder. 'I'll do better than that, Doris. I'll come round tomorrow morning and bury him for you.'

'Now there's an offer you can't refuse,' said George approvingly. He had been about to make the same suggestion but was relieved to have been forestalled.

'Where's Mr Freel?' Vera called after him anxiously as he pushed through the swing doors.

'Your guess is as good as mine,' he said cheerfully and bade them all goodnight.

As he groped in his pocket for his car keys he was not too pleased with himself. He knew he should have offered to drive the poor old dame home but that would have meant waiting until she had cleared up and as she lived in the opposite direction to the pub in St Ninians, a town ten miles down the coast, he would be late for Tony again. He reckoned it was safe enough to meet Tony there because the two towns had nothing to do with each other, the Glasgow-Edinburgh syndrome in miniature, though no less virulent.

He was about to switch on the engine of his battered but beloved third-hand MG when Jenny tapped on the window. He unwound it and tried not to sound too impatient as he asked, 'Jen. What's up?'

'It's Pa. Did he take the service? Has he left already?'

He shook his head. 'I haven't seen him since this morning.'

'Have you any idea where he could be?'

'He didn't say. Have you tried St Leonards? I know old Mrs Bridges is very ill.'

'She's dead. The matron rang to ask if Dad would come... I don't suppose you could come up, could you? Ma's a bit worried.'

Sam hesitated, thinking guiltily of Tony.

'Please, Sam?'

She was a nice kid, he thought, and so was her brother. Good kids. 'I'll have to make a phone call first.'

He locked the car and while they walked through the graveyard into the overgrown garden, he thought about what he would say to Tony. Sorry something's cropped up would not satisfy. My boss's gone AWOL would elicit the response, 'why don't you?' He even thought of lying. For the umpteenth time he wondered why he bothered with Tony. He was a mean little bastard really. But that was the trouble with Sam, he was always attracted to dangerous men. So far no one, apart from Francis, knew he was gay or so he believed, but he wouldn't put it past Tony to use a bit of blackmail just like Kevin had done. Kevin had threatened to tell his rector in his Chesston parish where he was a deacon, so he had told Francis at one of the diocesan meetings and Francis had been a saint, gone to Kevin himself and told him he would go straight to the police if he threatened Sam again. That was the last he had seen of Kev. And now there was Tony, with his glittering sexy eyes and pale undernourished body. Shamefully, he admitted to himself that it was the evil in these men that attracted him, the potential danger in the relationship that drew him to them. It had nothing to do with love. He dared not allow himself to think of love.

Once inside the vicarage, all thoughts of Tony receded as four pairs of anxious eyes turned to him.

'He's not usually as late as this, at least not without letting us know,' Ro said almost apologetically.

'He's had an accident. I know he has,' Minnie cried with tears on her cheeks.

'Rubbish! He hasn't got the car,' her brother said tersely in a crude attempt to comfort her.

'Oh Sam, please can you find him,' Jenny implored, her hands clasped together, a damsel in distress.

'How did he seem this morning?' Ro asked quietly. 'I gather he left the service early.'

He didn't try to brush aside their anxiety. Francis had walked out of the pulpit, gone into the vestry and not reappeared. He knew his rector's habits well enough to realise that something must be wrong, but then he had known that something had been far wrong with Francis for a long time, and had done nothing about it. 'Of course I'll go and look for him,' he said guiltily.

'Oh would you Sam? Shall I come with you?' Ro asked unsteadily.

'No,' he said firmly. 'Stay here with the kids. He'll probably walk in at any moment and want his supper,' he added trying to lighten their anxiety.

'What about you?' Jenny asked. 'There's some macaroni cheese."

'First things first. Maybe later,' he told her firmly.

Ro saw him to the door. 'Do you think we should contact the police?' she asked in a low voice, unwilling to further upset Minnie who was crying quietly.

'Early days. Give me a couple of hours.'

Night

Sam found it surprisingly easy to trace Francis' movements. A minister on the beach on Sunday morning was rare enough. A priest with his cassock flapping round his ankles, half in and half out of the tide-line was memorable and he had not gone unnoticed. Sam had asked first at the paper shop at the end of Parsonage Lane. Amar had been there more or less all day. Dicky had called for the paper as usual that morning and bought a bag of toffees. The minister had passed later in a hurry. Had someone died?

Vicarage Lane led on to Beach Avenue. Old Rossie, more or less permanent occupant of the three-sided kiosk, the front of which served as a bus shelter and the back as a windbreak, had certainly seen him. 'No time for the likes of me' he grumbled. 'That's yer modern faither for yer. Couldn't get by quick enough, like I was a bad smell.'

Which you are, thought Sam reeling from the stink that was only partly alcohol. He thanked him and went down one of the flights of stone steps that led on to the sands.

The wind had risen. The sea was a mosaic of grey waves darkening to the east under a sky that threatened rain. A tall thin woman whose face was vaguely familiar, with three tall thin dogs in tow, admitted that she had passed him on the sands that morning. 'Oh yes I saw him all right. I thought I'd been caught red-handed,' she said with a thin smile. 'I know I should have been in church but the boys do so love their morning romp.' She indicated the restless setters.

'Which way did he go?' Sam asked trying to sound casual but not succeeding for she immediately looked concerned. 'That way, towards the cave. I do hope he's all right. I did think it a bit strange that he didn't appear to notice me, and then I thought maybe he was just being tactful. Is there anything I can do?'

Sam reassured her and hurried off along the sands towards the cave set high into the raised beach about a mile from the town. He tried not to feel resentful as a few spots of rain stung his face. What on earth was Francis up to? He thought about Francis. He liked him, maybe a bit more than that, no, if he was to be honest, a lot more than that. Snapshots of his rector flickered through his mind; half-turned to spoon instant coffee granules into mugs at the weekly staff meeting in the rectory study; the nail on his forefinger blackened from some blow and the rim of his shirt cuff a little frayed, but always clean. He had once found him in the kitchen emptying the washing machine and folding the half-dry clothes. 'Makes them easier to iron' he had said unapologetically. Sam realised that he probably did that too. An ideal husband then. He remembered Minnie coming into the study with a bag of jelly babies demanding that he hide them. 'I just know the others will nick them;' and Francis had joked with her, 'are you quite sure you can trust me, not to mention Sam here?' and she had told him solemnly they could have one each. An ideal father then. He knew he was a good parish priest. Pretty well perfect all round. But there were other memories too, ones that he did not want to think about, like the time he had lost his temper with George Fenton, the other day when he had found him alone in the kitchen... He began to run, dodging the accumulating strew of rocks and boulders as his concern converted into a spasm of fear. Francis had not been himself for a while now. What the devil had happened to him? Suddenly he realised just how much he cared.

There were six caves in the space of three miles set into the raised beach well above the high tide line. The nearest had enjoyed countless years of habitation, culminating some fifty years ago in an eccentric couple who had opted out of conventional living to endure six months of damp squalor. Sam stood in the sandy entrance and peered into the gloom.

'Francis?' he called out tentatively, feeling ridiculous for he did not really expect to find him here. As he listened his eye was caught by a darker mass in the corner. His skin chilled as he stepped forwards to look more closely. With relief he saw that it was not a child, not a dead dog, only a coat. He stooped to lift it but it was not a coat either. It was a cassock.

The police officer who knew Francis by sight was kind and non-committal. 'Let's not jump to any hasty conclusions, Mrs Freel,' he said quietly after Ro with wretched eyes had assured him that the cassock had belonged to her husband. 'It's early days yet. The best thing you can do is to try and get some rest. Perhaps Mr Gardner would show us exactly where he found - the garment?' Cassock was not a word he was familiar with.

'Of course,' Sam said rather too heartily as he looked at the four stricken faces turned towards him for reassurance and hope. 'He probably went for a hike - just to get away from things for a while. He'll turn up good as new any time now.'

But he won't, Ro thought. There was a great gaping hole inside her head where the words 'he's dead' headlined across the void. Slamming shut the manhole in her mind, she forced herself to sound calm. Looking straight at the embarrassed policeman, she said briskly. 'Thank you for your help.'   She got up.' 'I'll show you out.'

'Try not to worry, Ro,' Sam touched her arm. 'If he's there, we'll find him.'

'Of course you will,' she said briskly for the stricken children's sake.

As soon as they'd gone Minnie began to cry again. Murmuring words of comfort, she gathered her into her arms and drew her close. Jenny flung herself into a chair and covered her face with her hands. 'What's happening? What's happening?' she muttered but it was not a question that expected an answer.

'He is coming back, isn't he?' Dicky asked her bluntly but Ro could only shake her head over Minnie's sobbing body. 'Make us some cocoa, Dickie,' she asked him, trying to sound normal.

'I'll help,' Jenny said unexpectedly rising from the chair. 'Come on, Minnie. Crying won't help.'

But Dicky wanted an answer. 'He will come back, won't he?'

Ro could not meet his eyes. 'Probably,' she said quietly, but she had no expectations and now that it had happened, she was not even surprised.

Dicky exploded. 'It's not fair. It's bloody not fair. What about you - us?' He was shaking with anger, fear and distress. Extricating herself from Minnie, Ro turned towards him and put her arms around him. It was a long time since he had allowed her to hug him so closely and she was surprised by his strength. He was no longer a little boy. 'He's got to come back,' he muttered. 'He can't just walk out of our lives - like any stupid kid. Make him come back.'

Suddenly Jenny was angry too. She clenched her fists. 'If that's how he feels about us, we can manage without him.' It didn't sound too convincing. When Ro reached out to draw her into a hug, she turned and banged her way into the kitchen. 'Cocoa all round then?' she called back brightly.

Chapter Two

Coolwater Bay: Monday May 26

Morning

I should have known. I should have known. I should have known. The words repeated themselves over and over in Ro's head, blotting out all logical thought, all hope of sleep, all ability to think. And of course now she did know what had been inevitable from the beginning. Oh Francis, Francis, how could you? A wave of fury swept over her and for a moment hatred overtook all else.

The luminous figures of the digital alarm clock shone out balefully. 3 10 am. Sleep was impossible. Flinging back the duvet, she slid to her feet, reached for her slippers and pulled on a cardigan over her nightgown. As quietly as possible, she opened Minnie's door. The moonlight was bright enough to show her face, tearstained, pallid, but she was comatose with her mouth open, deep in the sleep of hopeless exhaustion. She listened for a moment outside Jenny's, then Dicky's rooms and to her relief heard nothing, so she crept downstairs and into the tidy kitchen. This was not how she had left it. Good for Sam. He must have stayed on after they had all gone to bed, washed up and put everything away before going home. Thank God for Sam. She made herself some tea and took it into the sitting room. She needed to think. Francis would not be coming back, that much she was sure of, so what to do first? A list; that was it, make a list.

Firstly, let school know. But what exactly would she say. Francis is - has - what? He's gone away for a few days... I'm having a bit of trouble at home... sorry I won't be in for a few days. She could hear Sylvia pause, waiting for something more, but she was damned if she would say it. Not yet.

Back to the list. Contact the bishop. Hopefully Sam had already done that. Even so, she would have to speak to him some time, and, to him, she would certainly have to say something more. Sam would deal with the vestry. That dreadful little man, Fenton, who did his best to make Francis' life a misery...Francis' life. Oh Francis. How could you? How could you let that dreadful little man and all the others take control?

The washing machine. The bank. The police, though no doubt they would be here soon enough. Her father, good old Dad, what would he have to say? How would he cope from his sheltered house in Brighton? Her sister, though heaven knew what she could do in Australia. Suddenly she wanted Anna here, wanted to turn everything over to her, bossy Anna who was three years her elder and never let her forget it, who had always taken the decisions; Anna, whom she, Ro, as a student, could not wait to get away from; Anna now to take control, to tell her that all would be well. 'All will be well' – Francis' irritating mantra even when clearly things were not well.

Who else? What else? Only the children. Should they go to school, pretend nothing had happened? Surely that would be better than hanging around brooding all day. She flung down her pen and held her head in her hands. Brooding or mourning. Was it fair to let them go on expecting their father to come back when she knew, knew without a doubt, that he had gone? Then, suddenly, like a ray of watery sun after rain, a glimmer of hope lightened her mind. Perhaps he had left a letter.

Taking her list, she left the sitting room, crossed the passage to the study by the front door. Was it her imagination or did it seem tidier than usual? Impossible to tell because Francis was a naturally tidy person. The type-writer, mostly unused, stood on its own desk beside a neatly stacked ream of paper and other carefully assorted stationery. Francis still preferred to write his sermons and keep his records by hand. The duplicator sagged under a stack of old Church Times' in the corner. How she hated the bloody thing that covered her fingers with sticky black ink on the days when, at the last minute as usual, she had helped Francis print out the parish magazine. The roll-top desk that had belonged to Father George was open. One drawer was full of envelope files; the blue one was labelled receipts, a red one held outstanding bills, including the garage account with a final demand notice stuck to it, a fat yellow one labelled letters and so on. The central drawer held a well-thumbed lectionary, a stack of old church notices including the one for the current week which should have been pinned up in the church porch yesterday. Another drawer was full of gadgets, paper clips, stencils, drawing pins, etc. Yet another drawer contained old sermons neatly separated from each other in plastic envelopes and labelled with the date and Biblical text. The one below held insurance policies, all clearly marked including licenses, university documents, birth certificates and personal papers. There was something uncanny about the tidiness of his desk, almost as though Francis had been preparing himself and his affairs for what she was convinced he had done.

She turned her attention to the bookcases. Mostly they contained theological tomes many of which had belonged to Father George and a shelf of fishing guides. She remembered with a pang how Francis used to enjoy fishing with Father George. That never happened now. Come to think of it, since Father George's death at least a decade ago, Francis had changed, the nightmares had gradually become more frequent, the silence between them both deeper. He had taken the old priest's death badly which was hardly surprising. Father George had been the only family he remembered.

She scanned the cork clip-board above the duplicator with its notes and messages, some dating back for several weeks but there was nothing to be seen that she could possibly mistake for a letter. Oh Francis, Francis, where are you? Who are you? Why? Abruptly she left the room sick with the loss of him.

Perhaps he had left a note in the vestry. It was worth a look surely. The church would be locked. Then she remembered that Francis always opened it at 7 am to say his office first thing in the morning. Who locked it last night? He would never have left it unlocked. Perhaps he had come back too late to disturb his family. Perhaps he was there now. A finger of hope touched her darkness.

Pulling a coat on over her nightgown and thrusting her feet into a handy pair of welly boots, she slipped out of the back door.

Minnie awoke just as her mother went out. Her head and her eyes ached and her bladder was full. For a moment she thought she must have flu then she remembered, and, instantly alert, padded through to the bathroom. The house was silent, listening, empty the way it always seemed when Pa was out. She did not have to go to her parents' door to know that he was not there. She crept back to bed and pulled the duvet over her head.

Where was Pa? He had never - well hardly ever - not been there at night. Was he all right? Why had he gone to the beach? Then the awful thought: what had she done? She remembered the moment she had last seen him. He had been preaching in the pulpit. She had not been listening. That made her feel guilty because she never listened to Pa when he preached. Okay, at the children's services when he had asked easy questions like 'where was Baby Moses found' and she had delighted in shooting up her hand, clicking her fingers - something she was not allowed to do at school - bursting to answer 'in the bulrushes!' Yesterday she had been playing Hangman with Tim under the desk of the choir pew hidden from Sam's view. Pa had come out of the pulpit and gone straight into the vestry and that was the last time she had seen him. Had he seen her playing Hangman? Or maybe she had done something naughty on Saturday. She had gone on a bit about the pony. The pony. Screwing her eyes shut, she clasped her hands together under the duvet and muttered 'Please God, if I promise not to go on about the pony, will you send Pa back?'

Then she heard the bird. One clear, concentrated, urgent sound. Properly awake now, she crossed to the window, opened it wide and leaned her head out. In the pre-dawn light she could see only the darker shapes of the trees while the invisible dawn chorus grew in intensity and as she listened it seemed to her like a message of hope.

Slamming the window shut she dragged on yesterday's clothes with no thought of school and crept downstairs and out into the shouting dawn. She knew the names of every one of the birds for Pa had taught her their songs, their habitats and their food fads. She stood still just to listen, to draw comfort from their support. The sun had risen and as it touched the top of the great Wellingtonia redwood which stood at the foot of the short drive, she was for a moment filled with hope. 'I'll find you, Pa. Don't worry. I'll find you.' Without thought or hesitation she took the road that led to the shore.

No one was about although she could hear the milk float in a neighbouring street. Even Amar's paper shop was still shut The assorted houses, pre-war bungalows and pretentious Edwardian stone villas paid no heed to her, nothing stirred as the sun pointed its strong new beams at their blinded windows. It was like everyone was dead. Dead. The word boomed in her head. Pa was not dead. How could he be dead? The word was there alive in her head. Running, she could not escape.

She reached the water's frilly edges. So pretty with the new sun glittering on the baby waves. How could Pa be dead in such an intensely alive world? Okay, so Sam had found his cassock in the cave. Perhaps he had gone for a swim. Perhaps he had got cramp, whatever cramp was, but she knew it could kill you. Unlikely though. Pa hated the sea and never bathed with the rest of them.

Without consciously making up her mind, she began to run again.

A line of blue and yellow tape had been fixed across the mouth of the cave, attached to two triangular police notices barring her entrance. She stood still and stared. It was true then. Pa had really gone. Her legs felt heavy, her body leaden. She was aware of sea sounds behind her like little ripples of laughter while light-hearted clouds scudded across the sunny sky, impervious, uncaring, unaware of the horror inside her head. Two seagulls squawked and chattered to each other on a ledge above her. Closer at hand thickets of bramble clustered with tight buds, baby nettles thrust their shoots through crevices in the rocks. No-one, nothing, cared.

Peering into the depths of the cave she saw that it was as it always had been. Smelly, with suspicious bits of screwed up paper in the far corner, a bashed can of coke, the remains of a fire and the skeleton wing of a dead tern. Nothing of Pa.

Wind ruffled the water and a passing cloud momentarily dimmed the sun and turned the water grey. Too heavy-hearted to stand any longer, she sank down on a lichened boulder and looked at the water below her where greedy wavelets licked the barnacled rocks. Shivers of fear slid up and down her back. She did not like deep water. She hated seaweed. She would bathe only over sand where she could see her own feet wavering beneath her. 'Please not,' she whispered, 'Please don't be there.'

Then she heard the voice, very loud, very clear, very close. All it said was 'All will be well.' Scrambling to her feet she answered. 'Pa? Where are you, Pa?' They were Pa's words but it had not been Pa's voice. It was altogether different, a voice she could not describe, a voice she recognised but could not remember.

Scrambling over the jagged rocks and lichened boulders of the raised beach she could find no trace of the speaker in or out of the cave. Suddenly she tripped and her hand automatically went forward to break the fall and touched something wet and sticky on one of the boulders. Bird poo, she thought with a shudder, but bird poo was not normally rusty red, was it?

The Bishop rang at nine precisely.

'Rosamund? Paul here.'

'Bishop,' she replied shortly. Though he called himself Paul he did not like to be addressed by his Christian name. He preferred 'My Lord', would tolerate 'Father' from his Anglo Catholic clergy and accepted Bishop from strangers. Francis' wife was no stranger but she had always been bolshie. There were many sorts of bolshie; flirty bolshie he could handle and quite liked but at the other end of the scale there was impudent bolshie. Rosamund had always been on the cusp of impudence.

In his late sixties and a bishop now for twelve years Paul Arnot believed he had dealt with every possible problem his clergy could throw at him. Paedophilia fortunately had never happened, adultery and marriage problems occasionally, theft was rare and not always proven, debt and depression sadly too often, suicide twice and suspected murder only once, thank God. Complaints, poisonous letters and incandescent phone calls came almost daily, alas. Now this. And Francis of all men.

Truth to tell, Francis had always been a bit of an enigma. A good parish priest, he did not deny, a support on committees, unflappable, someone who presented well, a good listener, had the right appearance, - his Lordship did not approve of slouchers or beer bellies - his hair decently short, remarkably fine eyes, yes, a good appearance, and, from his Lordship's point of view, the right churchmanship, slightly left of evangelical, slightly right of Anglo Catholic. Middle-of-the road, or so he supposed. Come to think of it he was not completely sure what Francis' churchmanship was. Behind his good appearance and courteous manner he was not sure he knew Francis at all. You could never quite get to grips with the man. Private, he supposed you would call it.

'Would you like to tell me what has happened?' he asked gently.

'I don't know what happened,' Ro replied shortly. Her voice shook with anger. Aware that none of it was the bishop's fault she relented sufficiently to say, 'I thought Sam had told you'.

This was not going to be easy.

'Indeed. There have been no further - developments?'

'He's not come back if that's what you mean,' Ro had meant to sound sarcastic but it came out on a sob.

Plus Paul gestured to his secretary who brought over his desk diary. His first appointment was in half an hour. He pointed to it and raised his eyebrows but Joan shook her head. Too late to cancel the diocesan treasurer, a surly man at the best of times, who would already be on his way. She indicated his afternoon round of golf, arranged weeks ago with the diocesan chancellor and two of his legal colleagues on what was supposed to be his afternoon off.

44

Sighing inwardly, he nodded to Joan. 'I'll be with you round about 2.30,' he told Ro, adding uselessly, 'try not to worry too much.'

D I Ian Ross was no lightweight. He overflowed the kitchen chair both lengthwise and sideways. His presence may have appeared reassuring to Ro and to Sam, who had arrived on the doorstep at the same time as the two police officers, but inwardly he felt less than confident. Role reversal, he told himself with an inward sigh as Sam offered to make coffee for them all. Truth to tell, he had always been a little afraid of Mrs Freel, so forthright and competent when facing him and Ruth in Brian's busy class room surrounded by children's art. William Wallace last term, if he remembered right. Ruth enthused about her, Brian tolerated her, but he could never shake off the feeling of clumsy inadequacy in her presence, a hangover from his own primary school days when his fingers perpetually tingled from his teacher's over-generous use of the strap. Always too big for his clothes, his desk, his age, it had not been his fault that pencil boxes crashed to the floor, schoolbags stumbled over, toes mashed and doors crashed in his presence. He still felt too big for his surroundings and it was not much use Ruth saying it was one of the things she loved about him, she was the first to complain of his clumsiness.

Detective Constable Alison Pearson also knew the family. She had told him on their way from the station that she had been a Girl Guide in the St Ambrose church company and for a short time sang in the choir. 'The Rector was a nice guy,' she told him. 'Was?' he queried. 'Sorry' she said quickly. She was no more at her ease than he was.

And Francis Freel probably was a nice guy, or so he had seemed on the rare occasions they had met. He remembered a glue-sniffing teenager found dead in one of the beach pavilions. Coolwater Bay had its quota of misfortunates and Mr Freel had not been afraid to get involved. Not the type to go AWOL, he would have thought, but he had been long enough in the Police Force not to be taken in by appearances, not to make snap judgements. Suicide, stress, memory loss, murder or just plain escape from the daily grind were still all possibilities, though judging from the report on his desk this morning, the former seemed most likely. A sad business whatever. He had not yet visited the cave himself but the duty officer and a constable had sealed the site last night, the coast guards had been alerted, the local police stations informed, and the station sergeant was co-ordinating the search locally.

The coffee was hot and strong and the mugs large enough for his broad strong fingers. He gave her a moment to question him about the search but she asked him nothing. He saw that she was no longer Mrs Freel of Primary Five, alert, smart, competent, who knew his son probably better than he did, and certainly saw more of him. This was a small, dark, angry, distraught woman.

She did not look at him as she answered the routine questions. Francis had come in for a cup of coffee after the 8 am Communion Service, then disappeared as usual into his study to go over his mid-day sermon, and no, the children had not been up. No, he had not seemed more preoccupied than usual, he was always preoccupied on Sundays. No, he had not told her he would be late for lunch. No, he had not seemed particularly worried about anything, not that he ever discussed his parish affairs at any time and she had learned not to pry, and, no, she had no idea what he had preached about that morning. 'I don't have time for church,' she informed him sharply.

He tried again. He had not visited his doctor lately, as far as she knew. He had not mentioned going away and he would have had very little money on him, if any. Francis seldom had more than a few shillings in his pocket. Certainly they could examine the study, their joint back account, his desk diary, but she had already looked and had found nothing relevant, no letter, no note.

Mr Gardner, though obliging and obviously anxious to help, had little to add. Yes, he had brought back the cassock which was now in police custody and he apologised if that had been the wrong thing to do. Yes, Francis had seemed much his usual self when they had met briefly in the vestry before the mid-day service, perhaps a little more preoccupied than usual. He was a busy man. Yes, he could supply a list of all those who had been in church yesterday morning; yes, he remembered the sermon. Francis had preached on the Gospel for the First Sunday after Trinity, the story of the rich man and the beggar at his gate, pretty routine stuff. No, he had not thought to follow him into the vestry after he had left the pulpit for Sam was already on his way up to the altar to receive the elements from the servers as it had been his turn to celebrate at the monthly Eucharist, but yes, it was a little unusual. He assumed that Francis had gone to visit one of his elderly parishioners in the Residential Home who, so he had been since informed, had just died.

Suddenly Mrs Freel came alive. 'Questions, questions! Why don't you ask me outright what I think?' She was suddenly incandescent with anger, shaking from head to foot. Alison Pearson put her notepad down on the table, rose from her chair, stood behind her and ran her hands up and down her clenched arms. 'It's all right, Mrs Freel. Take your time. It's all right.'

'Well, Mrs Freel, what do you think has happened to your husband?' Ian asked firmly

'He's dead,' she said woodenly.

'You don't know that for certain,' he said gently.

'Oh but I do,' she said, and suddenly her anger dropped from her like a cloak. 'I just do,' she said sadly.

'Why do you think he is dead?' he asked evenly.

'He did it,' she answered woodenly.

'Why do you think that?' he probed her.

Alison left her side, returned to her chair and picked up her notepad.

After a while Mrs Freel shook her head.

Ro would have to tell them something, but what? What did she really know? His father...but dear old Father George was not Francis' father, was he? He was just the local vicar. Francis spoke of him as if he were his real father, remembered some sort of upbringing near Maldon in the Dales, but it was mostly a lie.

A couple of weeks before her wedding, Father George had come to see her. It had been a huge effort for him crippled as he was with arthritis. She remembered his phone call. 'I shall be in Chesston' - he did not say why - 'next week. Can you give me some tea, perhaps?'

She had been surprised that he should attempt to make that somewhat uncomfortable cross country journey from his remote vicarage but, not unnaturally, assumed he had come to see Francis who was finishing off a second curacy at Chesston Cathedral.

'Are you staying with Francis?' she asked, then remembered he was attending a pastoral course in Oxford the following week.

'I shall be staying in the Retreat House in the Close.'

Curiouser and curiouser, she had thought, but maybe he was trying not to be a nuisance to his son. Later she realised that he had chosen that week deliberately because there could be no chance of Francis being there.

When he was sitting in the easiest chair she possessed in her small flat - two rooms and a shared bathroom on the middle floor of a Victorian terraced house in the suburbs of Chesston - he came quickly to the point.

'I'm glad you and Francis are tying the knot,' he said firmly.

'I'm glad you're glad,' she said smiling her pleasure. It had all been so quick. Love at first sight for her and for him too, or so he said. Three months since they had met; eye catching eye at her school assembly which he was leading in place of the sick canon-in-residence, an instant recognition that this was the man she would marry, although at that point she did not even know his name, all far too quick her father had warned, her friends had advised, she herself had thought in her saner moments and probably his father had believed too. Francis had accepted a post in an inner city team ministry in Liverpool where there would be plenty of teaching opportunities for her. They both wanted to work in disadvantaged areas. Why wait any longer when they knew this was what they both wanted, so they argued with themselves and their families. She realised now that it had been simpler than that. They had wanted to sleep with each other and of course in the fifties that meant marriage.

'The thing is,' Father George said looking down at his swollen arthritis fingers, 'I'm not sure how much you know about Francis, how much he's told you about himself, his childhood?'

'Not much,' she admitted, thinking about it. In fact, he never spoke about his childhood at all. She was always rabbiting on about hers but when she asked him about his, he was vague, dismissive almost. She remembered him telling her about a birthday party and a cake with ten candles, and a massive tree at Christmas with real candles which had to be carefully watched. (Come to think of it, he still liked candles. He encouraged the parishioners at Coolwater Bay to decorate the church with candles everywhere at Christmastide.)

'It never happened,' Father George sadly, 'at least not to my knowledge.' He watched her with his wise old eyes. 'Francis is not my son. My only son was killed in France at the beginning of the war. Francis just turned up one day and stayed. He looked about fifteen years old. I had no idea where he came from and nor had he. All I know for certain is this that we care deeply for each other, and, I believe, he loves you.'

She stared at him. 'Then who is he?'

No one really knew. One theory at the time had him as one of two little evacuees from Liverpool billeted in the village at the beginning of the war with an eccentric aristocratic couple who lived in a huge rambling mansion house. The small boys were called Francis and Aloysius O'Brien. As homesick children they had not stayed long as evacuees but had returned to the city and shortly afterwards the family home had been bombed to extinction, the parents and Aloysius killed. Francis may have survived. He was sent to some sort of temporary orphanage but escaped and disappeared. It was suggested that he might have found his way back to the village, only to discover that the elderly couple he had been billeted on, were now dead; a thin story but the only explanation available. Father George had found Francis, if that's who he was, traumatised, injured and living rough, more dead than alive in the church graveyard.

She was surprised, of course, but not that surprised. There had always been something a little odd about Francis' reluctance - or inability - to speak about his past. 'What do you think?' she had asked.

'All I really know is that he was not my natural son.' Father George sighed. 'The O'Brien boy would have been about fifteen at the end of the war. He said his name was Francis. I wondered about that, though. He was sitting staring at my son's memorial stone in the churchyard when I found him huddled there shivering with pneumonia. My son was called Francis, Frank actually.'

So Father George had taken him in, nursed him, healed him, befriended him, loved him and after a while Francis had almost taken the place of his dead son.

'It was obvious of course that he had completely lost his memory.'

There had been anomalies. For a boy raised in Liverpool he had no trace of a regional accent. That could have been the influence of the aristocratic couple he had been billeted on as an evacuee, or so it was supposed. In those early days when he had been so ill he would rave in his delirium about someone called Ali.

'His brother, Aloysius?'

'So it was assumed.'

He still talked in his sleep, such troubled sleep, and she too had heard the name Ali, though he had no memory of it in the morning. In the early years of their marriage the nightmares had been less frequent but over the years they had not diminished and lately his sleep was broken more often than not, waking her up as he thrashed and moaned in the middle of the night.

It had occurred to Ro as she listened to the old priest that the grief for him who had lost his own son to the war and his wife to cancer must have been overwhelming. 'What about you?' she had asked reaching out her hand towards him. He had taken it and after a while said. 'I saw Francis as a gift from God, as indeed he has proved himself to be.'

When he had recovered, Francis had remembered nothing of a brother or of the orphanage, or how he had got there. Nor had the orphanage been much help. The boy had stayed for only a few weeks but no one really remembered him. Their records were scanty. 'Francis O'Brien's birth certificate told me he was fifteen years old. He had no relatives to object so eventually it was possible for him to become legally Francis Freel and although he could never take Frank's place, he became very dear to me in his own right.'

Ro had been astounded, 'Why didn't he tell me all this?'

The old priest had shaken his head. 'I don't know, Rosamund. I believe he has no memories at all of his own past. He knows he's adopted of course but he doesn't know who else he is. It was a terrifying experience for him and of course he was very ill with pneumonia. He also had a nasty wound to his head which had become infected. The doctors did what they could and reassured me that it would all take time. He would cling to me in those early days, never letting me out of his sight and the explanation was not hard to find. He thought that if I were to go out of his presence, I might also go out of his memory, as indeed everything else in his life had done. I gave him what counsel I could, but all that really amounted to was my reassurance and my love. He needs all the love you can give him, Rosamund. In the end he was able to cope with his memory loss by making himself into my son, my spiritual son if not my natural son; I always believed he became a priest to prove just that. You see my Frank had been called to follow in my footsteps. When I asked Francis if that were the reason, he did not deny it. I remember his exact words; "to make amends", he told me. I could not, indeed I would not, talk him out of it.' He paused. 'Does all this worry you?'

Ro thought for a while. Francis, dear, dark, enigmatic, loving, stormed into her mind and she was flooded with a tenderness that enhanced and enlightened her love for him. She would make up to him for all he had lost. She would become his family. Slowly she shook her head.

'There is something else' she said. 'Those terrible scars. Do you know what happened?' She remembered the first time she had seen him in an open-necked shirt, how shocked she had been by that jagged scarring of flesh that zig-zagged lividly around his neck, how she had touched the scars, kissed them and how he had stiffened in her arms. 'How was he hurt?'

'That happened before I found him, part of his forgotten past.'

'How could anyone forget a thing like that?'

Father George spread his hands. 'The trick cyclists called it deep trauma… Long ago I reached the conclusion that with Francis it's probably better not to probe too deeply. Sleeping dogs and all that.'

They were both silent, both assuming that he had tried to kill himself.

Before Ro could explain, the telephone rang. Sam who was nearest to the kitchen extension rose to answer. That rather intense woman who worked in the chemist, Mrs Shotton, was asking for Francis. Sam was both reassuring and non-committal. Almost immediately it rang again. George Fenton this time. Sam explained that Francis was unavailable and with a glance at the officers offered to disconnect the line.

'That might be best for the time being,' the Inspector said calmly. 'You were saying, Mrs Freel?'

Sam listened fascinated as Ro explained that Francis had been adopted, that something appalling must have happened to him in his adolescence and that he had blotted the memory out. He had these scars on his neck. Both she and Francis' adoptive father had thought he had tried at one time to - she could not bring herself to say it outright.

'But that's not what I thought,' Sam interrupted.

It had been one of the Tuesday morning staff meetings not that long ago. Sam had been talking about getting a dog. He'd been offered a Yorkshire terrier but his landlady had put her foot down. Would Francis be interested? He knew the children would like a dog.

Francis had made a face and fingered his collar. 'I don't get on that well with dogs.' He had been wearing an open necked collar at

51

the time and the scars were livid. Though he did not actually say so, Sam assumed that was how he had come by the injury.

He had, however, known that Francis was adopted. They had been discussing a choir boy, who, according to the organist, behaved like a holy terror. Francis had said, 'Not so holy perhaps. He was adopted. Like me.'

After a few more questions, the Inspector told them they had both been very helpful and perhaps he could have a look at the study. Then the door opened and Minnie came in.

'Ma,' she said. 'I'm hungry.'

Such a grubby forlorn little figure; Sam wanted to go over and give her a hug. 'A cheese sandwich do you?' he said getting up to make it while Ro held out her arms to the little girl. But DI Ross had noticed something else. There were rusty red streaks on her hands and down the thighs of her jeans where she had rubbed them.

'Marjorie, is it?' he asked quietly. 'Did you take a tumble then?' he asked, eyeing the streaks on her jeans.

'I tripped over a rock outside the cave,' she explained, as Sam handed her a glass of milk. 'But I didn't hurt myself. It's bird poo.'

'Where have you been, Minnie?' Ro asked tensely.

'I went to look for Pa, but he isn't at the cave. I promise you,' she said, turning to the policemen, 'he's not there.'

'Would you show us where you found the bird poo, Marjorie?' Alison Pearson asked, 'after you've had your sandwich, of course, oh, and maybe you would like to wash your hands and change first?'

'Sure,' said Minnie obligingly. She slipped off Ro's knee and joined Sam at the bread-board, while DI Ross went out to contact the station.

Sam was appalled. Though Minnie was begging him to cut off the crusts 'just this once', he still managed to overhear the constable's words to Ro. 'Can you give us Marjorie's clothing, Mrs Freel? We have to make quite sure…'

He knew exactly what they were thinking.

'I could walk out too,' Dicky thought. 'Why don't I?'

What had induced him to come to school? When Ma had woken him that morning at the usual time and after she had told him that Pa had not come back, she had given him the choice. 'It's up to you,' she had said evenly. 'If you want me to ring school, I'll do it. It's your decision.'

Odd really. Normally he would have jumped at the chance to have a day off, especially a Monday but he had not answered her. He had tried to turn over and go to sleep again but he was wide-awake now. To go or not to go? It was English Lit today. Lear for O-levels. He had thought over his timetable. RE, English Lit, French Language. Two periods of History this afternoon. Horrors, all of them. And now old Keir was going on and on again about Lear's madness, dementia, Alzheimer's... Pa. Maybe he had gone mad. 'Care-crazed' like Lear. People did, didn't they? Old people. Was Pa old enough? He didn't know any mad people except for Old Rossie down on the shore. Was he mad? Or was it just booze? Booze did that sort of thing to you. Did Pa booze? Ridiculous idea. Except of course for the Communion wine. Pa was supposed to finish what was left after the congregation had received but he usually got one of the sides-men to do it. Maybe that was just a cover-up. Maybe he had gone to the cave to have a drink and somehow staggered into the sea. He knew it wasn't a good idea to booze and bathe. Maybe that was it.

To walk out or not to walk out? To drink or not to drink...? To live or not to live.. ?

'Richard, read.' Old Keir commanded in his most Shakespearean voice. What the hell was he supposed to read?

He would walk out too. At break he would walk out... not walk out. Walk out...not walk out. He would have to be back in time for rugby practice at seven. Pa might even be home. Surely Pa would be home by then.

Jenny woke to hear a knock on her door, a sort of apologetic tap. Not again, she thought ungraciously. No way was she going to school. She had already told Ma. If Pa could go off without a word, she could stay in bed... But it was no use. Her insides were a great gaping abyss which had nothing to do with hunger, a worse edition of what she felt before a music exam which vaguely she recognised as what her piano teacher had called 'musical evening pains'. The same as when she had to go to the dentist. Only this was worse because there was nothing she could do about it, no exam to finish, no tooth to fill. It was bad enough having a father who wore that weird collar, who sometimes came to Assembly and prayed, prayed for God's sake! Left her in cringe mode all day. None of her friends would meet her eye, at least not for that morning. Mostly they were polite, distant and reserved, sorry for her. How humiliating was that. Worse still, the teachers were polite. And now to have a father who did God and then disappeared was totally blush-making.

The door opened and Ma stood there with a mug of coffee and a banana. 'I thought you might be hungry.'

Ma looked terrible, her mouth pale and pinched with no lippy and her hair like a bird's nest. She half sat up and removed her headphones while her mother put the small round tray with Canterbury Pilgrims prancing round the corners down on her bedside table on top of her Annabels. 'Ta,' she said ungraciously, remembered that her mother disliked her saying that and added in a small voice, 'Thanks, Ma'. Suddenly her eyes filled with tears. She seized her pillow and clutched it into her face to stifle the sobs that shook her whole body. 'I'm scared,' she cried between gulps.

Ro sat down on the edge of her counterpane with the Beatles splurged all over it and put her arms round her. For a while neither of them said anything, her sobs subsided and she was enormously comforted. The abyss inside her shrank down to the size of a hunger pang. She freed her hands to peel the banana.

Then Ro said evenly, 'We might have to get used to him not being around.'

Jenny was still. What did that mean? Had they had a row? Was it a divorce? One of her friend's parents were divorced, but ministers don't do divorce, do they? 'Did you have a fight?' she asked pushing away the banana and wiping the snot from her nose with the sleeve of her pyjamas.

Ro smiled forlornly. 'I wish,' she said. 'I think,' she said evenly, 'I think maybe he's just had enough'.

The abyss threatened.

'Enough of what?' She asked in a small voice. 'Enough of us?'

Ro took her hand and turned it over. Jenny wondered fleetingly if she would be angry about the pink nail varnish. It was worse. She never noticed. She lifted Jenny's hand to her mouth and kissed it.

'No, darling, not of us. I think maybe he just got tired of it all.'

'You mean he's gone off for a rest? Like that retreat place with the nuns?'

'Not exactly.'

Jenny felt her mother shudder. She put her arm around her narrow waist. There was no roll of flesh above her skirt band like she had. She shut out the perpetual worry about getting fat, as it occurred to her with a sudden shift of vision that if her father needed a rest, so must her mother. What did that mean? She would have to help out a bit more at washing dishes, making beds, looking after Minnie, keeping her room tidy, not arguing all the time. She dropped her arm from her mother's waist and twisted away.

'It's all right, Jenny. We'll manage.'

But now she was truly scared and being scared made her angry.

'It's not fair,' she blurted out childishly. 'How could he just leave us like that? It's so mean. I thought he was supposed to be a good person.'

'He was a good person, darling. Perhaps he tried too hard.'

She noticed immediately. The abyss widened. 'Was'. She knew what that meant. She stared at her mother aghast.

'Jenny, I don't know what's happened. I'm just saying we need to be prepared for...bad news.'

The tears came again, helpless, hopeless sobs. She felt her mother's arms tighten around her but this time she was not comforted.

By the time Sam and Minnie reached the cave a small group of people had already gathered at a respectful distance as close to the police notice as they could get to stare up and speculate as the forensics team in white overalls scrutinized the cave. Inspector Ross politely but firmly told them to stand further back. Minnie's hand crept into his. He gathered her small cold fingers into his warm grasp. He noticed the woman with the red setters to whom he had spoken the previous evening. Had she no home to go to? He distinctly heard her say knowingly, 'That's the daughter, poor wee mite. He's called Gardner, he's the assistant at St Ambrose. They've likely been searching all night.'

Before he could hear more, Alison Pearson came up to Minnie and asked her to show them where she had fallen. She took Minnie's hand but asked him to stay back. 'It's important to keep the scene as uncontaminated as possible,' she said apologetically, 'Marjorie will be fine with me.'

As soon as they'd gone, the woman with the dogs and the other on-lookers surrounded Sam. They all had questions. Sam fobbed them off as well as he could and moved away but he knew that soon some sort of statement would have to be made. The press would be on to it fast enough. Hopefully, the Bishop would know what to say.

He could see Minnie standing over one of the many lichen-covered boulders that had at one time tumbled down the cliff-side and now formed part of the raised beach between the cave and the high tide line. The forensics couple were bending down with their equipment. There was no doubt that they thought it was blood. But whose blood? A dog, an otter maybe? Someone had seen otters playing on the shore recently. A bird? Unlikely. Francis' blood? Perhaps he had tumbled over and somehow fallen into the sea. Sam could not believe that. If he had gone into the sea it would have been deliberate. A cat?

Suddenly Mrs Croft flashed into his mind. He was supposed to be burying Napoleon this morning. This afternoon then? But the Bishop wanted to see him so not this afternoon. Poor old soul, she would be worrying herself sick thinking he'd forgotten. He would also have to go up to St Leonards to arrange Mrs Bridges' funeral. Then there was Tony. Oh God, Tony. He would have to finish that relationship if Francis had really gone. Apart from the dangerous stupidity of such an affair there would be no time. Tony wouldn't care, bitch that she was. He wondered if Francis had told the Bishop about Kevin. He didn't think he had. He would have known just from the way the Bishop looked at him. Perhaps he should tell him. Telling Francis had been one of the wisest things he'd ever done. Shared the load, the guilt, the doubts and taken them away somehow. Oh Francis, I need you, where the hell are you?

Minnie was running back to him followed by the police constable who told him that they would be in touch as soon as possible. 'Will you take Marjorie home now? She's been a great help.'

Minnie looked up at him from Francis' eyes, those great green, dark-lashed eyes and slipped her hand back into his as they turned to go. 'Pa's all right, Sam. I know he is,' she told him confidently, suddenly hopeful. 'Someone told me. I heard this voice. I don't know who it was but I think it might have been God.'

Sam was deeply touched but he was not reassured. Far from it. If Francis was dead and somehow with God, then he would be all right wouldn't he, but what about the rest of us, Francis? What about the rest of us?

He grasped her small hand and they turned to trudge the mile walk back along the sands.

Afternoon

Doris Croft looked up at Jim's presentation clock. 2.10 precisely and she knew it was right by the BBC. When would Sam come? Maybe Rector was coming too or perhaps they had both forgotten. Everything was ready. Napoleon lay in state on the kitchen table. The spade was outside the back door. Perhaps they'd already been and found her out when she'd gone to the Co-op first thing to get a big enough box. She'd stuck it over with a sheet of pretty wrapping paper to blot out the label for tinned peaches. Then she'd wrapped Napoleon in the old matted shawl that had lined his basket and laid him in the box as well as she could. He was so light. The thought flashed into her mind that he felt just like her bag of knitting needles. Not a kind thought. But it was all right to think that because she just knew that he was not there any more. His soul had moved on. How much did a soul weigh?

She fixed the cardboard flaps with sticky tape, wrote his name on a purple condolence card with white lilies and sat down, folded her hands and said out loud, 'I'm sorry, Napoleon, for all the times I put you out in the cold, I was not there for you, gave you that horrible dried food ...'

Jessie had phoned at 10.30 full of commiserations. 'I can't talk now,' Doris had explained with one eye on the street. 'I'm expecting the curate.' Then the postie had called with a parcel from her catalogue. The milkman was next, needing paid. She'd missed him on Saturday. She hadn't felt much like dinner so had had a cup of tea and a KitKat at 12.30.

Just as she had looked up at the clock for the umpteenth time, the door bell pinged twice. 'Thank you, God,' she thought as she always thought when something good happened and hurried through the passage to let Sam in. But it was not Sam. She did not know the large dark-suited man on her doorstep though the woman, lassie really, looked familiar. For a moment she thought they might be Jehovah's Witnesses and arranged her face suitably. She had promised herself not to be nasty next time they called. Then discreetly, they both shown their badges and at the same time she recognised the girl with her short neat hair and navy blue costume. 'Alison Pearson!'

When the young woman smiled and nodded, she held out her hand. 'I never forget a face. Second row on the left of St Ambrose choir. You were one who knew how to behave.'

The large man interrupted gently. 'Mrs Croft, we're police officers. We would like to have a word with you if you can spare us the time.'

Her hand flew to her mouth. Napoleon, she thought guiltily as she led them into the parlour. Perhaps it was my fault. 'Can I offer you a cup of tea?' she asked falteringly.

'No thank you,' Alison said politely. 'We won't keep you long.'

Doris' heart began to beat fast. The police never had a cup of tea when they were on duty. She knew that from the telly. Oh, Napoleon. I didn't mean to neglect you. Her eyes filled with tears. 'The vet said it was natural causes. He had a growth. He was quite old. Sixteen is old for a cat isn't it?'

Alison touched her arm. 'I'm sorry about your cat, Mrs Croft,' she said kindly, 'but that's not why we're here. Perhaps we could sit down?'

The large detective took the largest seat which was almost the whole couch. The springs sagged alarmingly. The couch had been part of her life and her mother's before her, always in the parlour, mostly unused except for Christmas and New Year and when Rector visited of course. Alison chose a little beaded chair that no one ever used by the window and took out her notebook. Doris sat down gingerly on the edge of the rocking chair that Jim had given her for their tenth wedding anniversary where she felt safe.

'You were in church yesterday morning - ?'

'And evening,' she interrupted.

'Did you notice anything unusual?' he carried on as if she had not spoken. What did he want her to say? Guiltily she remembered that her mind had not been on the service. She had been thinking and praying about Napoleon. She looked at him blankly.

'Was Mr Freel there?'

'Rector?' So this was about Rector, not Napoleon. Thank you, God, but wait a moment, maybe this was worse. Two police officers were asking about Rector? He wasn't at Evensong last night, when Napoleon had died.

'Has something happened?' she asked falteringly. 'Is it one of the children?'

'The children are fine, Mrs Croft,' the girl said soothingly. 'We were wondering if you could tell us when you last saw Mr Freel?'

She told them all she knew, which was not much, how Jenny had come down looking for him, how Sam had taken Evensong. 'Rector's a busy man. I heard someone was dying up at the Home.'

She remembered he had missed Evensong when Jim had that stroke. He had come before the doctor and he had stayed till the doctor came. Said all those lovely prayers. Held one of Jim's hands while she held the other. By the time the doctor came it was too late for Jim and for Evensong. She hadn't noticed at the time, only weeks afterwards when she'd calmed down. 'No-one's indispensable, Mrs Croft,' he'd said. But some people are more indispensable than others and he had been indispensable to her.

'He's a lovely man. He's a good man,' she said warmly, feeling that nothing she could say was adequate. 'He takes a lovely funeral,' she added lamely and then, as the truth dawned, her eyes filled up. 'If he'd known about Napoleon he would have come, that's for sure. What's happened?' she asked.

'That's what we're trying to establish, Mrs Croft,' the big man said quietly.

'Somebody's ill,' she said firmly. 'That'll be it,' she added but they didn't look convinced.

'You liked your Rector, Mrs Croft?' the girl asked in a sympathetic voice. 'Was he popular with the congregation?'

'Oh, I did and he was well liked - by most, that is.' She hesitated, wanting to be truthful. 'There's always some. There's no pleasing everyone in the church.'

'Anyone in particular?' the detective asked casually.

Doris hesitated. She wanted to be truthful but she didn't want to speak out of turn. She tried to make it into a joke. 'Oh you know folk. They gossip - just for the sake of hearing their own voice...' But it was not funny and the two officers did not laugh.

'What do they say, Mrs Croft?' the girl insisted.

Why shouldn't they know? Everyone else did. 'They say he's lazy. They say he doesn't visit. The congregation's not what it was. The church is going downhill fast as an express train (George Fenton's words). They say his marriage is on the rocks, his children wild and his wife never comes to church. They say he drinks too much and that he's owing the wine merchant and the garage. But none of it's true. It's just what people say. They're a lovely couple

59

and they have three fine children and he's a good man.' She paused and added in a desire to be completely truthful. 'They say he's seeing someone else.'

'Anyone in particular?' the big man asked.

Doris hesitated. She knew, of course, how Vera Shotton felt about Rector and she supposed everyone knew. She sat in church gazing up at him, never missed a service volunteered for all the wee jobs that no one else wanted, was going to get confirmed, but she had no idea what he thought of her.

'It's all just hearsay,' she answered awkwardly and then added in a low voice, 'I suppose you could talk to Mrs Shotton. She works in the chemist.'

'Thank you, Mrs Croft. You've been a great help,' the lassie said and shut her notebook.

George Fenton decided to take the Morris Minor, not that it was all that far to Doris Croft's terraced house, nor because he had planned to plant out the impatiens and the begonia plants in the front beds that afternoon, but because he couldn't wait to tell her about what had happened. Sam had phoned at dinner-time.

'Sorry, George, to put this on you. I promised to bury Doris Croft's cat today but I can't make it. Could you possibly help out?'

'What about his Highness? Can't he do it?' he had protested, 'Or is his day off sacred?'

'I'm afraid Francis is not available,'

George was annoyed. This was the second time today he'd been fobbed off. Where was his bloody Reverence? 'What's up, Sam?' he asked shortly.

The curate was silent for a second. Then he said, 'I suppose I'd better tell you. It'll be common knowledge soon enough. Francis is missing. Hasn't been seen since yesterday noon. The police are involved.'

'What? Gone off with the church funds, has he?' George answered crudely, but inwardly he was stunned. 'What's happened?' he asked swiftly in a different tone.

Sam explained as briefly as possible and added, 'You'll be kept informed when we know more. Meanwhile I'm seeing the Bishop this afternoon. So if you could please help out with the cat?'

'Of course,' George told him. 'Anything else - just ask.'

60

A pulse of excitement throbbed in his temple. Always thought there was something fishy about that man. Too good to be true. Wait till he told Pam! Her idol had feet as clogged with clay as the rest of us. For once he regretted her absence from the house but this was her day at the Cottage Hospital, doling out tea and scones. Then he made three phone calls; first to the secretary of the vestry, a retired ex-army major who lived in a mansion on the outskirts of Coolwater Bay and who was always late with the minutes. He was out but his wife promised to let him know. Then to the snooty organist who sounded close to tears. Probably had a crush on his nibs like others he could mention. Enjoying himself, he decided he ought to let the other members of the vestry know. Mrs F.D. was the only one at home. 'Oh, that poor family!' was her first comment. 'I expect he was overdoing it, I'll contact the Rectory at once.' After pausing for less than three seconds to make up his mind, he rang the news desk at the Record where he left his own name and address. If there was any money in it he would donate it to St Ambrose... probably.

Then he put a spade in the boot of the car, donned his gardening boots and drove round to Doris Croft.

At 2.40 precisely Bishop Paul parked his navy blue Wolseley in the Rectory drive. It was beginning to need weed-killer. He was critical of priests who neglected their gardens. What else were they neglecting? He shut out the thought as Sam came out of the front door to meet him.

'How are they all?'

Sam shrugged. 'Stunned I think.'

'Give me a few minutes with her alone and then I shall want to see you about arrangements - presuming of course that Francis doesn't turn up.' He locked the car door, somewhat unnecessarily he realised, but he was in no hurry to see Rosamund.

'What do you think has happened, Sam?' he asked pausing on the doorstep. 'Stress is it? Or something worse?'

He listened appalled as Sam brought him up to date and explained that the police were now heavily involved. 'If it's Francis' blood they won't rule out foul play.'

'Does Rosamund know?'

'Ro is already convinced that he's dead,' Sam said forcing out the unpleasant words.

Plus Paul closed his eyes for a moment. God give me strength, he thought, I'm too old for all this. He had decided he would stay on in the diocese till his seventieth birthday in the autumn. Perhaps that had been a mistake.

The study in this modern custom-built Rectory was next to the front door. Paul looked about him. There seemed to be nothing of Francis in this room. He glanced at the wall of books. Mostly commentaries and religious tomes. An old Hooker among them. He pulled it out and looked at the name on the fly-leaf. George Freel, Francis' father. Indeed most of the books probably belonged to that saintly old man whom he once met conducting a retreat he had attended some twenty years ago at Oxford. That was the main reason why he had welcomed Francis into his Scottish diocese. Wait though, George had not been Francis' birth father, had he? Not that Francis had told him much, just that Father George had taken him on, nothing about his past life, those formative years. 'I'm told I was a Liverpool evacuee,' he had explained briefly. 'Father George is the only father I remember.' Bishop Paul had not pursued the matter. Perhaps he should have. He sighed.

Rosamund was looking dreadful. He walked straight over to her and took her in his arms. For a moment she stiffened, then suddenly relaxed and allowed him to hold her.

'Was he unhappy?' he asked

Instead of answering she crossed the room, opened one of the desk drawers and took out an orange folder marked with a label printed Complaints stuck on the outside.

Inside was a sheaf of letters, some hand-written, some typed, some signed, some anonymous and all of them unpleasant.

Paul glanced through them. Some he must have already seen for many were marked at the bottom Copy to the Bishop. One sentence, neatly scripted in black ink, caught his eye. 'I came to you for living water but instead you gave me a stagnant puddle...' dated a year back. He skimmed roughly through the rest of the pile. He could well understand how the relentless drip of criticism could bring a sensitive soul to the edge of despair but was it enough to provoke him to walk out of his life?

'Were you in debt?' he asked gently.

Ro sighed. 'Not more than usual - as far as I know.' she answered.

'Might you not know?' he pressed her.

'I don't think I knew Francis at all,' she said slowly, 'but no, money was not the problem. We had a joint account and I have a reasonable salary. The police have already taken the bank statements.'

'Have you any idea why -' He groped for the right word. 'why he's gone?'

She shook her head. 'All I know is that Francis had a past history. He would never speak of it, perhaps he had genuinely forgotten it. But those scars on his neck. He's obviously tried it before. This time it looks as if he's succeeded.'

'You don't know that,' he said gently.

She turned her back on him. 'No,' she said harshly 'I don't know. I've told you, I don't think I knew Francis at all, what he thought, what he felt, what he really believed. No one, not even Father George knew Francis. How could we know him when he had no idea who he was himself?'

She began to weep. He put a hand on her shoulder and left it there until the sobs subsided sufficiently for her to speak. 'What are we going to do? What will happen to us?'

Now he was on firmer ground. Taking a neatly folded handkerchief out of his breast pocket, he handed it to her. Practicalities were his forte. Whether or not she took in his reassurances, he told her firmly it was too soon to make big decisions. Whatever happened there was no need for her to leave the rectory immediately.

'We'll give it three months,' he told her. 'If Francis has not returned by then, we will have to think again.' Meanwhile his stipend would be paid into their account as usual and Sam would take care of the parish. She was not to worry unnecessarily. The diocese would look after her.

He was pleased that she had felt able to thank him.

Ma was still with the bishop when the doorbell rang. Jenny and Minnie looked at Sam questioningly. 'Better let me go,' he told her.

'No,' Jenny said firmly, 'I will.' Since her conversation with her mother and that flood of tears, she was full of good intentions. She wanted to prove to her mother that she was mature enough to 'handle the situation', as her English teacher would have put it. Having Sam around helped. He had always treated her like an adult. Now she needed to prove to him that she was worthy of his trust, his notice, his admiration even, so she washed coffee cups, wiped down the draining board, decanted the milk into the blue and white jug and kept the kettle simmering on the Aga.

'I'll come with you,' Minnie jumped up from her seat at the end of the table where she was tracing a palomino. At the same time, the telephone rang. When Sam rose to answer it, the doorbell shrilled again.

'Mrs F-D,' Sam mouthed his hand over the receiver and waved them away.

'Maybe someone's seen Pa,' Minnie said hopefully as she followed Jenny down the corridor to the front door.

Two strange men stood there, one with a camera which he immediately raised, pointed and flashed at the two girls.

'You must be Jane - and this must be Marjorie?' The older one said ingratiatingly. 'We're from the Record and we'd like a word with your mother. Perhaps you would invite us in?' He had a short, grizzled beard and a greying pony tail and Jenny's immediate reaction was 'Yuck.'

'She's busy,' Jenny protested but by that time both men had crossed the threshold and stood in the porch. The one with the camera who was younger and quite a dish was still snapping away.

'I said she's busy,' Jenny protested, reddening with anger and embarrassment. She knew her mother's opinion of that particular paper. She would be appalled if Jenny let them in. She moved quickly to stand with her back to the half open inner porch door.

'Your dad's missing. That right?' said the older man looking at her appraisingly, changing tactics. 'You know we can be a great help finding him. Fetch your mum, pet.'

'She's with the Bishop,' Minnie pointed to the study door indignantly. 'You can't interrupt.'

'We can wait. All we want is a simple statement and perhaps a photograph of your dad, is that so unreasonable?' the younger guy asked her. 'After all, you do want to find him, don't you? We can help.'

At that moment Sam came to the rescue. 'They're from the Record and they want to know about Pa,' Jenny explained trying to sound calm but she could hear the tremor in her voice.

'There are already rumours,' the older man said calculatingly. 'I'm sure Mrs Freel would prefer we printed the truth.'

Sam, who knew a little bit more about how press could make feeding the five thousand controversial, said quietly, 'You'd better come in then.' He led them both into the sitting room and at the door turned to ask her. 'Perhaps you'd make us some coffee, Jen?'

Thank goodness for Sam, she thought, and then she tapped on the study door.

Ma had been crying; her face was wet and blotchy. The Bishop turned his head prepared to be annoyed until she explained, 'Two reporters are here from the Record.'

'I'll deal with them in a minute,' the Bish said firmly. 'Thank you, Jane,' he added dismissively when she still hovered, 'I'll see you all presently.'

She shut the door thankfully and went back into the kitchen. The old mugs would do, and they could bloody well share a teabag.

'We haven't any biscuits left,' Minnie remarked.

'Tough,' she said and catching her sister's eye was filled with a fierce love for her.

'Pa's all right, you know,' Minnie said in a small voice.

'Of course he is.' She arranged the mugs on a tray and poured sugar into a bowl.

'That's salt,' said Minnie

'Oops, so it is.' Guiltily the sisters laughed.

The pharmacist waited until Vera had finished serving a customer, then called her aside. 'Two police officers are waiting for you in my office' he said curiously.' I hope everything's all right at home? '

Vera liked her boss, a plain earnest young man who always treated his staff with respect. 'So do I,' she said with that slight frisson of fear and guilt. Had she given someone the wrong medication? Had she recommended the wrong cough mixture? Had something happened to Bob?

The Inspector's bulky frame she knew by sight. His wife was always in the shop inquiring about some new diet product. She could see why. DI Ross's bulk took up most of the tiny office space. She wondered briefly what it would be like to have such a large lover. Bob had been skinny, a bag of bones – she put it down to all that exercise in bed, for he spent the rest of his time in his car with the back of his estate car filled with beauty products. A woman in every town, he had boasted when it had come to the final show-down. Maybe something had happened to Bob   She had some cousins in Birmingham whom she hardly knew. Her parents were dead and she had been an only child. It had to be Bob. She braced herself for the news.

So when the Inspector asked her when she had last seen Francis, she was astonished. 'Oh don't say something's happened to him?' she cried spontaneously

'We don't know that, Mrs Shotton. We certainly hope not,' the policewoman said smoothly. 'Maybe you could tell us when you last saw Mr Freel?'

As she answered the routine questions, it occurred to her dimly that the clergyman they were asking her about and the Frank of her fantasies were two very different people. All they had in common was a face.

'I don't see how I can help you,' she said at last, 'He was kind to me when I was ill. I've become a member of his church, but I hardly knew him,' Realising that sounded a little like a betrayal she added, 'but I do like him. I like him a lot and I hope nothing's happened to him. Mrs Croft will be very upset.'

The two police officers regarded her closely.' You have no idea then where he might have gone?' Inspector Ross asked keenly.

My God, thought Vera. They think he's with me. If only…

'No,' she said reluctantly and added with feeling. 'I wish I could help.'

'Thank you, Mrs Shotton,' said the policewoman and shut her notebook.

Vera followed them out of the office. She wished she could have been in a position to help. A new and delicious fantasy had already started to run itself through her head. Francis leaving his pulpit, leaving his family, leaving his home - for her. How she would cherish him. And then another thought came to her. Perhaps he was out on the cliffs lost and alone. What if she were the one to find him…

Meanwhile a new customer had come to her counter with items that needed to be packaged. For the rest of the afternoon, between customers, she felt awed by her new fantasy. What if she found him hurt? What if she brought him home, what if he became hers? Then as she was tilling up, it occurred to her that maybe she had been the reason why he had left home. Why should the police have come to her otherwise? They must have thought she was somehow involved. The thought was both sweet and terrifying.

66

Just as she was leaving, her boss, who always locked up himself, hoped she had not had bad news.

'The minister at St Ambrose where I go to church is missing,' she said briefly.

'Ah yes,' Mr Williams replied,' A strange business that. I gather they are interviewing everyone who was in church yesterday.'

Vera was both disappointed and relieved. It had been a daft fantasy, the idea that she would go looking for him. There were plenty others better qualified to do that. Reluctantly her thoughts turned to what she would cook for supper.

The back door crashed shut behind Dicky. 'I've got rugby practice in five,' he shouted as he dumped his school bag on the utility room floor. 'Is Pa back?' he asked as he opened the kitchen door. Jenny turned from the sink

'You're not thinking of going to rugby are you?' she said reprovingly. 'Who's going to take you? Ma can't.'

'Why not? ' he asked defiantly though he knew the answer perfectly well.

'Why do you think? Pa's not back yet.'

Dicky slumped down on a kitchen chair and tilted it back He felt angry with Pa and angry with himself for not walking out of school as he had intended in some sort of protest. Now he was angry with Jenny. Who the hell did she think she was ordering him about. 'I don't see why my life has to stop just because Pa has decided to take a day off,' he snarled at her.

Jenny turned from washing coffee cups to look at him, but he would not meet her eye. 'Don't take it out on me,' she snapped. 'It isn't my fault.'

'Sorry,' he muttered as his anger collapsed and misery took its place. They were both silent for a while.

'The thing is,' Jenny said quietly, 'Ma thinks Pa won't be coming back.'

Anger, misery and now fear. 'What does that mean? What's happened?' he asked resentfully.

She told him about the police visit, Minnie's jeans, the press interview and her conversation with her mother.

'Oh God,' he said, and was immediately aware that his father would not have approved of his language. 'Why?'

'Ma thinks maybe he's had enough.' Two large tears flooded her eyes. 'I'm not going to cry. I'm not,' she insisted as the tears spilled over and fell down her cheeks.

Dicky got up and self-consciously put an arm round her and gave her a rough hug. 'Enough of what? It doesn't make any sense.'

Jenny did not reply. Her body convulsed in a sob.

Dicky squeezed her shoulders. He felt like crying himself. The reality of the situation was bleak. Even rugby seemed unimportant. He was filled with an aching tenderness for his mother and his sisters. 'Where are Ma and Minnie?'

Jenny wiped her face on the tea towel 'Ma's gone upstairs to lie down for a bit. She got really upset when the Bish was here.'

'The Bish has been?' he interrupted. Then it must be really serious.

'He was here for hours, first with Ma and then with Sam. He's only just gone. Actually he was really nice.' She told him what had been said and arranged. 'And he was very nice about Pa too.'

I hate him, Dicky thought with a surge of anger, How could he do this to them all, especially little Minnie. All she wanted in life was a pony. Fat chance of that now. 'Where's Minnie?' he asked aloud. 'Through in the sitting room. Actually she's acting a bit oddly. She refuses to believe anything bad has happened to Pa.

She says God told her he was okay.'

'He is okay.' Minnie said defiantly from the door. He wondered how long she had been standing there. 'I know he is.'

'Let's hope so,' Dicky said shortly, 'but the point is he's not here with us, is he?' It was hard to keep the anger out of his voice.

Two large tears spilled down Minnie's cheeks. Jenny held out her hand. Minnie ran to her and buried her head in her sister's jeans.

'It's okay, Minnie. We'll look after you,' Jenny comforted. 'It's not the end of the world.'

But, thought Dicky, it was. Even if Pa came back, things would never be quite the same again.

At that moment Sam came into the kitchen stinking of vinegar and carrying a plastic bag with five portions of fish and chips from Mario's café on Beach Avenue.

Dicky found himself ravenously hungry. Even Jenny who was so militantly vegetarian eyed her portion covetously.

'I'll tell Ma,' said Minnie wiping her eyes on her sleeve.

'Wait a second,' Sam said. 'Put the chips into the oven, Jen. Let's wait for your mother.'

What now? All Dicky wanted to do was eat but Sam was asking them to sit down. Oh Lord, thought Dicky squirming in his chair, he's going to pray. He remembered that Sam too was a priest and tensed himself for some embarrassing moments. He caught Jenny's eye and knew that she was on the verge of giggling. He swallowed hard.

But Sam did not pray. All he said was 'I think I need to warn you that it's going to be tough on all of you for the next few weeks.' Dicky stared at a round heat stain on the table. Jenny's eyes filled up again. Only Minnie was looking at him as he tried to continue. 'The papers are not going to let this go. You're going to have to be very strong because you will have both your own feelings to handle and the press to deal with, not to mention the congregation and the curiosity of your friends.'

'Pa's all right, you know,' said Minnie still in that false bright tone. It had become like a church chant.

'I expect he is,' said Sam gently, 'but he's not here, is he? That's the hard bit.'

'We know that,' said Dicky harshly. 'What good is it talking about it?' He'd heard enough. He just wanted to eat and go to his room. Rugby practice seemed like part of a lost world.

'Sam's only trying to help,' Jenny said appeasingly which irritated Dicky even more and also loaded him with guilt.

'Sorry,' he muttered.

'No,' said Sam firmly. 'I've probably said more than enough, but I thought I ought to warn you. It might be an idea to go back to school tomorrow and carry on as normally as you can. I always think it best if you have something difficult to face to get on with it. The more you put it off the worse it becomes.'

'What could be worse?' Dicky heard his voice break. He could see Jenny's eyes were filling up. Minnie looked from one to the other and burst into noisy tears.

They all crowded round to comfort each other and in a moment Sam joined them. The weight of his arm on Dicky's shoulder was immensely comforting.

At that moment Ro opened the door. Minnie ran to her and flung her arms round her neck. Her mother hugged her and then said in a falsely bright voice. 'Do I smell chips?'

69

'You do indeed,' said Sam heartily 'and Mario's best battered haddock.'

'I hope there's no vinegar on mine,' Jenny said opening the oven door.

They had barely started when the doorbell rang. For a moment no one said anything. 'Leave it,' said Ro.

It was Minnie who spoke the words they were all thinking, 'It might be news' and Sam who went to the door.

He came back with a huge hamper full of food, a cold roast chicken, salads, a trifle, chocolates and wine with Mrs F-D's compliments. She would not stay.

Night

'What on earth have you done to yourself?' the stranger's educated voice had sounded disapproving. 'I suppose you're drunk.'

Through his half open eyes caked with dried blood he had seen her; first her stout boots caked with chicken shit, then her shapeless dungarees, finally her sharp-featured wrinkled face haloed by a thicket of wild white hair. He had tried to sit up. His hands were scratched and bleeding, his black trousers streaked with mud, his black shoes clogged in cow dung by the stink and his head throbbed from the gash across his brow. The old trout looked like a tinker but she did not speak like a tink. A hen cackled irritably behind his back and he saw that he had been lying on the overgrown grass beside the wire netting that enclosed a hen coup. He had closed his eyes.

'Can you stand?' the voice insisted. 'I can't leave you out here all night.'

When he had tried to rise, a grey mist descended and he was no longer himself.

Judging by the state of his clothing, she must have dragged him into her home and somehow got him on to this hideous hard sofa, for he had no memory of how he had got indoors from the hen coup.

He looked at the cased clock that tick-tocked loudly on the mantelpiece above an ash-cluttered iron grate. Nearly nine o'clock. Morning or evening? He had no means of knowing for it was grey and overcast outside the unwashed,uncurtained window, neither dawn nor dusk, as far as he could tell.

His head ached abominably. Putting his hand to his temple, he felt elastoplast. He must have taken a tumble. As he struggled to sit up, waves of giddiness washed over him. He held his head in his hands. After a moment he staggered to his shoeless feet. He had to get home. Papa would be worried sick and where was Ali?

Swaying a little, he clutched the mantelpiece for support. The cat wound between his legs and mewled persistently. Hungry, no doubt. When he attempted to stroke it, his head swam dizzily and he realised just how hungry he was himself.

He staggered to the door, through piles of old newspapers, an assortment of old magazines, a clutter of clothing, and, opening it, called out a tentative 'Hullo?' The stench of cat in the passage was overwhelming but the house felt empty so he was not surprised when there was no reply. The old dame was probably out bedding down or waking up her hens. He staggered back to the sofa and closed his eyes…and opened them an hour later. He felt a bit better. Still no answer to his call. Where was she?

He opened the front door and called out. He could hear the hens clucking and the cat streaked out between his feet but there was still no reply.

The kitchen was stone-flagged with a bottled-gas ring and a rusty double stone sink with a scrubbing board on one side and an ancient wireless, the sort that needed batteries, on the draining board. The ceiling was hung over with bunches of herbs and on the table among the clutter of pots and plates and candles, there was a bowl of unwashed eggs. He also noticed a pair of gleaming newly-polished black shoes neatly arranged on old newspaper beside an empty cat bowl near the back door. His? It seemed unlikely but they would certainly match the mud-caked black socks on his feet and these weird black trousers.

He could not think clearly until he had had something to eat. He hoped she would not mind if he helped himself.

The three scrambled eggs without butter or milk stuck to the pan. But he scraped it clean. Now for a cup of tea… The kettle, thick with grease, took an age to boil on the low gas flame. Meanwhile he found a stack of tins of Kit-E-Cat in a cupboard that was stocked with sardines and baked bean cans and a tin opener in a drawer full of ancient cutlery and filled the cat bowl. There were two identical caddies on the shelf above the cooker. Both were black, decorated with Japanese ladies in parasols, but their contents were different… very.

There was no telephone, no electricity and getting decidedly chilly. Where the heck were his proper clothes? These filthy black trousers were obviously not his. And where had this weird collarless white shirt come from?

The other room across the lobby was the old dame's bedroom. An old-fashioned iron single bedstead with a horsehair mattress like his own at home took up much of the space. The bed had been made and covered with a white linen counterpane that was grey and brown-spotted with age. A brass oil lamp with a blackened chimney sat on the bedside cabinet. An assortment of female clothing was heaped untidily on a chair and the wardrobe door was ajar. Opening it, he found it stuffed with old-fashioned coats and dresses, including male suits and jackets and trousers that might have belonged to his grandfather. Though he searched carefully he could not find his own flannel bags or his tweed jacket and grey collared shirt he was sure he had been wearing. What had she done with them?

Back in the kitchen he switched on the radio. The local news programme told him that it was 10 pm. Among the other items of news he heard that the Reverend Francis Freel (41), minister of St Ambrose, Coolwater Bay, last seen on Sunday morning, was still missing. Anyone who may have seen him was invited to get in touch with the nearest Police Station.

It meant nothing to him except that he now knew that it was night. Though he listened to the end, there was no mention of any accident at sea. Oh Lord, Papa would be worried sick.

The outside privy was clean enough, he was glad to see but apart from the kitchen sink there was no other way of washing. Nor had he a razor. Oh well, no matter. He would be out of here in the morning provided the old dame came back and gave him his clothes. He ran the tap over his fingers and picked up a bar of coal tar soap.

It was then that he noticed his hands. They looked used somehow, and these nails so neatly trimmed had not been bitten. He remembered the looking glass in the old dame's bedroom. It was getting dark now but it was still light enough to see his face... that was not his face. Dear God, what had happened to him?

PART TWO

Chapter One

St Magnus Isle: Wednesday May 1 1946

Morning

Six o'clock and the early sun had already pierced the most easterly of his three narrow windows causing the dust to dance. Aidan glanced sleepily round his room at the top of the tower which had once been the watch chamber of the 16th century modest-sized fortalice that was his home. He loved his room, though Kristy had begun to girn over having to trundle the carpet sweeper up the narrow turnpike stairway, a storey higher than the main block where the rest of the family slept. She had not openly suggested that he take over Magnus' room below, but he knew they were both thinking of his brother.

'I can do my own room, Kristy,' he assured her and though he had meant it at the time, he could not imagine himself wielding the clumsy sweeper over his threadbare carpet. The idea made him feel slightly ridiculous.

'Aye, that'll be the day,' she had grumbled.

Though he loved Kristin and would follow most of her instructions, he would never leave his look-out post in the tower, still less move to Peedie Magnus' room. It would be like - unthinkable. He could well imagine Ali's fury at the very idea. And Ali would be right. Oh well, at least Kristy would have three months relief with him away at school. The horror of what was about to happen swept over him anew.

If, as he had planned, he was to walk round the island, say goodbye to every rock and strip of beach, not forgetting his cave and be back in time for breakfast at half past eight, he would have to get up now and getting up was getting harder and harder the older he became. Why was that? When he was little and sleeping in the night nursery with Nan, he couldn't wait to be out of bed and out of doors...

His overnight suitcase was more or less packed, just washing and shaving kit to go in. He was shaving three times a week now and found it a frightful bore. Ali was lucky with his fair hair; at twenty he still had hardly any beard at all, whereas with black hair and pale skin he would soon be forced to shave every day and he was not yet

73

fifteen. He had thought he might grow a beard but Ali had said absolutely not. They were strict about that at school, strict about a lot of things, he'd have to watch himself, so Ali said. He shut off the chilly threat of school and pulled on his oldest flannel bags and a much darned gansey on top of his shirt for although the morning was bright and sunny, for once windless, the nip of night was still in the air. He clumped noisily down the spiral flight of stairs taking the shallow main staircase two steps at a time, through the great hall and out into the porch where he pulled on his gumboots and the first available coat which happened to be an old hacking jacket of his father.

Then, poking his head round the door of the adjacent gunroom, he called to the two spaniels who having heard him clatter down the stairs were already snuffling and scratching to be released.

'Hi Odin! Down, Thor! Good boys!' He bent down to caress their silky ruffs. 'Behave yourselves, and no sheep baiting!' He found their leads, for the lambing had started and most of Erlend's sheep lived off seaweed on the shore.

Scrunching over the gravel with the dogs at his heels, he raced them round the side of the grey stone walls of the castle towards the stable block. No horses kept these days but he had his pick of an assortment of vehicles ranging from a rusty temperamental motor mower not in use during petrol rationing, to the Standard Big Nine which Luigi kept in immaculate condition, despite its many dents and scrapes, redundant tricycles, scooters, go-carts, fairy cycles, bicycles, and, on its own in one of the single stalls, Magnus' motor bike which Ali had inherited and allowed no one else to touch, as Aidan knew to his cost.

Meanwhile it was his custom to grab the first bicycle with hard tyres and working brakes, provided of course it was not Ali's. His own bike was as usual punctured, so he took the old bone-shaker which had belonged to his father and which Luigi occasionally rode.

Taking the dirt track to the beach, he was careful to keep to the grass verges, avoiding the ruts and stones that were death to thin tyres. Whitemaas screeched above him, oystercatchers foraged in the grassy links and terns swooped low over their nests on the shingle as he dumped the bike against the stone dyke that separated the cultivated fields from the grassy sand dunes. He could hear a skylark singing high above him in the shimmering blue. A little cloud of misery gathered over his head and threatened to spoil the morning. How could be bear to leave this place? Why did he have to go? Enough…

There were only two directions to choose from, right or left. 'Davy-davy-knick-knack, which one will ye tak,' he muttered to himself going through the rhyme on his fingers and ending up turning left and south. The tide was nearly high as he stepped down on to the beach. The wide sands were white and dry, blowing a little on a rising wind. A perfect sailing day. He prayed tomorrow would be as fine. A small lift of excitement quickened his steps as he thought of the sail. It was decent of Ali to agree to take him. You never could tell with Ali. Some days he tolerated his brother, but mostly he couldn't be bothered with him, and Aidan did not blame him for that. In Ali's presence he was conscious of his own inadequacies. He became gauche and clumsy, and irritating, the way Ali saw him, a boring, whining, spoiled brat. Oh well, tomorrow would be his chance to prove that he had grown up a bit, was reliable, sensible, trustworthy. He knew how much Ali missed Magnus. Before the war, Peedie Magnus had been his friend, his constant companion on and off the water, his idol really, and why not? Peedie Magnus was everything that he, Aidan, knew he could never be; reliable, kind, funny, the best of companions. Since Magnus had gone, Ali had changed. He was aloof, unsmiling, morose when he was sober; critical, intolerant and even more impossible to please with a drink in him. Maybe though, just maybe, things would be all right after tomorrow's sail.

He decided there was not enough time to follow the shore right round the head of the bay to where Melvick Lighthouse stood. He was sorry not to see Earchie the keeper to say goodbye and to taste one of Mistress Earchie's cheese oatcakes but 6.30 was a bit early to call. Instead, he leashed the two dogs and cut across the neck of grassland where pregnant sheep, with the occasional tiny lamb, cropped the short grass between the buttercups that were just beginning to turn the fields yellow, and into Melvick Bay.

Ali had taken *Good Shepherd* out of the boat-house the previous day and there, bobbing expectantly in the water, she waited, tethered to the short wooden jetty in the bay. What a good job Ali had made of scraping, cleaning and painting her and he had done it all himself. Aidan's offer of help had been rejected and he could see why. The one and only time he had been allowed on board, he had tripped over a pot of blue paint on the deck. In spite of turps and

75

scrubbing brushes, the stain had never entirely disappeared. He wasn't usually quite so clumsy but the truth was, Ali made him feel nervous. He rather wished Luigi was coming too tomorrow, or better still, Erlend, but Luigi was hopeless in a boat, seasick in a millpond and Erland was busy with the lambing. At least he, Aidan, was never seasick.

Releasing the dogs, he threw a stalk of seaweed into the wavelets and both bounded after it, only to demand that he do it again and again. When he refused to play any longer, they retaliated by shaking themselves all over him, so he took to his heels and ran half in and half out of the busy surf, while the excited dogs bounded ahead.

Beyond the arch of the bay the cliffs rose steeply, curving jaggedly round to the east, skirted with great boulders that sheltered pools of sea anemones and baby crabs but there was no time to explore them today. Leaving the beach he took the steep cliff path bordered with primroses. Almost immediately he was aware of the cacophony of nesting birds in the rocky ledges below, kittiwakes, razor bills, guillemots, and those deceptively innocent fulmars with their vicious vomit. Behind him on the moorland he could hear the warning tuk-tuk of a nesting bonxie and see silhouetted against the glorious sky its huge unmistakeable outline. Both dogs knew better than to investigate further and stayed close to his heels. A curlew's faint but ghostlike cry reflected the way he felt. Sad.

After ten minutes of jogging along the curving cliff edge he reached one of his special places. Magnus had first brought him here when he was six, made him promise never to come alone and he had kept that promise until Magnus had joined the army. Magnus knew all the island birds, collected their eggs, one of each species only, blew them and preserved them in a special glass fronted box now kept in Ali's room. He coveted that collection but dare not say so. Maybe he would start his own.

Just below the cliff edge, which was pockmarked with nesting burrows, the precipice shelved shallowly in ledges for about a metre to a flat rock where it was safe and sheltered to sit. Crouching down, he could see half a meter below him a projection of rock which was a favourite roost for puffins. There were seldom less than five smart little gentlemen taking the air and this morning was no exception. The sight of them so dapper, so jaunty, filled his eyes with tears. 'You be here,' he said fiercely. 'You be here when I come back.'

But now he had a decision to make. If he jogged on he would come to the Gloup. He had not been to the Gloup for over two years now, not since before Magnus had.... All he had to do to avoid it was to track inland for some quarter of a mile past the ruins of the old burial cairn, thus missing the dreaded chasm.

A fault line in the cliffs running inland had formed a long narrow cavern some hundred and fifty metres long. Over the centuries the inner roof of the cavern had fallen to expose a great gaping mouth into which the sea surged furiously and noisily and then retreated with a retching noise which echoed and reverberated upwards from the dark hole. Although fenced off to safeguard the sheep, it was still a dangerous place and as children they had been forbidden to go there. This had not stopped them however. On the contrary. It had become a place of mystery and magic, a doorway to Valhalla, until Magnus had turned it into a place of horror.

Today he would not avoid it. If he faced that horror nothing else would seem so bad, not even the thought of school. Five minutes later he was there. Leashing the dogs again, he tied them to one of the fence posts, climbed over the wire and inched close enough to look down into the mouth of the Gloup. He found he was trembling as he peered down into the gloomy depths and heard the sinister gulp of the sea as it swallowed and regurgitated spume through the narrow black tunnel of rock seventy feet below. Magnus why? he cried out in his soul, but part of him could understand, part of him wanted to fall too. Part of him wanted it all to be over. Suddenly, with an echoing flap of wings, a black shag which had been roosting on a ledge below, inches above the water level, rose, and, spreading its great wings, flew across to the near side of the chasm which was invisible to him. It was enough to rouse him to reality. He turned and climbed backwards to safety.

But where was safety? Where was there escape? With the dogs still leashed, he ran for another quarter mile until the rise of the cliffs began to drop and he was at shore level again and on to a pebble beach with a small wooden jetty where Old Beelock kept his lobster pots and an ancient dilapidated rowing boat generally considered by the Islanders to be more like a rookle o' bones than a seaworthy vessel. Beelock lived in a bothy close to the shore in comfortable chaos. In exchange for rent he kept the castle supplied

77

with crab and lobsters. But as Kristy said, there was a limit to how many lobsters she could tolerate screaming in her kettle, so he did all right with the Kirkwall hotels.

Aidan had a decision to make. If he visited Beelock there would be no time to go to the King's Cave on the other side of the island, so called for it had once given legendary shelter to Saint Magnus. This was the most special of his special places, his refuge, his retreat and from earliest childhood, his delight. He would have to make time to go there later. Meanwhile smoke belching from the bothy chimney told him that Beelock was up and about and would be offended if he passed him by. Tying the dogs to a solitary post, all that was left of a hen coup, for Beelock's chickens knew no boundaries, he picked a path through a wilderness of flotsam and jetsam, the result of years of beachcombing, interwoven with vicious young nettle shoots, lifted the latch and found the old man pouring two mugs of tea.

'Beuy, Ah'm fair blide tae see thee. So ye're aff the morn's morn?' he said after he had poured evaporated milk from a tin into two mugs of black stewed tea and sugared them liberally.

Aidan was silent. The combination of misery and smoke from the hearth fogged his throat and filled his eyes with fresh tears. He could not speak.

'Aye, aye.' The old man sighed. 'Thoo've a journey to make, richt enough, but thee'lt be back. Ah'm hopin' Ah'm spared to see the day.'

For a wild moment Aidan wanted to laugh. The old man punctuated every utterance with the same proviso. In the respectful silence that followed, Aidan's swallowed laugh unexpectedly emerged as a sob and he found himself saying what he could tell no-one else, what he had not dared to whisper even to Nan. 'I don't want to go away. Why can't I just stay here? What's the point? I don't want to leave the Island. I don't want to say goodbye. Why do I have to leave my life behind?'

Beelock took a slurp of tea, nodded several times. 'Beuy' he said after a while. 'Thoo canna leave thyself ahint. Ye tak yersel wi' ye, wherever ye gang. Thoo'lt do chuist fine.'

It was a sort of comfort he supposed.

'So this'll be your last day, then.' Nanny looked closely at the lad with his untidy mop of black hair and those great glaikit green eyes that sometimes saw you but sometimes not, so unlike his brothers, Magnus who had been sandy-headed like his Pa, and Ali - there was only one word for Ali - a daft name for a lad right enough – and that was bonnie, just like his Mam. He should have been a lassie with that golden hair he kept close cropped and those cornflower blue eyes. Her loons, and she loved them all, but Aidan had been her bairn right from the day he was born.

'Worse luck,' he was saying in that voice that was almost broken but not quite.

'Aye, weel, thoo'lt be wanting thee half-croon no doubt,' she said dryly just to get a rise out of him and reached for her purse. It never failed.

'That's not why I'm here, Nan,' he protested.

She relented. She knew that was not why he had come. He visited most days, hungry for the girdle scones and pancakes with raspberry jam that she made mostly for him, or content, as he was now, to sprawl back in the hooded Orkney chair in front of the range that summer or winter gave out a fearsome heat, facing her smaller cushioned version with the drawer under the seat that held her knitting. A child's version of the same chair had been relegated to the corner of the room. He and his brothers had all sat on it and plucked its pleated rush back with their peedie fingers till it frayed. She sometimes wished they were all small again. Come tomorrow there would be no bairnies left at the Castle.

'When does Ali go back to that college of his, then?' Impossible to believe that Ali was twenty now and poor Magnus - God rest his soul - would have been a grown man if he'd been spared, and here was her bairnie in long trousers with pimples on his chin about to go to his big school away down in England. 'So this time the morn's morn thoo'lt be on the ferry.' She sighed deeply.

'No', he said with a wide grin, 'if the weather's okay we're sailing the *Good Shepherd*. Ali's taking me. He's got plenty of time. He's not due back to college for another fortnight.'

'Is that right.' It was not so much a question as an expression of disapproval. 'And what does the Major say to that, then?'

When he blustered defensively that his father would not mind, that he would be all for it, she knew he had not asked permission. She also knew that Aidan was probably right. Major Melvick was all for proving yourself a proper man. He had climbed mountains all over the world, gone up the Amazon, hunted tigers, killed Jerries in the

Great War. If he had any sense he would put a stop to this daft caper. The Pentland Firth was never safe, not even for Ali who had been demobbed from the Navy last summer. 'Thoo'lt ask him first,' she told him firmly. 'Now.'

'Yes Nanny,' he said meekly and then spoiled it all by grinning again and making a face at her. 'Don't worry, Nan. Ali's a brilliant sailor.'

'Aye,' she grumbled, 'if he's sober.' She had not meant to speak so bluntly but it was no secret on the island that Ali took a drink. It was the war made him like that, she excused him to herself. He and his brother, they had both come back damaged.

'He knows what he's doing,' Aidan placated her, 'we won't go if the weather's bad.'

'Aye weel, maybe,' she sniffed her disapproval.

Major Melvick had wanted all his sons to follow him into the army, sent them to that army school with all those ferry-loupers down in England. Peedie Magnus had done his duty, joined the Gunners in 1940 when he was barely seventeen, seen action in Africa and Italy and paid the price. Not everyone was born to be a soldier. Poor Peedie Magnus had tried, hadn't he? Done his bit. You could say the war had killed him as surely as if he had been shot by the Jerries. And now here was Alastair training to be an estate manager just to please his dad, when all he wanted to do was go back to Africa. No good would come of it. 'Ah don't like it,' she said firmly. 'Hid's too early in the year fer sailing. Thee canna trust that water.'

'Oh, Nan, you're such a fuss-pot,' he said affectionately. He climbed to his gawky feet to gave her a hug. 'But I love you, and I'll miss you.'

'You take care then.' She held him at arm's distance examining the scar on his neck which had delayed his start at public school by a couple of terms. She said nothing for she knew he did not like to speak of it, nor was there any need, for it had healed well. 'Thoo 'lt be back in a blink,' she said drawing him close again. For her it would be a blink. It used to be the more you had to do, the quicker time passed; now the less busy you were, the faster it flew.

'Where's Gibby?' he asked at the door.

'Sleeping it aff. He was out on the tiles all night. It's a wonder you nivver heard 'im. Ah'll tell him thoo wert asking'.

She kissed him loudly on his cheek. 'Write to me frae that grand school or ah'll skelp yer bottom.'

'See you when I see you,' he said dodging her raised hand and laughing.

She came to the cottage door to wave. As soon as he had gone, the tears came. Since Peedie Magnus had passed away, since Aidan had had that accident a year past, it seemed that she was always weeping for her family. Impatient with herself, she wiped her eyes on her pinny. Inside, a big black tom cat stalked tail high into the kitchen, demanding her attention. At least there was always Gibby to cuddle, bad lad that he was.

Alastair slept late and, thank God, missed breakfast. He'd had a late night, met up with an ex-naval ordinary seaman who had spent the war at Scapa Flow and they'd had a jar or two in Kirkwall away from the prying eyes of the Islanders. He'd already forgotten the chap's name, nice bloke though, quite a bit older than himself, who missed the navy like hell. Ali had told him all about Mombasa. 'Sounds like you had a cushy war,' the guy had said enviously. He supposed it was true. Escorting convoys through the Indian Ocean had been relatively risk free and shore leave plentiful. God, how he missed Africa. The girls, the wild life, the sun and the sailing. In reverse order though; he missed the sailing most, just the four of them, himself, his mate Mike, Sheila and Dora. All he wanted was to go back to Africa, make a bit of money running boat trips up and down the coast, and eventually get a farm up country somewhere in the Nyali district. Dora's dad had a place up there. Dora's dad had no sons. She would inherit the farm, Golden Ridge it had been called, a dream place in the foothills of Mount Kenya... but it was all a dream only to be enjoyed when he was pissed. He realised that studying estate management might bring that dream a little closer which was why he had reluctantly agreed to go to college. The reality for him was the Island. He hated the Island. When he compared its incessant winds, its treeless landscape and the cold castle with Kenya, he raged inwardly for with Peedie Magnus gone, the Island would inevitably become his responsibility, a life sentence and there was no one who understood. He had tried telling his father, but he would not listen. 'There have always been Melvicks at the Castle, m'boy,' he had told him and that was all there was to say on the matter. He had once tried to explain to

Erlend but his solution had been too easy; 'Hiv another pint, beuy' of his obnoxious home brew. If only Mama had not died. Nanny told him that she had too had hated the Island, but she had done her duty, stuck by the Major, put up with the incessant wind, the darkness of winter, the ever-present sea for the sake of the family. He could see no escape.

Driving back over the barrier last night in the old Standard had been a risky business. A bit 'wavy navy' he had thought at the time. He had had to pull up twice because he was laughing like a drain... He was not laughing now. His head ached and his gut felt squeamish.

Outside, he took the short cut across the south field to the jetty. It was a perfect May morning but he neither saw the oyster catchers nor heard the lark, for his mind had turned to more immediate matters. The boat trip tomorrow.

He had not told his father that he had agreed to take Aidan. When he had first spoken of sailing to the mainland after he had worked so hard on making the sloop seaworthy, he had had his father's ready approval and respect. He well understood his son's passion for sailing. Alastair had not, at that time, considered taking Aidan. He had not believed his brother would care for the idea, but he should have known better. Aidan had always annoyingly and unswervingly wanted what he wanted. 'Can I come with you? You know I'm a good sailor, Ali,' he had nagged and he supposed it was true. They had all three boys been taught to sail at an early age. Peedie Magnus had always allowed Aidan to tag along since he was five years old and what a nuisance he had been, getting hurt, breaking stuff or arguing. He was not quite sure why he had agreed to take him on this trip, but he was almost pleased with himself for not refusing outright, his usual response to Aidan's everlasting requests. He knew he was not nice to Aidan. His irritation with his younger brother had become, if anything, stronger since the war, partly, he supposed, a reflection of his own dissatisfaction with his future. Everything about Aidan annoyed him, even the way he breathed through his nose. Why then had he saddled himself with his maddening sibling tomorrow when he could not abide his company for more than a few minutes let alone his inane chatter?

The decision, of course, had had nothing to do with kindness. For a while he had been looking for an opportunity to tell Aidan some home truths out of earshot of the Castle. Why was it so urgent to inform him at all? Why on the boat? Why could they not just cross the barrier on their bikes and go down to the pub in Stromness or take a walk along the shore and tell him there? Why did it have to be on a sloop in the Pentland Firth? The excuses were always ready at hand. He did not want Aidan anywhere near the pub, there was no privacy on the Island, he did not want Aidan to go blabbing, possibly blubbing, to Kristy or Nanny, for he knew that what he had to say would hurt his brother. No chance of tale-telling if he were on a boat on his way to school, out of sight and earshot for three months.

Surely, he argued with himself, Aidan deserved to know the facts. He should have been told a long time ago. Perhaps if Mama had lived it would have been different or if Peedie Magnus were still here, his father would have done it, but his death and then Aidan's stupid accident had changed his father. It had changed them all. For the umpteenth time he told himself that it was important for Aidan to know what everyone else on the Island had probably always known. Certainly it was common knowledge at the Mains for Jennet, after swearing him to secrecy, had told him months ago. Just because Aidan had nearly died last summer was no excuse for keeping the truth from him any longer.

For days now he had pondered and slept on his decision. Reluctantly he realised the truth that he wanted to be the one to tell Aidan. He wanted to hurt him, prick that bubble of self-confidence, put him firmly and once for all in his place. In which case instinct told him that he should not be the one to do it. Then he remembered that Aidan had rights too, and he, as his remaining elder brother, surely had responsibilities, or so he managed to convince himself.

He sighed. No amount of dressing up his motives disguised the fact that although Aidan was his brother, he did not really like him nor he did not want his company on this or any other occasion. He remembered him as a squawking infant, a demanding destructive toddler who had taken up everyone's time and attention and affections, an annoying schoolboy. From his arrival it seemed his mother had been always ill until her death four years later. He knew logically that blaming his mother's death on Aidan was unfair. She had died of cancer, which was surely nothing to do with the clumsy brat's existence, was it? Although his logical mind said no, of course not, his heart shouted yes; Aidan killed my mother.

He reached the small stone barnacled slipway. The Bermudian Sloop named *Good Shepherd*, acquired by his father second-hand in 1938, looked bright and clean on this fine May morning as if thankful to be out of the boathouse where he had been painting and scraping her throughout the Easter vacation. As she bobbed expectantly on the quiet waters of Melvick Bay, the sun slipped behind a fluffy white cloudlet and a puff of wind ruffled and darkened the waves. He looked up and suddenly it occurred to him that the weather would make the final decision. How simple was that? If the forecast was good and they were able to sail he would tell Aidan the truth that surely he deserved to know. If not, Aidan would go by the St Ola ferry and he would keep quiet for the time being at least.

As he prepared to spend the morning checking finally that all was shipshape and stowed in the proper places, he felt light-headed with relief, so much so that he was confident that one hair of the dog wouldn't hurt.

Major Magnus Melvick sat at the round table in his study, chartroom, as he called it, pouring over a map of the estate as it had been in 1752. He was engaged in writing a detailed history of the Island parish in the 18th century. Consequently the table was a clutter of documents, ancient account books, maps and stained tea cups; also an upright Remington typewriter and sheaves of paper mostly scribbled over on one side. He hated to see waste of any sort as much as he hated idleness in himself, his tenants or his sons. Since his gammy leg, badly broken some twenty-five years earlier from a fall while on a training expedition in Nepal, had grown so much more painful that it now prevented him from enjoying any activity, he had exchanged his passion for hard exercise with an obsession for history. When not documenting the 18th century records, he was editing his diaries of the recent war years on the island. He was also engaged in detailing the many reasons why the Churchill barriers should continue to be maintained. It took up most of his time and kept him from moping, as he put it, to John Shearer, a gentleman farmer, close friend and his nearest neighbour across the Sound or South Barrier as it now was.

Nevertheless his infirmity had been a hard cross to bear, as hard as it had been to leave the Gunners, as hard as coping with the devastating death of his eldest son, a deal harder indeed than the loss of his wife some decade ago, for he could admit now that theirs had not been an entirely successful marriage. Poor Davina. Put up with a lot from him. She had disliked the Island, its climate, its isolation, but she had stuck it, never complained. A good woman; realised where her duty lay and. encouraged him in his. Sometimes she had gone beyond the call of duty, not that he had ever regretted it. He could say that now and mean it.

As for himself, he had never considered living anywhere else other than the Island that he had inherited from his father shortly before he had been forcibly retired. He had taken over the running of the estate from his factor and found much contentment in coping with the tenants, the three farms and the accounts. The war years were particularly satisfying for he had also been responsible for the Civil Defence of the Island which had, for a while, housed a number of Italian POWs. He had formed an unusual friendship with their commandant who had been remarkably supportive over Magnus. He missed the bustle and busy-ness of that contact now that most of the prisoners had been repatriated, except for the few who had preferred to remain behind, some for reasons he had not queried, others because they had married local girls and chosen to find work in Kirkwall; Luigi, for instance, had married his housekeeper Kristin, and had more or less taken over from old Beelock as handyman on his estate, a lazy blighter on a wage he could ill-afford. He knew that his servants, tenants and children considered him tight-fisted but there was very little capital left, no dividends during the war and the boys' education to pay for, money the estate could ill afford. The Castle urgently needed essential repairs and where would he find the cash for the expert labour required; the home farm barns needed re-roofing and the fences were always more than old Beelock, let alone Luigi, could keep up with. Perhaps he should have sent Aidan to Kirkwall Grammar School as he had requested. It had an excellent hostel for boarders, so he had been told. He hoped it would not come to that for there were good reasons why Aidan in particular should leave, reasons, he supposed, he would have to share with the boy sooner or later...He shied away from the thought.

If only Alastair were more interested in the estate, but he had come back from the war restless and uninterested. Wanted to go back to Africa. He could understand that. He had wanted to settle in India but he had done his duty, hadn't he? No doubt Ali would settle down given time. At least he had agreed to study estate management, but he knew his heart was not in it. He sighed and attempted to submerge his own worries in those of his ancestor, the fifth Magnus. He had had to cope with fire, a year's harvest gone up in smoke and most of the cattle cooked but he had survived.

His thoughts were interrupted by a knock on the door. What now? 'Enter.'

It was Aidan, and by the look on his face he wanted something. He hoped to God it was not money. He had already given him his allowance for the quarter and a small account book to register every expense. Five pounds which he could ill afford was a more than generous sum. No doubt Ingrid would cough up another quid. Most of it would have to go on fares of course, but it was a generous allowance. In his day it had been a guinea a term.

'Well Aidan. All packed up?'

'Yes sir,' he hesitated. His fine black hair flopped untidily over his brow and down his neck.

'You need a haircut,' he said more abruptly than he meant.

'I know, sir. Kristy's doing it later.'

'Good! Good! Seen Cousin Ingrid?'

'Tea at four.'

'Excellent. Should be good for a guinea! Was there anything else?'

'Yes sir... I was thinking of sailing to the mainland with Ali tomorrow, if that's all right with you?' It came out in a rush and Magnus knew he had been expecting an argument. 'It would save the expense of the ferry ...and the petrol to Stromness,' he added hopefully when his father was silent. 'It'll depend on the weather of course.'

But Magnus did approve. He had sailed the Firth himself as a boy often enough and the one thing he had taught all his sons was how to row, sail and swim long before the Churchill Barriers had been built and boats were essential to the Island. Both boys knew what they were doing. If it hadn't been for this bloody leg he would have gone with them. 'I don't see why not. I'll give *Good Shepherd* the once-over this afternoon and I'll check the forecast myself. Go ahead. Finished your packing?'

'Most of it. Luigi took the trunk to Stromness yesterday. Just my suit-case.'

86

'Good! Good!' He paused 'You all right now? Neck giving you any bother?'

'I'm fine, Papa, thanks.'

'See you at dinner then.'

When the door closed Magnus turned back to his documents. He felt happier. Aidan and Alastair seemed to be hitting it off at last. Good boys really.

Kristin added a peeled potato to the lentil soup simmering on the range. She should never have used that bacon bone as stock. It was far too salty and the Major would be demanding pots of tea all afternoon. She hoped the tatty would do the trick.

Fortunately lunch was a grab-and-swallow meal. The boys came in when they felt like it, helped themselves from the soup pot, took a couple of bere bannocks from the baking tray which she made fresh each morning, a hunk of cheese or ham depending on what was available and a mug of home-made ginger beer or a glass of the Major's ale if her back was turned, specially Ali. He was a devil for the ale.

She still missed Magnus, his company, his chatter and his drawings. She could see him now lounging in the basket chair with his sketch pad propped against his knee, his fingers quick and deft as she baked, scrubbed shirts at the wash tub or stirred pots on the range. Her room, which she now shared with Luigi up the back stairs, was papered with his sketches. Not flattering really with those huge ham-like arms, fat round cheeks, big bosom and big bum, but they made her laugh. 'One day I'll make you famous, Kristy,' he would say. He had always called her Kristy. When he was just a peedie wee lad it was always 'Will you marry me, Kristy?' 'Ah'll give thee first refusal,' she had joked. She remembered how he had been the first she had told when Luigi had proposed. 'If it's fine by you, of course,' she had said and he had kissed her and told her to watch out or he'd claim droit de seigneur whatever that meant, but he had smiled. It was the first time she had seen him smile for a long time. It was the last time too. A fortnight later Luigi had found him at the foot of the Gloup.

She wrenched her mind away from the memory. She loved the other two boys, of course she did, fiercely and protectively but Ali for all his fair looks was a dark horse and he was drinking too much. She had removed the bottles she had found hidden in his wardrobe and said nothing, not even to Luigi. Maybe she should have told the Major, but she was all for giving him another chance now that he was training to be a farmer. It was high time Ali took more interest in the estate with his brother gone. In her opinion he should be learning from the Major, not from all those high falutin' folks at that college of his in Edinburgh. But, she told herself firmly, he was a lovely boy really, a lovely boy, his poor mam's pet. He and Aidie, they were both lovely boys even if they were chalk and cheese. She put the soup bowls out on the table.

Which reminded her; where was Aidie? She had promised to cut his hair this morning before lunch... Speak of the devil.

'Sorry I'm late,' he burst into the kitchen and flopped down in one of the chairs. 'I was with Papa. Ali and I are sailing *Good Shepherd* to the mainland tomorrow!'

'Thoo're not!' Kristin was appalled. 'And the Major agrees?' What could he be thinking of letting his two sons loose on the Firth.

'Papa thinks it a good idea,' he said truculently. 'Why shouldn't we?'

'Well if thoo don't know, Ah'm no' the one to tell thee,' she said firmly.

He was silent while she rooted in a drawer for the scissors. She knew they were both thinking of Magnus. Then he said placatingly, 'It all depends on the forecast, so don't get your knickers in a twist.'

'Ah'll worry if Ah choose,' she told him tartly as she tied an old towel round his neck and privately determined to have a word with the Major. Ali and Aidie together was not a good idea. 'Sit still!' she ordered him. She often wondered why it was that the two boys had never been pals, not as Ali and Peedie Magnus or Peedie Magnus and Aidie, if it came to that.

She remembered that first Christmas she had come to the Castle. The mistress had lit all the little red candles herself on the big tree in the hall. Peedie Magnus, a big boy now at twelve years old, had been allowed to climb the steps to put the star on top. Ali, pernickety even then, had been arranging the parcels round the base when Nanny had brought in the two-year old toddler. What a monkey he had been. He had staggered over to Ali and reached out curiously to tear at the wrapped parcels. The next moment, he was screaming, his high pitched yells echoing up to the rafters in the hall. He could not yet speak to tell tales but Kristin, standing at the door, had seen what had happened. Ali had pinched him hard on his plump little thigh. At eight he should have known better. Aidie had always striven to keep up with the big loons. Peedie Magnus had been amused by him and tolerated his destructive behaviour but he had annoyed Ali. She remembered him complaining to her before some outing or other, 'Does Aidan really have to come too? He's such a pest. He spoils everything.' She had put it down to childish jealousy.

Not that they had seen so much of each other with Ali at boarding school and then those two years away in the navy. 'He can't help being six years younger than you,' she used to tell him tartly. 'You be nice to your peedie brother.' Poor Aidan, always so determined to be with the big boys, worshipped them and still did. No doubt he had pestered Ali to take him on the boat. Normally she would have been happy for him that Ali had relented, but on this occasion she wished he hadn't. She had too much respect for the sea to think it could be tamed by two lads.

'Penny for them, Kristy?' Aidan asked her as she snipped away at the hairs on his neck.

'No' fer sale,' she snapped back.

He was silent. Then she saw a large tear fall on to the towel tied around his neck and her own heart wrenched. She did not hold with boarding schools and had told the Major so on many occasions over the years, not that it made any difference. He had dismissed her opinions without a second thought. For a moment she hated her employer, but it would not do to notice the lad's tears.

'Ah've made up a peedie parcel for you, a few sweeties and things.' Half a pound of his favourite Highland toffee and a poke of mint humbugs which had been her and Luigi's sweet ration for the month and a couple of pots of last year's raspberry jam made from the wild berries that he himself had picked for her, and a tin of Melting Moments.

'That's thee, then,' she said forcing herself to sound cheerful.

'Thanks,' he muttered not looking at her, as carefully she gathered up the towel with the strands of silky black hair and gave it to him to shake outside the back door. When he had gone she found the broom and swept up the scraps of hair from the flagged kitchen floor. But she kept back one little snippet to put in her Bible along with the sandy curl taken from Magnus before he was laid to rest.

'Please let it be all right.'

Aidan knelt on the kneeler embroidered in blue wool with a white dove somewhat shakily by a great-great aunt some fifty years ago. It was the custom for Melvick women to work at least one kneeler for the little chapel dedicated to St Magnus and built by his great-great-grandfather, Magnus Melvick umptreenth baron of Castle Island in 1865. A fervent Puseyite, he had designed and furnished the ornate little building when the Oxford Movement was at its height. In those days the estate had employed a private chaplain to minister to the spiritual needs of the family and their servants who were expected to attend prayers twice daily. Nowadays it was served by the Episcopal priest from St Olaf, Kirkwall, who held a Communion service once a month for the few who still attended. His father and brother (sometimes), cousin and himself sat in the front on bubble-backed upholstered chairs and shivered for the stonework though handsome was extremely cold.

Aidan had always believed in God which was not to say he had always liked God. He remembered Mama reading him Bible stories from a big book with pictures and what he chiefly learned was that you had to watch your ps and qs where God was concerned. You had to be good, otherwise you might get washed away in a flood or sacrificed on a stone altar or thrown into a lion's den. You had always to remember to say please and thank you to God, and, even more important to say sorry, even if you didn't quite know what you had done wrong. Even then, bad things still happened, like Mama dying. Nanny had told him that God wanted her to be with him. That was a bit selfish of him, wasn't it, he had wondered. No, Nan had said. Aidie was the selfish one wanting to keep her on earth when she had the chance of Heaven. He had sort of understood, but secretly he had wondered if God had taken her to punish him. He had never thought much about Jesus when he was young. Nan didn't mention Jesus much. It was the stern old grandfather God she believed in.

Then he had had the accident. For a moment he had been flying through the air. It had seemed endless but it couldn't have been more than a second. That was when he had seen Jesus, well maybe not seen him exactly, more a brilliant light, a bit like the Burning Bush, so how did he know it was Jesus? It was the voice. It didn't sound cross or stern or loud. It sounded like Jesus and it said 'All

90

will be well'. That was all he remembered until he awoke up in hospital. That was all he ever remembered.

He never told anyone about it, partly because for ages he couldn't speak and partly because it sounded a bit silly, and maybe it had all been in his head anyhow, but when the minister had come to visit him and had blessed him, he knew that he had been blessed by Jesus and he had put God the Father to the back of his mind and from then on thought about Jesus the Son. Since the accident he had always been very careful to say please and thank you and I'm sorry, not because he had to, but because he wanted to.

He didn't stay long in the chapel. There wasn't time, but he stopped for a moment to look at the brass plaque at the west end of the church where the deaths of his forebears, all called Magnus, were recorded. The last name was that of his brother. He supposed his father would be next. Then there would be Alastair. He sighed.

'Please let it be all right,' he whispered again as he went out into the warm sunshine.

Noon

Jennet moved along the settle to make room for him between herself and her sister. They were all in the big Mains Farm kitchen drinking tea with their pieces for it was dinner-time at the farm. Jimmy Flett and Marie his wife, their two lassies Jeannie and herself, Jennet, and old Joe the ploughman with his younger brother Eric, the cattleman were there when Aidan came in.

'Well, mon, I hear you're for the off?' her Da said heartily after Aidie had squeezed himself in. He was considered one of the family. Sitting close to him, she could see what looked like the tear stains on his cheeks.

'It's ham,' she said encouragingly as she pushed the plate of thick-cut sandwiches towards him while her Mam poured him a cup of thick black tea, liberally creamed and sugared. Rationing was unheard of on the farm.

'Ah heard thoo're taking the boatie. Is that right?' Old Joe said putting into words what they had all been discussing before he came in.

'Aye, mon. Ali and me,' said Aidan with his mouth full, 'If the wind's right.'

It made her want to giggle when he tried to talk rough, because he never got the Orcadian dialect quite right. Like the Eyeties.

'Aye weel,' said her Da tactfully. He had already had his say on the matter and Jennet knew he did not approve. He had seen too many disasters on the firth to be happy about this particular outing.

'I wish I could get to go,' she said longingly. She was two years older than Aidan and at sixteen thought herself in love with Ali. She kept his tiny photo, carefully cut out of a group snap taken last harvest, in the locket round her neck.

The idea was so preposterous that no one bothered to answer. She expected no more. Everyone, except probably Ali, knew that she fancied him rotten; they also knew that Ali was not interested in her which was, of course, a challenge but not a disaster. She was working on it. She knew she was pretty in a bubbly sort of way and she had plenty of other admirers on and off the Island. She enjoyed a certain amount of teasing from her sister who at twenty-one was walking out with Sweyn Oag, Old Joe's grandson, abroad in the merchant navy. She also suspected that Aidan fancied her, but he was just a laddie. Wouldn't know a French kiss from a pair of French knickers. She knew a lot about French kissing because of the Eyeties who had worked on the farm. She liked kissing. She daydreamed a lot about kissing Ali,

'Go on, take me with you,' she teased Aidan while the men folk talked among themselves. She poked him in the ribs with her elbow.

He blushed scarlet. She loved to make him blush. That pale skin of his would flame into colour and he would be stuck for words.

'Leave the loon alone,' said Jeannie sharply and for once Jennet held her tongue. She was sorry for him on his way to that big school away down in England. Jeannie had told her how much Peedie Magnus had loathed it. Jeannie had been sweet on Magnus. She had a picture he drew of her on the rocks hidden in her bottom drawer which she was forced to keep secret because she had no clothes on. Jennet had sneaked a peek one day when Jeannie was out. Sweyn would kill her if he ever saw it.

'Where's Ali?' she asked him when the men folk had started talking about something else. When Aidan, still scarlet, mumbled with his mouth full that he didn't know, she added suggestively, 'Tell him I've got something for him, something nice.'

'Gi'e 's a hand wi the coos, Aidie?' Eric interrupted with a wink to her ma, for everyone could see the boy's embarrassment.

He wiped his mouth hastily with the sleeve of his jacket. 'Aye', he said with relief and climbed quickly out of the centre of the settle. 'Are we getting them out the byre?'

'Early days,' Eric said. 'Best no' to rush it.'

'Early days for the boatie too,' her da warned but Aidan was not listening. He was already pulling on the pair of dungarees kept handy for him by the back door.

She was giggling as she too got up from the table. 'Wait for me, Aidie. I'll gi'e ye a hand.' But he was already out of the door. 'Och, well. I'll no bother, shall us?' she shouted after him.

'Behave yourself,' Mam told her sharply, 'and clear those dishes.'

Afternoon

'You stink of cow,' Ingrid said, looking up from the spread of cards on the table in front of her as he opened the door letting in a guff of the byre along with a draught of fresh air into the stuffy drawing room that already stank of nicotine and dogs.

'Sorry, Cousin Ingrid,' he said unrepentantly and looked round for a seat free of her yappy Yorkshire terriers.

'You can put Daisy down,' she told him indicating the upholstered chair opposite the card table where she had laid out a line of Patience.

'Sevens?' he asked as gingerly he pushed at the plump disgruntled creature who growled and snapped at him as she relinquished her cushion with a bad grace. She knew he disliked her dogs. He had once asked her how many she had and she had replied 'Good gracious me, I never count them,' but she did, all the time and there were seven. Somewhat pointedly he turned the cushion over and sat down. That was his one fault, she thought. He did not really get on with 'the children'.

'You finish it,' she told him handing him the cards and sat back while Daisy looked up at her soulfully and was allowed to leap on to her lap.

So far it had been a good day. The children had been out all morning. She had taken them as far as the north barrier and they had chased rabbits and seagulls and done their business. Now here was Aidan. Good. She was glad she had made a Victoria sandwich for tea. It had turned out better than usual.

She watched him closely, quick to point out where he had missed a build or cheated as he turned over the pack, three cards at a time.

Dear Aidan. In spite of his obvious dislike of her dogs, he was by far the best of the bunch. She intended to leave the house to him, well not the house, it wasn't hers to leave, the Dower belonged to the estate, but most of the contents were hers. A bit shabby now, but those Indian prints were worth a bob or two and the miniatures, though she supposed they would have to go to Evie since they had come from her father. Evie…The thought of her was like St Paul's thorn in the flesh. It continually jagged her mind. How long now since she had seen her? Must have been the beginning of the war. She sighed. What a hash she had made of Evie. But when did one's children become responsible for their own actions? Evie was an adult now, nearly thirty years old which in her opinion was quite mature enough to know that her mother had only done what was best for her at the time, but Evie hadn't written for months. Last she had heard was to inform her that she was now in the WRNS about to be posted overseas but she was not allowed to say where. Must be somewhere fairly civilised because she had once sent a food parcel - dates and currants, sugar and tea - for the whole family. Although she herself had written regularly, once with the dreadful news about Peedie Magnus, and posted her letters care of the Admiralty Office, there had been no reply. Surely she would have heard if anything had happened to her. Surely now that the war was well over she would get in touch.

Meanwhile there was always Aidan. They had so nearly lost him too. She peered closely at his neck as his fingers turned over the cards. The scars had healed nicely, only a little redness left, but it had been touch and go. Yes she would definitely leave what little she had to Aidan. It might not be much but it would help him take care of the children. She knew she could trust him to find good homes for them if only for her sake. Not that she intended to shuffle off the mortal coil just yet. She reached for the ever-handy packet of Woodbines. Smoking the smaller cigarettes made her feel noble. The only trouble was she smoked more of them, far more than was good for her. Her cough was getting worse.

'Stuck,' said Aidan and swept the cards together, tapped them. 'Again?'

'What about backgammon or chess?' She could hear the eagerness in her voice. Poor Aidan, she thought with an inner smile, closeted indoors on this fine May afternoon with his aged relative but he didn't appear to mind. No groans or sulks. Magnus was sometimes good for a game of chess on a wet winter evening but Peedie Magnus had preferred his pencil while Alistair sulked; always such an ungracious child for all his good looks. Aidan was decidedly the best of the bunch.

'Backgammon,' he said with a grin. 'Usual stakes?'

'Very well,' she sighed,' so long as you don't cheat.' She suspected that he rigged the gambling because she never understood it.

As they set up the board she asked him if Luigi was taking him to the ferry.

'I'm sailing in *Good Shepherd* with Ali,' he told her. She could hear the pride in his voice. 'It should only take a couple of hours.'

'You're not?' she exclaimed sharply. She could hardly believe it. Alistair may have been a good sailor but he was not to be trusted with Aidan. Been jealous of him right from the start. What could Magnus be thinking of to let them go together? Was he blind? From the very earliest years Alistair had pinched his little brother, pushed him, punched him, lashed him with his sarcastic tongue and refused to share his toys. Although no one else agreed with her, least of all Aidan, she was convinced that the accident had been Alistair's fault. Why could no one else see it? 'I don't approve,' she said shortly and made up her mind to telephone her cousin as soon as Aidan had gone. She rattled her dice in the red box.

'Why not?' He looked up at her with those huge green eyes. She noticed he had had his hair cut, very badly too.

'Who cut your hair?' she grumbled changing the subject abruptly. She knew perfectly well that Kristin had cut it. 'It's a mess as usual.'

'Double sixes,' he cried triumphantly as his dice tumbled out on to the board. 'Give up?'

'Certainly not.' She threw a six and a one. 'There you are!' She moved her pieces to the conventional squares. 'I have a block.'

'Too late,' he crowed. 'Nothing to block. The bird has flown.'

She hoped it was not an omen.

Aidan glanced up at the carriage clock on Cousin Ingrid's over-crowded mantelpiece. Half past five. There would be plenty of time to visit the cave before dinner if he stepped on it.

'I'll have to go,' he told her 'The Shearers are coming for dinner. Thanks for the cake.'

95

'Wait a moment. I owe you - what?' She groped behind her chair for her handbag. How well he knew that old bag made from the skin of the Egyptian crocodile shot by her husband years before he had died of malaria in India.

'One and six.'

'I hope you didn't cheat,' she said as she always said for he always won.

'As if I would!' He grinned as she counted out the shilling and a tanner.

'You'd better have this too, I suppose,' she said reluctantly and gave him a pound note. It was a game they played. She reluctant, he eager. But in reality they both knew it was the other way round. She was the eager one, eager to please him, to protect him, to love him, but not able to show it; he reluctant to take what she offered because he knew she had very little. He loved his old cousin but would die rather than be soppy with her, the way he could be with Nan. Come to think of it, the only person he could remember ever kissing and hugging was Nan. He would like to kiss Jennet, but the thought of it made him blush all over.

'I'm off then,' he said after he had told her that they intended to sail at seven in the morning. 'I know it's early but Ali hopes to dump me ashore and get back before dark. Gives me time to catch the Stromness ferry at nine if the weather's no good for sailing.'

'Hmm,' she said. He knew that although she would do her best to stop him sailing, she and the dogs would be there at the slipway to wave goodbye.

The sun was still shining and the sky still unclouded as he picked up his bike, walked down the stony drive between the few scrubby wind-bent bushes, out of the old iron gates and on to the main tarmac road that ran like a spine through the island, linked since the war by the Churchill barriers north to the mainland and south to another larger island. Leaving his bike by the northern barrier, he realised it would have been would quicker to have returned to the Castle from the Dower House and walked from there past the southern barrier to the cave, but he had already determined to walk right round the Island one last time. He had done barely half this morning and the easy half at that.

Thankful he had not brought Thor and Odin, for Erland's sheep were all over the shore, some with lambs, he jogged along the links enjoying the sun, the smell of the sea and the anger of the terns as they swooped and dived at him. He supposed he had better pop into Erland's cottage to say goodbye to him and his wife Inge and Angus, their eight year old son. Erland Tait was one of his father's tenants, a shepherd by trade whose flock thrived on seaweed and neglect, or so his father said. Flat-footed and with a serious eye defect that had kept him out of the forces, Erland had not been able to join up like Sweyn and Magnus and the other Island lads. Perhaps because of that, he looked a seriously scary guy especially with a dram in him, but Aidan knew from long experience that he was really as soft as a big teddy bear.

Tall at six foot three and broad to go with it, at not quite thirty years old, he was already famous for his home-brew which he made in a shed behind the cottage. No one emerged from a session with Erlend completely sober. Peedie Magnus had been initiated by him and since his death, he and Ali had become mates. He had helped Ali with *Good Shepherd* and Aidan knew that some evenings they went off in Erlend's old army jeep, picked up for a song, to the pubs on the mainland.

He was not included nor expected to be. Come to think of it, he had no real mates on the Island. The kids were either much younger like Angus, or older like Jennet and Jeannie. The few lads who had been at the primary school on the mainland with him, had gone on to Kirkie Grammar but since his accident he had lost touch with them. He sighed. For the umpteenth time he wished he were going there too, anywhere but down to England.

Leaving the shore, he crossed a well-nibbled field and the sheep pen where several very pregnant sheep watched him impassively. There was no sign of anyone, not even the collies, as he lifted the latch of the gate, passed through Inge's despairing attempts to make a garden - a freshly dug potato patch and the stalks of last winter's Brussel Sprouts - and opened the cottage door. The kitchen smelled of cooking. They were at their tea, Erlend overflowing his chair at the head of the table with a pint mug of a dark frothy vicious-looking concoction in his hand. Aidan had forgotten it was tea-time.

'Come awa' in, Aidie. We're fair blide tae see thee, are we no?' said Inge from the foot of the table where she was doling out great dollops of mince and mashed tatties.

'Hi, Aidie,' Angus greeted him with a shy grin. It occurred to Aidan that the lad probably looked up to him in the same way he looked up to his brothers, so he took time to speak to him and ask

97

how he was doing. 'Fine,' he replied with a fork full of mince in his mouth.

'I'm just here to say I'm off the morn's morn,' he told them, slipping clumsily into the vernacular as he hovered by the door. Though he tried to sound cheerful his heart was not in it.

'Pull up a chair, beuy,' said Erlend impatiently. 'Ye're givin' me neck ache.'

But he didn't want to stay. It was too painful, Inge with her mass of chestnut hair loosely escaping from the knot on her nape, Angus her spitting image, Erlend with home-brew froth on his dark unshaven chin and the two collies stretched out in front of the range.

'We got a lambie,' Angus told him. Right on cue he heard the feeble bleat as the new-born creature struggled to its spindly feet to peer over the rim of the cardboard box on the hearth between the snoring dogs. 'Its mam deid.'

He looked at the little creature but could think of no helpful comment. 'I'll just say cheerio then,' he said and heard his voice crack.

'Not until ye tak a peedie taste.' Erlend gestured to Inge who disappeared into the scullery and came back presently with a mug of the notorious home brew. It was a first-time honour he found hard to appreciate having heard Luigi comment on its potency, but he did not like to refuse.

Taking it gingerly, he pushed aside a pile of un-ironed clothing and sat down on the only available space, an old kist under the window.

'Slainte!' said Erlend lifting his mug. 'Here's mud in yer eye.'

'Slainte!' he said and took a sip. It was just as disgusting as it looked. After several sips to Erlend's slurps he realised he would never reach the cave or anywhere else before dinner. A warm feeling of couldn't-care-less came over him. Several minutes later he found himself feeding the lamb with a baby's bottle much to Angus'delight, while Inge clattered the dishes together on the table and Erlend watched him with what passed for a smile snarling his ugly face.

And after a while he found himself telling them all about the boat trip. 'Can ye not get to come wi' us the morn's morn?' he asked Erlend.

'That'll be the day.' Inge with a laugh turned from the sink. 'Ali's already been at him. Erlend's no' one for the water.'

'Beuy, there's the lambin',' he explained ignoring her and launched into a long complicated tale of how he had shot the black backed gull that had pecked out the mother's eyes.

'He missed,' Inge said good-humouredly.

'Wheesht yer mouth, woman,' he told her without malice.

Before Aidan knew it the hands on his watch had moved up to an unbelievable seven o'clock. He shot to his feet and staggered to the door. They all came with him and Inge hugged him while Erlend lifted his mug. 'Here's tae ye, beuy! We'll mak a mon o' ye yet.'

Evening

John and Meg Shearer's old Austin clattered into the long Castle drive. He was doing less than twenty, partly to conserve precious petrol but mostly in respect to the old girl's dicky suspension. The surface of the lane was terrible. They had intended walking the four miles or so from their home on the mainland but with so many gardening jobs to do on the first fine day in weeks, they were both whacked.

'Careful! That's Aidan,' she warned as John stopped behind a bicycle that was wobbling dangerously from side to side of the narrow lane 'What on earth's wrong with him?'

'Silly young pup!' he exclaimed. 'Showing off, no doubt,' he told his wife, but he suspected that Aidan was drunk. He hoped to God he was not going down young Alastair's path. It was common knowledge that Alastair took a drop too much. Not that he entirely blamed the lad. He'd probably had a tough time of it in the Navy and that tragic business with young Magnus and then Aidan's accident can't have helped.

He hooted and Aidan promptly fell off into the reeds by the burn at the side of the narrow lane.

'Better see if he's all right,' Meg said anxiously.

'He'll be fine,' her husband told her. 'They always are.'

She looked at him uncomprehendingly.

'Drunks,' he said shortly as he opened the car door.

'Surely not!' He could see she was shocked. Meg was always being shocked by something. He closed the door behind him.

'All right, Aidan?' he asked brusquely as he watched the lad struggle to his feet.

'I think I've bust the bike,' he tried to say only it came out as 'biked the bush'.

99

'Better get in the car. I'll take you round to the back so you can have a wash and you'd better ask Kristin to make you some black coffee.'

'Thank you, sir,' but that came out differently too. John had to smile but he turned his head so that the lad would not see.

'Home brew, was it?' he asked as he opened the back door for him.

Suddenly the boy turned green. He wrenched himself away, staggered to the kerb and vomited.

'Feel better now?' he asked minutes later when the attack had passed. The boy still looked pale. 'Better come with us,' he said firmly. With downcast eyes Aidan squeezed into the back seat.

'I'm sorry,' he muttered.

'Don't worry about it,' Meg said stiffly.

They drove the half-mile or so in silence. He took the left fork which led past the stables and outhouses directly to the kitchen entrance at the back of the castle. 'I'd better take him in and have a word,' he murmured to his wife who nodded shortly.

He waited while Aidan struggled to his feet. He was looking green again as he pushed ahead of John, opened the back door and disappeared through one of the doors in the long stone passage which John presumed must be a lavatory. He could hear him retching. He walked on and into the kitchen where Kristin and Luigi were preparing dinner. Briefly he explained. Luigi laughed and muttered something in Italian, which, knowing the Eyeties, was probably sympathetic, but Kristin was angry.

'Thank you, Mr Shearer,' she said in careful English but she could not contain her feelings. 'The poor laddie, he's heart sick' she burst out. 'He should never be going away to thon place. He's chuist a bundle of misery but there's no telling him upstairs.'

John Shearer's eyes hardened. 'The boy has to be educated,' he told her firmly.

Her eyes sparked and her plump arms shook as she folded them across her large bosom but she said nothing. He knew exactly what she was thinking, what probably all the Islanders were thinking. What was wrong with the local school? He however agreed with Magnus. The boy needed to get away from the Island, now more than ever. Too many memories. Too many bad influences.

'How is he?' Meg asked as he got back into the car to return to where the drive forked and arrive as usual at the front of the Castle.

100

'He'll be all right,' he answered with a sigh. 'Probably best not to mention this little incident to Magnus.'

'Of course not,' she agreed. 'Do you think Aidan knows …about himself?'

He shrugged. 'Not our business to mention it.' He suspected however that Aidan must know what was common knowledge on the Island. All the same perhaps he should have a quiet word with Magnus. He sighed again.

Alistair came to the door to greet them. He was very affable and relaxed as he welcomed them in but John caught a whiff of peppermint as he took Meg's coat; perhaps it was just toothpaste. All things considered, perhaps he and Meg were fortunate to have no family. Sons were such a responsibility…and daughters.

It was well into the long May twilight by the time Aidan reached the cave. It had been easy to escape after the meal because the Shearers and his father enjoyed a game of Bridge and Ali had been roped in to make up the four. It could just as easily have been himself but on this occasion Papa had let him off the hook. 'You will no doubt have a lot to do, so I'm sure John and Meg will excuse you,' he had told him to his relief. His head still throbbed but he did not think his father had noticed his state.

He had hardly touched his meal which was a waste because Kristy had made his favourite food, Shepherd's Pie with proper black treacle tart and lashings of custard for pudding. He was rubbing his temple when he met Luigi in the corridor on his way to clear the dining room table. He laughed. Luigi was always laughing. 'You need something to take away sore head?' He was still grinning. 'Ask Kristy, she give you something. Tell her I told you.'

Kristy took one look at him and tutted significantly. 'Luigi told me you'd have something,' he explained.

'Aye,' she said, 'and he should know, 'where are thee aff tae, then?'

'Out,' he said after he had swallowed the aspirin.

'Thoo watch it then. Thoo're in no fit state for gallivanting about. We're not wanting another accident. Mind and take a torch'.

The cave was situated to the south west of the Island some mile and a half from the Castle and set between the high tide line and moor-land into a raised beach so that the sea no longer entered its dark mouth. It was an easy scramble down through clumps of thrift and birds' foot trefoil as long as he was careful to avoid the colony of roosting fulmars whose oily vomit had ruined more than one gansey over the years...

Out of doors in the crisp air he felt better and debated with himself as to whether to take the dogs and decided against it. As Kristy was never tired of warning him, no more accidents and he was more afraid for them than himself on the cliffs. His headache eased and he began to jog over the field towards the moor which was strewn with rabbit warrens, bog cotton and last year's withered heather.

The cave was deep and dark and dry, a shelter in northern or easterly gales where you could crouch in relative comfort and watch the sea lashing the boulder-strewn shore below. Tradition had it that Saint Magnus himself had sheltered here and you could just make out a cross scratched into the back wall. Earlier still, Stone Age man had left his midden of clam shells around the mouth. Smugglers were known to have stashed whisky here when the excise-men were about. Tinkers had sheltered here and more recently an escaping POW had found temporary haven. It was a place of safety from the sea, of refuge from men, a hermit's sanctuary, a place of silence although strictly speaking it was never silent for the sound of the sea and the cries of seabirds were an unending symphony.

It had been Peedie Magnus' special place. Magnus had first brought him here, and now that Magnus had gone it had become his refuge. Magnus had brought Ali here too but Ali never came here now. He knew that because Nan had told him. His memories of Peedie Magnus were still too raw. Strange that brothers should be so different. He - Aidan - came here for the same reason that Ali stayed away.

Facing the sunset he sat down on his usual boulder in the mouth of the cave half way between darkness and light and marvelled at the glorious gold and green and fragile blue of sky and sea. There was no knowing where heaven ended and earth began for that glittering golden pathway led directly to the sun. Was God in the sun? If so, tonight, the gates of paradise stood wide open. This island, this familiar world of family and friends, sea and seals, rock and sand, field and sheep, moor-land and peregrine were linked by this glittering pathway to God. Awareness of all that he was about to lose brought the tears back to his eyes. One by one they dropped like hot nuggets of gold on to his clenched wrists. The darkness behind him exaggerated by the brightness of all that lay before him threatened to overwhelm him. The immanence of leaving felt like slipping backwards into the darkness of hell. Why? Why? Why do I have to be me? It seemed to him that everyone else's life was ordered, content, simple in comparison to his. His father closeted in his study with his maps and documents; Ali occupied with his boat; Kristin and Luigi content in their warm kitchen; the Shearers busy in their garden; Erland safe with his family, his sheep and his home brew. He turned away to face into the depth of the cave behind him. Dazzled by the light, he could make out no shapes, no edges, no scratched cross on grey stone. Nothing familiar. His future was like that, dark, unseen, unknowable.

The sun sank leaving a burnished sky. The golden path vanished. After a while he scrambled up to the top of the cliffs, disturbing one of the fulmars who hissed and spat missing him by a centimetre. It grew dark, if you could call it darkness, for although the moon had not yet risen, the stars shone like candles in the cloudless sky. He had a sudden memory of his mother lighting red candles on a Christmas tree. It was his earliest memory, also his last clear image of her, his only remembered image of her and of the dark tree ablaze with living lights; just as this sky was tonight.

It was unusual to see the night sky without the hint of a cloud. He flung himself down on his back on the scratchy heather and gazed upwards. Quickly he identified Orion's Belt and the Great Bear and the Seven Sisters. Peedie Magnus had taught him their names. Magnus, are you up there? Suddenly the sky took on a three dimensional perspective. He was aware for the first time of the immensity of space, the smallness of himself, the fragility of flesh. Oh God… he prayed, as he had been praying all day, but he had no words left.

PART THREE

Chapter One

Coolwater Bay: Sunday May 24 1987

Morning

Marjorie pushed open the glass fronted doors that led from the porch into the church. No Mrs Croft to whisper a greeting and offer a hymnbook. The sides-man who flashed her a wide but curious smile as he handed her Mission Praise and a news-sheet was a stranger to her. She slipped into a pew at the back and almost immediately the choir emerged from the Vestry led by the crucifer, another stranger, singing *New Every Morning* ...Two of the choir women and one of the three tenors she recognised, all looking greyer, bespectacled, and, in the case of one of the women, a good deal plumper, but there were very few children. Four in fact, one of them no more than five years old by the look of him, poor little mite. She remembered hours of tedium as a chorister, relieved only by pencil games and sign language and the occasional uncontrollable fit of giggles when an organ stop stuck on one note, or, as on one memorable occasion, the senior choir-man's robe was inside out.

Ahead of her near the front she saw the Fentons looking smaller than she remembered and not in the least intimidating and there was nice Mrs F-D, an old lady now, who had always been so kind especially during that dreadful time... but she would not think of that, not yet. She wondered if, after fifteen years, any of them would recognise her. An immense sadness settled on her. This was where she had last seen Pa.

Then Sam, robed in a green chasuble and flanked by two servers, appeared and now there was no escape. Though the memory of that summer was always with her, a black-edged card on the windowsill of her mind, she managed most of the time to keep it hidden behind the curtain of day to day existence. But here now in this quiet place, overlooked by those unchanging, unsmiling window saints while the words of the Eucharist, once so familiar, flowed over her, the mourning card opened wide.

She had always intended to come back. It had just taken longer than she had meant, what with school, the Dick Vet college at

Edinburgh, six long years of study and practical experience on farms and surgeries followed by another year specialising in ornithology and finally finding a suitable post in a bird sanctuary on the Kentish coast. She was due to start there in three weeks time so when Ma suggested she have a proper holiday first and gave her a generous cheque - she was broke as usual - she had decided to come north. She didn't tell Ma where she was going first, though. Ma would not have approved. She sighed. She and Ma had never agreed about Pa. Ma was convinced he had drowned himself. So, she soon learned, was everyone else, including the police. Their inquiries had never been more than half-hearted, or so she believed. She learned eventually to keep her thoughts to herself and had given up arguing, for it was all too painful. But the voice she had heard at the cave was still as clear in her head as it had been that dreadful day and she still had no idea who had spoken. Had it been God? She still believed in God, the more so since that she had studied the beauty and intricacies of the animal world, not perhaps the God that Pa and Sam represented, the God of the church, but everyone had their own idea of God, hadn't they? There must be as many opinions on the nature of God as there were human beings. She believed in the creator God, the loving God, the father God, just as she believed in her natural begetter, her human creator, her loving father. It was that love she believed in and still trusted. Her human father could no more have chosen to desert his family than her heavenly father... Her God had a human face.

Mrs F-D was the first to recognise her.

'Marjorie! It is you, isn't it? How nice to see you.' She hugged her and turned to the others crowding round her the back of the church. 'Look! It's little Marjorie Freel all grown up.'

The warmth of the welcome from those who had known her and the smiles and nods of strangers took her completely by surprise.

'You'll join us for coffee in the hall, I hope?' Old George Fenton said. 'My wife will want a word.' It was probably the first time he had ever smiled at her, a tight little grimace, as if he was not used to smiling much. Remembering the glares and complaints about the bad behaviour of the choir children in her day, she marvelled.

Over in the hall, clutching a cup of the too-strong, half-cold Nescafe, she answered their questions. Yes, her mother was fine, about to retire from teaching. (She much preferred the small village school where she had finally found work to be near her now dead father's care home in Brighton to Coolwater Bay Primary, but that Minnie kept to herself.) Yes, Richard was fine, doing well, a PE teacher only a few miles away from Ma. (He hated his school but that too she kept to herself). Jane, married with two children, was fine too. (The fact that she was not fine and was contemplating divorce, was nobody else's business.)

A strange woman appeared out of the hall kitchen. Her long white-blonde hair and careful make-up failed to conceal the fact that she was on the wrong side of fifty. Marjorie had no memory of her, but when she said 'I knew your father well,' in an insinuating tone and asked her to pop in for a cup of tea that afternoon and gave her the address, she thought she might go.

'That would be Vera Shotton,' Sam explained afterwards as they walked together up the path through the old familiar gravestones to the Rectory. Sam had invited her to lunch. 'She had a bit of a thing for your father.'

'I didn't know that,' she said as a host of new possibilities entered her mind. She would definitely go and see this Vera Shotton.

'What about you?' she asked shyly. Sam was so nice looking. His fiery red hair had toned down a bit and she supposed he looked his forty-five years. 'I should have thought someone would have snapped you up by now.'

'I'm gay,' he said opening the back door and ushering her into the kitchen 'You know the way,' Aware of her surprise he added,' Didn't you know?'

'No.' she said quietly. So that was why he and Ma had never got together. They had seemed so close at one time. She had always thought that it was because deep down inside herself Ma still believed Pa would come back. 'Did - does my mother know?'

'Of course. So did your father. He got me out of one or two scrapes. Everybody knows but no one talks about it, at least not to me. It's all right to be gay in the church as long as no one acknowledges it and you keep your nose clean.' She could hear an edge of bitterness in his voice.

'Does that mean you have no one?' She knew the question was on the edge of impertinence but in the old days she had always said exactly what she liked to Sam.

'Too busy,' he said shortly. 'What will you have to drink?'

'Just orange, thanks.' She knew that he had said all he wanted to say on the subject.

Lunch was lamb casserole which Sam had put in the oven before church and she remembered how good a cook he was, all those meals he had made during the days after Pa had gone. He had more or less taken over the housekeeping and everything else, dealt with the press, the congregation and the parish. Jenny had had a crush on him. Dicky had admired him because he played rugby. He had somehow held them all together. Looking at him now as they ate his excellent casserole she realised that she liked him all over again and in reply to his questions told him about her new job.

'Why birds?' he asked. 'I thought it was always ponies.'

'I love ponies and I always will. I got my pony you know. She was called Polly.' She had come from her grandfather's legacy and Minnie had stabled her at a nearby farm. Somehow the whole experience had been a disappointment. Now, she realised, nothing would have pleased her at that time and no one would let her talk about Pa. She was glad she would never have to be a child again. 'But birds are something else. Especially puffins. Do you know....' She was about to launch into the life cycle of a puffin but stopped herself. Why should he be interested? Nor did she tell him about that morning she had gone to look for Pa and had heard that amazing dawn chorus for the first time. Somehow birds had become associated in her mind with her memories of her father. He was the first to teach her their names. 'It just had to be birds,' she ended up brightly. 'What about you. Why did you come back here? I couldn't believe it when I heard you were Rector of St Ambrose. I thought you liked your parish - in Glasgow, wasn't it?'

'Because it was time I moved on,' he told her. 'Because I was asked to come.' He had been in his inner city Glasgow parish for ten years which in his opinion was probably long enough when he had received a letter from the secretary of the vestry. After the tragic disappearance of her father, St Ambrose had gone through a restless period. Two priests had come and gone and, faced with yet another vacancy, the vestry had sought the bishop's permission - a new bishop - to invite him to apply for the parish. It had been as simple as that. 'Better the devil you know and all that...' he added, 'but it did seem strange at first to come back to this house after everything that had happened here. I missed you all. Particularly your father.'

They were both silent for a while then she said, putting out her hand to touch his arm, 'Sam, what happened to him? No one will talk about it at home. They all look at me sadly when I tell them that he would never have done what they say. I just know. Ma gets so angry with me and thinks I need counselling.'

He took her hand and held it between his strong warm hands. 'I don't know, Minnie Mouse. I just don't know.'

Her eyes filled with tears. 'Nobody calls me that any more.'

He got up, came over to her and put his arms round her and hugged her. 'You can talk about it as much as you like to me if it helps, little Minnie. Tell me why you're so sure.'

She dried her eyes on the paper napkin, thanked him and told him about the voice. 'I didn't dream it but I don't know who spoke. I used to think it might be God.' But that wasn't quite true. She was convinced it had been God.

'And who am I to doubt that, but perhaps he was trying to give you another message,' he said with his arm still around her shoulders. 'It's not always easy to interpret what God is telling us.'

'Is that what you really think?' she asked, pulling away from him.

'No,' he said. 'I believe that Francis is dead, but I agree there are other possibilities. Maybe he lost his memory. It wouldn't be for the first time.'

'Exactly,' she said. 'So he must be out there somewhere.'

He shook his head. 'If he had lost his memory I think that he would have been found. He would have turned up somewhere, either in hospital or the police station. They did look for him, you know. We all looked for him. I honestly do believe that he ended up in the sea. How or why that happened, we probably shall never know.'

'You mean someone else might have been responsible?' she asked in a low voice. It was the one question she had never dared to ask.

'No,' he said firmly. 'I don't. Put that idea right out of your head.'

'But you agree it is a possibility? The blood on my jeans matched his, didn't it? Please, Sam, help me here.'

He moved away from her and started to clear the table. 'I'm sorry, Minnie, I can't really help you. I can only tell you what I think. I know no more than you do and I have a baptism at three.'

Afternoon

Sam could have told her more. He could have told her what he really thought. When she turned to wave at the garden gate before entering the graveyard, he could have called her back. The reason why he held his tongue was because the other obvious possibility never seemed to have occurred to her. It was perhaps too painful for her to contemplate and he did not want to hurt her any more than she was already hurt. If Francis had not drowned himself, if he had not been murdered nor lost his memory then perhaps he had chosen to disappear. He had wanted out of his life, but that did not necessarily mean death. Ro knew. Ro had said to him some weeks after the event that if he was not dead, he must be hiding, which meant that he did not want to be found, in which case, she had no desire to find him. All during those six or so months before she and the family left Coolwater Bay she had been angry. He thought perhaps she was still angry. If Ro had not thought to suggest the possibility to her daughter, if she had thought it kinder to let her children think him dead rather than alive and in hiding, it was not for him to interfere. Was that kindness or cowardice on his behalf?

Robing for the baptism in the vestry, he tried to put Francis out of his mind. Most of the time he gave him little thought, but his daughter had brought the memories storming back. Her pure green eyes were a reflection of her father's, her red-gold hair was so like his own that she could have been his child. His child with Francis. Ridiculous thought, but he had loved Francis, had he not? Not at the beginning when he was so besotted with - what was his name - Kevin. And there had been others. Finally there was Tony, but he too had only been transient, they had all been transient, there just for the sex. It was Francis he loved but it was only after his disappearance he realised how much.

It had started that day he had found Francis alone in the house. The children were at school, Ro teaching at Coolwater Primary. They had arranged to meet here in the vestry to sort out the register for the synod returns, but Francis, usually so punctilious, had not turned up, so he had gone to look for him. Peering through the kitchen window on his way to the back door, he had seen him sitting at the kitchen table, his head in his hands.

When he went in without knocking, Francis seemed not to have heard him. It was only when he called his name that he looked up,

109

bewildered, startled, his green eyes bloodshot, unfocussed, unrecognising, his pale face unshaven,

'Are you all right?' he had asked. Stupid question. It was so obvious that all was not well. 'Can I help?'

Suddenly the older man's expression changed. It was as if he had come back into his right mind.

'I think I'm going mad,' he said quietly.

Sam, feeling inadequate, sat down on a chair opposite him. 'Why?' he asked.

The explanation had been garbled; not sleeping, not daring to sleep, nightmares, and almost-memories on the tip of his mind. 'I think I must have done something unspeakable, but I can't remember what it was....I keep getting little half-forgotten glimpses of - I don't know - faces, water, noise, water, noise of water - I don't know who I am anymore – I don't know myself - I can't get away from this self to find my true self. I don't think I can stand much more of it.'

He dropped his head in his hands again and Sam knew that he was weeping.

Aghast he rose, and, without thinking, took Francis in his arms and held him. His body shook and trembled. He bent his head, and, because he could not help himself, kissed his hair. The white threads among the black filled him with an agonising tenderness. It was then that he knew that he loved him, overwhelmingly, achingly. Words of love sprang to his lips and as quickly died unspoken. Abruptly he let him go and moved away to stand by the window. How dare he put another burden on this already over-burdened soul?

After a moment, Francis raised his head and apologised. 'I'm sorry, Sam. I didn't mean to bother you with this. It's my problem.'

'You've been overdoing it, I expect, what with Lent and Easter,' he murmured awkwardly. He was so shocked by the discovery of his own feelings that he could not look at the priest.

Francis attempted a smile. 'Stress. Is that what you're saying? I wish it were that easy. ...What have I got to be stressed about?'

Sam mentioned one or two names that included George Fenton's but Francis dismissed the idea. 'Poor old George. Goes with the territory, I'm afraid. If he can't take his unhappiness out on God, there's always his servant.'

'Does Ro know?'

110

'Of course,' he replied dismissively and got to his feet. 'What was it we wanted to talk about?'

The subject was changed.

It was not long after, maybe ten days or so that he had found the cassock in the cave. He had been wracked with guilt for he believed that he could have done something to prevent what had happened. He could have spoken to Ro. He might have been able to persuade Francis to see a doctor. He should not have told the police about the incident for his statement had undoubtedly influenced their actions. Although he was logically convinced that Francis had drowned himself, there was part of him, admittedly a very small part, which still hoped, like Minnie, that he might still be alive, might find his way back. That was one of the reasons he had come back to Coolwater Bay.

'Someone to see you, Mrs Croft', the carer said brightly. 'You've got a visitor. Aren't you the lucky one?'

She opened her eyes, fumbled for her spectacles dangling from a cord around her neck and peered up. 'Drat it,' she said loudly. She did not want that woman from the church with her everlasting 'let's tell Jesus about it.' Jesus was supposed to know already that she was sick and tired of having legs that wouldn't walk, hands that couldn't hold her knife and fork, ears that couldn't hear and eyes that saw only dimly.

'Hullo, Mrs Cee,' the visitor said. It was a strange voice, a young voice. She peered up and saw a blurred face and what looked like a red gold halo. Couldn't be, could it? No such luck. But she looked like an angel. 'It's Marjorie. Remember me? Minnie Freel. You used to baby-sit for us.'

She had a sudden clear image of three bairns sprawled round a coffee table squabbling over Ludo. What were their names again? Another girl and this Minnie and there was a boy... Nice children they were. 'You liked liquorice allsorts,' she remembered.

'I know,' the lassie said, 'so I brought you some.'

She took the packet between her gnarled arthritic fingers and began to fumble with the plastic. Dratted unopenable packets, she thought irritably. 'Here, you do it,' she told the lass. It was a while since she'd had a nice sweetie. That Jesus woman from the church always brought pan-drops.

'Find me a blue one. I like the blue ones best,' she said as she watched the lassie tear at the package with her teeth.

'So do I.' The lassie laughed. Hearing that laugh, she remembered exactly who she was.

'Rector!' she exclaimed. 'Your father was that nice rector.' Her voice faltered. 'He left us though didn't he?' It was beginning to come back to her. 'Sad, it was so sad. I'm so sorry dear. I don't expect you want to be reminded of unhappy times.'

What a tactless old biddie she had become. The girl leaned towards her and put her hand over hers. Dimly she could see the pretty pink hand with painted pink nails covering her old brown claw. 'I'm ninety-four you know,' she said hoping that her age would excuse her tactlessness. 'Here, have another sweetie, she said,' offering the packet with her other hand.

'So you remember my father?' the lassie asked her, so it was all right to speak about him.

'He was a nice man, a real gentleman. When my Jim was dying he sat with him all the time. He saw him off. I may be ninety-four but you don't forget a thing like that. I even remember what he said. 'Doris,' he said (he always called me Doris), 'Look at it this way. Your Jim has just gone through a door. He'll be waiting for you when it's your turn to go through.'

The lass was quiet. Had she said too much? 'I'm sorry. Maybe I shouldn't have said. Me and my big mouth.'

'I'm glad you told me,' she answered but by the sound of her voice she could tell the girl was upset. She felt the easy tears of age slip into her own eyes.

'It's just a door, pet. He's still there on the other side.'

'You think he did it then, drowned himself?'

'That's what everyone said, isn't it?' She frowned and helped herself to another sweetie. 'Mind you, I was never convinced. He was a man of God, your pa was and he would know it was the wrong thing to do. Here's what I think,' she added, more sure of her ground now. She had said it at the time and she still believed she was right. 'It was just an accident, a terrible accident and accidents do happen.' She held out the bag of sweeties.

'Thank you, Mrs Cee,' the lassie said quietly. 'You've been a great help, and, yes thank you, I'll have a pink one this time.'

She told her about working with animals and they talked about Napoleon for a while. 'Your pa once told me that animals go to heaven.' It was her dearest wish to have Jim meet her with Napoleon in his arms. Maybe not, though. Jim was not that fond of Napoleon.

'Maybe he's grown to like him,' the lassie suggested. 'Maybe pigs can fly,' she replied and they had both laughed. They had another bit of a laugh remembering her baby-sitting days. The boy, Dicky he was called, had twisted her round his little finger. She knew she had not been a proper baby-sitter. 'Too much telly and too many sweeties,' she had confessed.

'You were the very best,' Minnie told her, kissed her and after a while she kissed her again and said goodbye.

Would she come? On her way back from church that morning Vera Shotton had bought a Battenburg from the Co-op which was open on Sundays and laid out the best china, her mother's best tea-set, on the coffee table in her sitting room,. The imitation coals in the electric fire were glowing for it had grown chilly outside.

By four o'clock she had almost given up hope when the door-bell rang. What a pretty girl she was. Mind you, she could do with toning down that red hair, blonde it a bit, but she had beautiful eyes, her father's eyes. After fifteen years her heart still fluttered at the memory of those eyes.

'Come away in,' she said warmly.' Take a seat - Marjorie, isn't it? - You'll take a cup of tea? It's all ready.'

The girl sat down in Frankie's chair - she still called him Frankie in her fantasies. She noticed that her hands were trembling as she poured tea into the small rose patterned teacup. She had to use both hands to lift it.

His daughter was sitting there just as he had done! While her tea grew cold, her eyes searched the girl's face eager to find more of the father in the child. The truth was she scarcely remembered the real Francis. Her fantasy had taken on a life of its own. She could see little of her creation in this girl, apart from the eyes of course. Nevertheless she found herself saying, 'You're very like your dad.'

'Am I?' she replied with a polite smile. 'I'm glad. There are so few people left who remember him.'

'He's not forgotten here. No indeed. Ask anyone. He was loved, your father was.' If she spoke a little more hotly than she intended, no matter. She wanted his daughter to know.

Her expression softened. 'Did you love him, Mrs Shotton?'

113

'Vera,' she said automatically, 'call me Vera,' but she did not answer the question. Instead, after a pause, she said, 'I saw him, but you would know that.'

The girl's expression changed. 'No, I didn't know,' she said sharply. 'When?'

'Didn't they tell you? I told the police.' What an ordeal that had been. She had been only one of many, for apparently there had been dozens of sightings in places not only locally but as far away as Edinburgh and Aberdeen. Folk had been ringing the police station at all hours to say they had seen him. Hadn't the girl known that?

No, she had not.

'Seemingly it's quite common when people go missing. People say they have seen whoever has disappeared, but it's just wishful thinking. The police have to look into it, and in my case they did, or at least so they said.'

The girl was sitting there, her hands clasped tightly, her eyes intent. 'Where did you think you saw him?'

'Think? I didn't think - I saw with my own two eyes. I'm not daft, whatever the police may have thought.' Aware of the girl's interest, she told her exactly what had happened.

It had been on the following Thursday afternoon, early closing day in Coolwater Bay and she had taken the bus up to Glasgow to have a look around the shops. She had bought some new tights and a few groceries at Littlewoods for a change, had had a cup of tea in Sauchiehall Street and was hurrying to catch the five o clock bus from Buchanan Street which was crowded at that hour. She had been waiting in the queue and had reached the bottom step of the bus when she saw him over the heads of the long queue. 'Get a move on,' someone had grumbled behind her so she had got off the bus and tried to push her way through the crowds. She had even called his name. 'Mr Freel!' she had shouted several times. People must have thought her daft because though she pushed her way right round the bus station twice there had been no sight of him. 'I know it was him,' she had insisted to the police. 'I'd know him anywhere.' 'We'll look into it, Mrs Shotton,' they told me, polite as pie but I could see exactly what they thought. Another daft woman wanting in on the act.'

The girl had been listening as if spellbound. 'Where do you think he was going?' she asked.

Vera shrugged. 'I don't know. He could have been leaving the station or gone off in a bus for all I knew, but I tell you this. I saw him whatever the police may have thought.'

'I believe you,' she said. 'How did he look? Was he all right, do you think?'

She remembered exactly how he had looked. 'Unshaven. A bit lost, or so I thought. There was a plaster on his head, here.' She pointed to her temple.

'Did you see what he was wearing?'

Indeed she had, improbable though it was. 'A donkey jacket,' she admitted reluctantly.

The girl's expression changed.

'I know it sounds unlikely, Mr Freel in a donkey jacket,' she added, 'The police didn't believe me either.'

The mind can play weird tricks, she knew that, especially when you love someone. 'I got confirmed, you know, because of him,' she said apropos of nothing. Somehow she felt it might draw them closer, and if he ever came back... but that she kept to herself. It sounded really daft.

'What do you think happened to him?' the girl was asking intently. To her surprise, Vera could see that her answer really mattered. They had all gossiped so much about the disappearance at the time, and still occasionally did, everyone with their own theory, no one paying much attention to anyone else, least of all to hers, but this was different. She chose her words with honesty.

'I don't know, pet. And that's God's truth. I thought I saw him at the bus station, but I suppose I could have been wrong. I loved him so much you see, it could have been wishful thinking.'

It was the first time she had admitted so much to anyone.

'So did I,' she said in a small voice. 'That's why I'm here. I was only ten at the time and no-one would talk about it.'

Not to her perhaps but in the town it had been a different matter.

'Is there anyone else who I could see. Anyone else who might know anything?'

Vera thought for a moment. 'I suppose you could have a word with the Fentons. He had a lot to say at the time,' she added tartly. She disliked George Fenton intensely, reckoned that he was partly responsible for whatever happened to Frankie. He had a nasty tongue on him, but the wife was a different matter. 'She's a nice soul. Works hard for the church. I suppose they both do.' She looked at her watch. Half past five. 'He'll be off to the evening service but he should be back by seven-thirty.'

A few minutes later the girl rose. Don't go, she wanted to say. 'How's your mum?' she asked, not because she wanted to know but to detain Frankie's lovely daughter for a little longer.

'She's fine, thanks,' the girl told her while moving to the door. How could she be? Losing her husband like that, how could she ever be fine again?

'How can she be?' The agonised words slipped out and as soon as she'd said them she wished them unsaid, but the girl was not offended. She stopped in the narrow hallway and turned back, her eyes reflecting the same pain.

'I don't know,' she said shaking her head.

Vera immediately regretted her outburst. 'I'm sorry. It's none of my business.'

The girl touched her arm. 'Thank you for caring,' was all she said. Seconds later she had gone.

Evening

The sisters still got together on Sunday evenings. There were only two of them now as Lydia had succumbed to lung cancer half a decade ago. Only Violet remained to keep Pam company and smoke themselves to death on Sunday afternoons in the sitting room. Which of the two would be next? George half-hoped it would be Pam, and was rather ashamed of himself for the thought. Pam snored, though she denied it. He would like the bedroom to himself but so would she. She complained of his farting which was a lie. Neither of them stated the obvious solution because neither of them wanted the other to sully their son's room. Even after thirty years that was still sacred space, a temple to his memory, so they had to put up with each other. He had walked slowly to Evensong and even more slowly home in the hopes she would be gone. Vi was a pain, a mirror image of Pam at her most annoying.

The first thing he noticed as he turned into the terrace was the green Mini jammed in between his ancient but immaculate Morris Minor and the next door neighbour's filthy white van. He stared at the Mini angrily. Must belong to those tinks across the road. It had better be gone by morning or he would have something to say. Car spaces were jealously protected in the terrace.

116

His hip was giving him gip as he opened the garden gate. A damn nuisance his hip these days, but he was not bad for eighty-two. Still managed to keep a tidy garden, best garden in the street, he reckoned. Next door was a midden. In comparison, his newly planted blue lobelia, white alyssum and red anchusas were a work of art. Sam had once called his garden a patriotic work of art. He liked that description - a patriotic work of art indeed!

He could hear voices in the sitting room. Vi was still there, damn it. He crept past the door intending to go out the back and clip a bit more off the roses, but he had been heard. Pam caught him changing into his boots in the kitchen. 'That girl's here,' she hissed.

'What girl?'

Then he remembered. Marjorie Freel, the one they called Minnie. He had completely forgotten that over coffee in the church hall he had asked her to call. He had been stuck for something to say so he had issued the invite. Never thought of course that she would take him at his word.

'You asked her. You can at least speak to her.' Pam turned her back on him and began to fill the electric kettle.

'What's she want?'

'You won't find out standing here,' she replied sharply.

Still he hung back. The memory of those days flooded back. The bishop had not been best pleased with him; nor had the congregation. Complained he had said too much to the press. In future all press interviews had to be done through the secretary of the vestry. Although that wily reporter had invented half of it, his name had been used. 'Mr George Fenton, 67, Treasurer of St Ambrose Church said... .' Cost him his job as treasurer. Kept him away from the church for several years. It was Sam had got him to go back. Told him he was needed at St Ambrose. Sam and Pam together. Queer as a coot, Sam was, or so they said, but he wouldn't hear a word against him. 'I take as I find,' he told them at the Bowls.

The girl was sitting on the edge of the settee reading last month's church magazine. She put it down and looked up at him eagerly. All he saw was Francis. Gave him a jolt, that did.

'Pam'll be back in a moment - just making a wee cup of tea,' he said. ' I see you're reading the 'two minutes silence' eh!' He rubbed his hands together, cracked his knuckles and could think of nothing to say. She'd already told him about her family and her job this morning.

'Mr Fenton,' she said. 'It was nice of you to invite me to come. I wanted to ask you about my father.'

'Oh, yes?' What on earth was on her mind. She must know how much he had disliked her precious father.

'What do you honestly think happened to him?'

Hadn't she read the papers at the time? He had made it pretty plain what he had thought. A sham, that was what he had said then and still thought. High and mighty Reverend Francis Freel with his posh voice had just upped and run away. Wanted out. Probably a woman involved. Would have been that Shotton tart if she'd had her way. He was probably living the life of riley in Spain or even South America by this time. For all he knew the wife had colluded, done it for the insurance. He heard she'd come into money, but he could hardly tell his daughter what he really thought. Pam would have his guts for garters.

'How would I know?' he answered her and then added before he could stop himself, 'You all did pretty well out of it, I gather.'

It was as if he had struck her. Her pale skin flushed. 'What do you mean?'

'Insurance paid up, didn't they?'

'Is that what you really think?' Briefly she explained that her father had no life insurance. If her grandfather had not died and left the family his savings they would have been homeless. After seven years Francis had been declared officially dead and the church now paid her mother a tiny widow's pension. It had helped pay Minnie's way through university. 'Is that what you meant?' she asked on the verge of tears.

It was his turn to feel embarrassed. Pam came in with a laden tray.

'Please Mr Fenton just tell me what you think,' she persisted. 'I was so young when it all happened, I need to make sense of it.'

In spite of Pam's warning glares from behind the teapot, he decided to be honest. It was a relief to say what he really thought.

'Your father was a sham. No better than the rest of us in spite of his posh accent and la-di-da ways.'

'George!' Pam said. threateningly.

'No,' he said without looking at her. 'The young lady has asked. The young lady shall be told....You know your dad was adopted?'

118

She nodded.

'Well I bet you don't know this. He was the son of a Liverpool Irish Catholic. Who did he think he was, lording it over the rest of us? He kept his past pretty dark, didn't he.' It all sounded rather nasty even to his own ears, but guilt made him bluster on. 'I don't mean to be unpleasant but you did ask.'

'Don't you pay any attention to him, pet,' Pam interrupted soothingly. 'Your dad was a lovely genuine man.'

She paid no attention to Pam. Her green eyes never left his face. 'I know all that,' she said in a small voice. 'I just wondered if you thought he might be still alive.'

Her meekness irritated him more. 'Who knows?' he said roughly,' It's quite likely. As I said, he was a sham in life, your dad, so why not in death.'

She stood up to go. 'I'm sorry to have troubled you,' she said politely and turning to Pam thanked her for the tea.

She had reached the doorstep before he relented. 'It's the police you should be speaking to, not me' he told her, his anger gone as quickly as it had come. 'That detective who was in on the case, Iain Ross. He's retired now. Lives just round the corner at number 15. Why not have a word with him?'

'Thanks,' she said evenly. 'I'll do that.'

'Bye, pet,' Pam said on the doorstep. 'You take care.'

Ian Ross was in his front garden watering the annuals which he had planted that afternoon. Ruth was still out at Brian and Doreen's. She was expecting her first and Ruth couldn't wait to have a grandchild. Brian was an under-manager at Safeways, steadily working his way up the supermarket ladder, doing well for himself. He had met his wife Doreen on the till. Iain was thinking he would go round and plant some pansies for them in their strip of garden. Doreen said she liked pansies. Nice new three-bedroom semi they had, built in that new housing scheme on the outskirts of the town near the golf links, but it was a big mortgage with only one wage coming in. Ruth was thinking of offering to baby-sit to let Doreen back to work but he was not too sure that was a good idea, he'd seen too many latch-key bairns get themselves into trouble; in his opinion a mum's place was in the home.

Then he saw the girl; lingering with intent or so it seemed. Trained to notice, he had seen her park her Mini across the street and out of the corner of his eye noticed that she had walked hesitatingly back and forward past his garden gate three times. 'Can I help you?' he asked straightening his back with some difficulty. He had managed to shed 21 lbs since his retirement but it not enough.

The girl said. 'I'm looking for Detective Inspector Ross.'

'Well you've found half of him,' he told her drily. 'Iain Ross but not the DI. He's retired.'

When she smiled he recognised her. The minister's girl all grown up. He had not thought about that business for a long time.

'I wanted to speak to you about my father,' she said

'Oh aye?' he answered carefully trying to draw together the details in his mind. She stood there expectantly so he added, 'you'd better come in, then.'

He led her round the back and in at the kitchen door where he took off his garden boots and puffing a bit, pulled on his house slippers.

'I'm sorry if I'm a nuisance,' she said.

She was, but he was intrigued. His mind groped back searching for the facts.

There had been such a stooshie at the time. Journalists, toffs, church folk, wife, family, all at him to find their minister. No body was ever found, none of the sightings, of which there had been many, had led to anything, though there was one incident which had left him wondering. Would he tell her? He supposed there could be no harm after all these years.

'Can I get you anything?' he asked. He was longing for a beer. Well why not? Ease the tension. Loosen the tongue. He allowed himself two cans a night and he had only drunk one so far. He had only half promised Ruth to cut down.

He went to the fridge took out a can and turned to her inquiringly.

'Okay,' she said. 'Thanks.'

'What did you want to ask,' he said after pulling out one of the kitchen chairs for her. Ruth didn't like the smell of beer in the living room.

She leaned towards him earnestly, her green eyes greedy for information. 'What do you think happened to my father?'

So he told her the official verdict was that he had probably tripped, knocked his head, and while the balance of his mind was disturbed gone into the sea.

'I know the official verdict,' she said, 'but what do you really think?'

'I keep an open mind,' he told her truthfully. 'No body was ever found, and usually in a case of drowning so close to the shore the body is washed up on the beach. As far as I'm concerned it's still a cold case.'

'What about all the people who thought they saw him, Mrs Shotton for example?'

He remembered the immaculate blonde from the chemist, her mascara running down her cheeks as she reported her sighting. 'The inquiries led nowhere.'

There was nothing else he could tell her, except – he hesitated 'There was one other thing.' Was it really worth mentioning? He decided to tell her. 'About a year after your father's disappearance, a lady rang the Station. She had inherited this farm cottage, Thorny Brae. Do you know it?'

She shook her head...

'It's nearer St Ninians down the coast than Coolwater Bay, a remote place at the best of times. Seemingly this lady, a Mrs Wright, was the only relative of the previous owner, an eccentric old body by all accounts, who had dropped dead of an aneurism in a telephone box in St Ninians at about the same time as Mr Freel had disappeared.' It had taken months for the lawyers to trace her next of kin, a distant cousin by the name of Wright, who then came up to clear the house. 'Mrs Wright phoned us to say she had found an IOU for £20 in a biscuit tin which still contained some £500 in cash, the old lady's savings, no doubt. The IOU had been signed by someone calling himself Aidan, no surname, just Aidan. Mrs Wright had wanted to know firstly if she was entitled to the cash and secondly if we could shed any light on this person. 'There was no real reason to connect the man with your father but we made the usual inquiries.' Mrs Wright had promised to let the police know if she ever heard from the man but she had not been in touch.

The girl listened intently. 'You think there might be a connection between this person called Aidan and my father?'

He shrugged. It sounded so thin but he had always had a gut feeling about that note, so much so that he had had the handwriting examined by an expert. The result had been inconclusive. The note had been wildly printed. The minister's handwriting was small neat and controlled.

121

'Was the IOU ever repaid?' she asked.

'Not to my knowledge. I've been retired for over a year now, but I believe I would have been told. Mrs Wright let the house out for some ten years but she's been living there with a son for the past five years since her own retirement.'

'Would it be okay for me to speak to her?' she asked.

'I don't see why not.'

When he had sketched out a map for her on the back of a used envelope, she got up to go.

'What do you really think, Mr Ross?' she asked impulsively.

Given Mr Freel's history of adoption and loss of memory and in spite of Mrs Freel's obstinate conviction that her husband had killed himself, he had never been totally convinced. 'I was trained to keep an open mind,' he repeated truthfully.

The small guest house where Minnie was booked in for the weekend had a private telephone booth in the hall. She had promised to keep in touch with her mother and knew the call could not be put off any longer. Anxiety was one of the unforeseen consequences of her father's disappearance. Ma would be worrying herself sick unless she rang. She could imagine her pacing from sitting room to kitchen, smoking endlessly, picking nervously at the grains of tobacco at the base of the cigarette

'Where are you?' her mother asked after the usual preliminaries which included reproach for the lateness of the hour - barely 10 pm. It was the question she had been dreading.

'Coolwater Bay,' she replied evenly and waited for the predictable reaction which began calmly enough.

'I thought you had planned to go to the Northern Isles, Orkney, Fair Isle and if time Shetland. See some birds. What on earth are you doing in Coolwater Bay?' She asked evenly but Minnie could hear the edge in her voice.

'It was on the way north,' she prevaricated.

'Hardly,' her mother said coldly.

'I wanted to see my old home, see Sam again. He sends his love by the way. Why do you mind so much?'

'Mind?' her mother said, 'why should I mind? I just happen to think you're making a mistake.' She paused. 'You won't find your father there, you know.'

She was wrong. Pa was everywhere, in the hearts and memories of everyone she had met. In her. In this conversation.

'Ma.' She changed the subject. 'Did you know an old farm cottage called Thorny Brae somewhere close to the cliffs between St Ninians and Coolwater Bay? I gather it was owned by an eccentric old woman called Agatha Wright. Does the name mean anything to you?'

'No. Should it?' she answered so quickly that Minnie realised she was determined to give it no thought. 'You won't find your father there, darling,' she added gently. 'Much better stick to your original plans. You haven't got that long.'

'Jen and Richard all right?' she asked.

The subject was changed long enough for her mother to tell her that Jane and her husband were still together and that Rich was thinking of answering an advert for a school which encouraged rugby. But her mother was not fooled.

'Darling, I'm really not happy about what you're doing. It's not good for you. You really do have to accept that your father has gone.'

It was somehow easier to say it over the phone than face to face. 'What if he hasn't, Ma? What if he's out there just waiting to be found?'

'Don't you see?' she said with a sigh of exasperation. 'Whatever happened to him, whether he's dead or still 'out there' as you put it, he left us. Left us, Minnie! You have to accept that if he's still alive - and it's a very big if - he doesn't want to be found. Don't you think it's better, kinder even, to let him go? '

She had never said so much, spoken so freely. No wonder she had always been, and still was, so angry. But there was something else that Minnie had not realised. Ma was not sure either that he was dead.

Morning

She had always planned to visit the cave. Now there was the added incentive of finding the cottage, Thorny Brae. Although she knew with her logical mind that the possibility of her father having been there fifteen years ago was slight, she could not help feeling excited and optimistic. Mr Ross had already warned her that the walk from the shore would be difficult. The cliffs were high and access from below impossible at high tide. Nevertheless she was determined to try. If her father had found refuge there, he must have walked from the cave. She supposed she should have telephoned this Freda Wright to warn her of her visit but decided that she would prefer to arrive unannounced if she arrived at all.

The shore was much as she remembered it, sandy below the paved esplanade with its scatter of dry seaweed, broken shells and driftwood along the high water-line. The tide was midway, going out, a comforting background susurrus to her mind-full of memories. Here as children they had dug moated sandcastles, created rivers and dams, spent long sunny afternoons lost in a miniature geography of mountains, canyons and lochs. Beyond the bay, rocks cradled small pools lined with frilly anemones where baby crabs scuttled through underwater gardens of pink and emerald weed. Golden lichen decorated the older rock, long ago abandoned by the tide, while mussels, limpets and barnacles clung to those that were still washed daily by the restless water. Sun shone from a blue and feathered sky.

On she walked while the cliffs soared up above her, pocketed with thrift and bird's foot trefoil. Nothing had changed since the last time she had been here except that now she now knew the habits and habitat of the pair of lesser black back gulls that stared at her stonily as she passed their nest on a high rock stack that poked a few feet out of the water, well clear of the highest of tides, the wheeling herring gulls intent only on food, and, roosting on ledges in the cliffs beyond spitting danger, some half dozen fulmars. As she watched, one took off soaring into the sunny sky, a miracle of engineering, economy and beauty. And some people, her tutor included, scorned a creator! Let them try to make anything half so perfect and then imbue it with life. It had been a running battle with her contemporaries through most of her college days, creationism versus Darwin. Why not both, she would argue, for this was what she had been taught by a wiser man... Oh Pa, I will find you.... It occurred to her that the battle she had waged in university was in some ways similar to the battle she had fought for fifteen years with her mother. It was all to do with faith.

The cave, situated half way between the shore and the cliff top looked smaller, dirtier and less significant than she remembered. Hardly a cave at all, just a tapering hollow the sea had once washed smooth. Panting a little from the climb she sat down on the boulder just inside the entrance and thought about the voice she had heard all those years ago, or thought she had heard. 'All is well.' She had gone over it so often that she could no longer be sure that it had come from outside or within her mind. At the time she had been so sure she had heard it that she had risen and gone out to look for the speaker. Although she would still insist that she had heard it to those who questioned, she could no longer be sure. She might be remembering wrongly.

Once again she opened up her mind and listened but all she heard was a little wind, a lot of sea and the harsh deep chatter of a peregrine. Instinctively she rose, stepped out of the cave wishing she had brought her binoculars and there it was with its long wings winnowing the air above her. For a moment, as she watched the bird until it soared out of sight, she forgot her father, until, glancing down, at her feet, she recognised the rock where she had found the blood. His blood, that much at least had been proved. Touching it tenderly with her forefinger she fancied she could still trace a faint rusty stain.

For the first five or six miles the shore walk was difficult as she leapt from boulder to boulder or scrambled over smaller stones some slippery with seaweed. If the tide had not been on the ebb she would never have been able to go on. It was an exhausting trek but finally some four hours later she reached a small gravel bay bisected by a burn which had carved a deep cleft through the cliffs. The steep sides of the valley were overgrown with bushes of golden whin and thickets of thorny bramble, while umbrella handles of sprouting bracken poked through patches of primrose and wild hyacinth, but she could just make out a path of sorts beaten upwards through the jungle of undergrowth that clothed the ancient sea-abandoned cliff line beyond the burn. This must be the place.

Stung by vicious young nettles and torn by brambles, she struggled up the path and over a barbed wire fence to find herself at the top of the cliffs in a field with two ponies. For a moment, her quest, her scratches and her weariness were forgotten as she coaxed the pretty creatures to come to her. Willingly they allowed themselves to be talked to, stroked and loved. Sadly she remembered that a pony was all she had ever wanted in those long ago days, and how, overnight, the agenda had changed.

The ponies accompanied her across the field to a wooden gate which opened into a forestry ride which led her through a wide stand of close stunted pine which provided shelter from the prevailing west wind for the white-washed cottage which stood in a well-tended but obviously recently-designed garden. Everything about the place except the building itself seemed new and hopeful. This must be Thorny Brae.

Standing at the garden gate she felt suddenly shy, stupid and hungry. She wanted not to be here but the thought of the long trail back was daunting. She tried to imagine her father bleeding and disorientated arriving at this place all those years ago and found it hard, but not impossible. No, not impossible. With that thought in mind she entered the wooden porch and pressed the bell. She could hear its chime ding-donging 'Rule Britannia' inside the house.

A plump little woman came to the door. 'Ghastly, isn't it!' she said unexpectedly. When Minnie looked blank, she explained. 'Those chimes. My son fitted them and I didn't have the heart to complain.'

She was about to explain who she was, but the woman already knew. 'You must be Marjorie Freel' she said warmly. 'I'm Freda Wright. Come in, dear. That nice policeman - retired isn't he? - phoned me this morning to tell me about you. Just look at you, all scratches and stings! I expect you'd like to wash and put some Savlon on those cuts. Did you climb the cliff? I'm afraid the old path is completely overgrown. Are you hungry? I've made some sandwiches.'

Minnie could not get a word in, but hey, who cared? She liked this bustling little woman and she was starving. 'Thanks,' was all she needed to say.

The bathroom was sparkling with mirrors and gleaming tiles and one of those round baths in avocado which she had always wanted to try. After washing her face, dabbing antiseptic cream on her

126

arms, she looked at herself in the mirror. Her hair, like the burning bush most of the time, was wilder than usual. Her usually pale freckled face had a healthy flush and her eyes were excited. She had a good feeling about this place. Back in the immaculate kitchen which sported every gadget imaginable, she found her hostess ready with the kettle, 'Tea or coffee, dear?'

She opted for tea, 'I think I could drink a gallon.'

'We'll take this into my den, dear,' Freda said picking up the tray laden with ham-filled rolls and sponge cake. 'It's more me.'

The sunny porch at the back of the house was a clutter from floor to ceiling of magazines, papers, photographs, knitting and embroidery materials and an ancient treadle sewing machine which looked a bit forlorn. 'It came with the house, dear. I hadn't the heart to get rid of it.'

Minnie touched it briefly. Perhaps Pa... She cut off the thought before it could take a proper shape.

'We're doing up the house to put on the market. Everything gets dumped in here,' Freda explained. 'You should have seen it when we took it over. No electricity, no hot water would you believe, just an ancient Calor gas cooker. My poor old cousin lived in a midden, not that she didn't have pots of money, literally; we found it everywhere, in biscuit tins, tea caddies under the bed, inside the cushions and in the bank. We were the ones with no cash.' She laughed. 'Gerry and me. That's my son. He lives with me. Has a few problems,' she tapped her head significantly, 'but he's great with his hands. He's a good lad, really. Lad? What am I talking about? He'll be forty next birthday. He looks after the ponies. We stable them for a couple of sisters in St Ninians. Gives him something to do.'

When she could get a word in, Minnie explained why she had come.

'Yes, dear' she said nodding. 'I heard all about it. A sad business. I gather your dad was never found. I remember when my man left me, on account of Gerry being the way he was, but that's another story...' She paused for breath and then asked. 'Did you think your dad might have come here?'

Minnie did not answer. Instead she asked about the IOU.

Freda explained. 'It was in a biscuit tin full of cash. I could show you if you liked, but there was no indication of when the money was borrowed. It could have been any time.'

'Was it ever repaid?' Minnie asked.

'Oh yes, dear, in three ten pound notes, the extra ten to cover his expenses here. I suppose I should have told them at the Police Station but Inspector Ross had retired and I never got round to it. Such a nice letter, it was. It took a while to come because he was not sure of my old cousin's address. It's a wonder it got here at all. The Post Office is wonderful, don't you think, dear?'

'He?' she asked

'I don't think he had anything to do with your dad, dear. His name was Aidan, Aidan Melvick, if I remember right. I still have the letter somewhere. I sent him a thank-you card. Would you like to see the letter?'

She nodded, unable to speak, eat or think while Freda routed through a mound of papers on a table by the window.

The letter had been type-written, the post-mark blurred almost beyond recognition. With careful fingers she took out the short undated note written on paper headed 'The Castle Island' and addressed to 'Miss Agatha, the Cottage on the Cliffs, by St Ninians'. It contained a graceful apology for the delay, a warm thank-you for her hospitality, the hope that the sum was sufficient to cover his expenses and the sum borrowed. It was signed 'Aidan Melvick'. What more she had expected, she no longer knew, but she could not help the rush of tears to her eyes.

'I should go,' she said still clutching the letter, for although there was no hint of her father in the single typed page or in the sprawling signature so unlike her father's neat hand, she could not bear to part with it.

Conscious of her brimming eyes, Freda patted her hand and told her indulgently to keep the letter, if she liked. 'It would just go into the bin here.'

Freda insisted on giving her a lift. 'You've walked enough for one day, dear. Give me five minutes and I'll drive you back to Coolwater Bay. I have to pick up Gerry. He goes to woodwork classes in the school there.'

After Freda had left the room to get ready, she studied the postmark on the envelope more carefully. Although the date was smudged beyond recognition, three letters were just legible. Stro- might be Stromness, in Orkney, she thought, how weird. She had planned to drive north the following day.

Evening

Sam watched her from the kitchen window as she walked up through the garden to the back door. There was a lightness in her step that he had not noticed yesterday. Poor little Minnie Mouse. She had so obviously never come to terms with Francis' loss and perhaps never would. None of them had been able to settle. According to Minnie, Ro had become nervous and perpetually anxious. Jane found relationships difficult and Dicky was restless and unhappy in his work. Perhaps the least damaged was this small young woman with her flaming hair and eager eyes. She lived in faith and in hope. What more was one expected to do?

He opened the door and kissed her welcome on both her scratched cheeks. 'You 've been in the wars!' he joked.

She explained about her walk from the cave. 'I've just come to say goodbye. I'm off tomorrow.'

'Home?' he asked, 'or twitching?'

'I want to look at puffins in Orkney and if there's time do Shetland and the Fair Isle too. There's a ferry I can catch the day after tomorrow.'

She told him about the people she had visited and he laughed. 'I already know all about it. Pam Fenton phoned to tell me and Vera Shotton told me in the chemist. I gather you also saw Iain Ross?'

'But you won't know about Freda Wright.' After she had told him about her visit to Thorny Brae, she took the letter out of her shoulder bag.

He read the bland sentences and the scrawled signature which in no way resembled Francis' neat controlled writing and his heart sank. 'Is this why you're going to Orkney?' he asked.

'I was going anyway,' she said truthfully. Then she turned on him. 'Sam, for the last fifteen years I've been praying every night on my knees beside my bed to find my father. Don't you think that God listens? Don't you think this just might possibly be an answer? Don't you believe in what you preach anymore?'

He thought for a moment. It was a question that had often been hurled at him by unhappy parishioners.

'What you have to remember is that God can see the overall picture. Perhaps you're not listening to him because you don't want to hear the truth. Perhaps he's trying to tell you that it's time for you to get on with your own life. You're a lovely young girl. Have you ever fallen fall in love.'

She shook her head. 'Not really.' There had been several students she had liked, one quite a lot, but it had never really been love, or not what she understood as love. 'First things first. I still believe Pa might be alive and that I might well find him. I have to try.'

He said nothing. Looking down at the letter in his hand, he supposed she could be right. What then? God help them all.

'Sam,' she said after a pause, 'what was my father really like? I've sort of forgotten. I don't suppose I ever really knew him, did I?'

Now was not the time for platitudes. 'I don't know if I'm the right person to ask,' he answered thoughtfully. 'I saw his professional side and you couldn't fault that but I wonder if anyone really knew Francis. I sometimes wonder if he knew himself. I remember your mother saying that she never knew what he was thinking. We're all of us at least two persons, Minnie. The one we present to other people and the one inside our heads. Mostly you can get glimpses of the inside person from time to time, but with your father it was different. His inner person was a complete mystery to me…. at least most of the time.' He hesitated.

'Most of the time?' she prompted.

'He had his demons – as we all do.' He decided to tell her about the time he had found him in the kitchen. 'I know it's a cliché, but he seemed like a lost soul. He was at the end of his tether, which was one of the reasons why your mother - we were all so sure he had put an end to it.' He watched the tears gather in her eyes. 'I'm sorry, Minnie, You wanted to know about your dad and I haven't been much help. All I can tell you is that I loved him too, but I can't say I ever knew him.'

'Poor Pa,' was all she said. He gave her back the letter which she folded carefully and put back into her bag.

He offered her something to drink but she refused. 'Keep in touch,' he said as he hugged her goodbye.

Jane counted the rings, four, five, six. Who on earth …at this time of night just when she was trying to get Amy to settle. Furiously she snatched up the receiver. 'Yes?' she snapped.

'It's me. Not a good time?'

Her rage fell away like a heavy cloak. 'Marge! I'm trying to get Barbie to settle. She's being a complete pain in the ass.' She could say outrageous things to her sister, who knew that it was only her way.

'I'm sorry. I'll ring back.'

'No you bloody won't,' Jane said, then with her hand over the receiver turned to her elder child. 'For heaven's sake shut up. Barbie. You'll wake Amy. I'll finish the story later, I promise.' Her daughter pacified, she turned back to her sister 'You're the first civilised person I've spoken to all day. Where are you?'

When Marge told her she was silent for a moment as memories hurtled into her mind. 'Why that God-awful place?' she asked contemptuously, 'Get a life, Marge.'

'Sam sends his love.'

'Who needs it,' she answered shortly.

'Mrs Croft's in a home. She sends you her love. Mrs F-D has become a little old lady. Mrs F-D! Old Fenton was very Mr Fenton-ish.'

'I'm not interested,' she told her sister dismissively but she was and she knew that Marjorie knew it.

'Remember that weird woman with the sexy voice who worked in the chemist? She reckons she saw Pa in Buchanan Street Bus station just a few days after he went away.'

Barbie was whining again, 'I want a story.'

'For God's sake!' Suddenly she was angry. For fifteen years she had been battling with anger, losing it temporarily in the arms of lovers of whom there had been more than she could remember, from the first on a flat gravestone at St Ambrose with a youth in a Beatles T-shirt who stank of cigarettes, to the last who had come to fit new blinds and left her with Barbie, though she could not be sure of that. She was still sleeping with Tom, who was still her husband after six rocky years but not for much longer, or so he threatened. Sometimes she wished he would just go. Anything was better than this see-saw relationship, on, off, on-shore off-shore. The only good thing about it was the money. Turning back to the phone she told her sister, 'I really don't need this right now'

'I'm sorry,' Marge said and added after a pause, 'How is Tom?'

'Still on a rig in Norway. Due to come back next week, but who knows? Who cares'

'He'll be back, you'll see. I'm sure he loves you, Jen, and the girls.'

The silence that followed spoke for itself. Pa loved us, didn't he? But he left us.

'Jane,' she said quickly as if she knew that her sister would not want to hear what she had to say, 'What would you think if I found Pa?'

Barbie started to sob outright.

'Look, Marge, I'm sorry, I really do have to go,' she shouted over the noise but the question hung over her long after she had replaced the receiver. What would she say to him? Could she ever forgive him? Not until she had told him that everything in her life had gone wrong after he left. Was it really all his fault? Of course not, it only seemed that way.

After a while Barbie settled. She was only three. She kissed her and looked in on her other little daughter, five-year old Amy who, thank God, was deeply asleep in a scatter of toys and books. As she tidied the room on silent feet, anger lent a new purpose to her fingers and energy to her tired body. Was it better to have a father who deserted you or not to have a father at all? The little girls barely knew Tom. Perhaps it would be best if he left now rather than let them grow to love him.

'I've been trying to get you all evening, Richard. How are things?'

'Fine,' he said swallowing the last dregs of his first beer of the evening, 'Just fine, Ma.' What else was he expected to say? Things were not fine. Lucy, his girl-friend of three years, who was on the English staff at the school he endured had written him a 'Dear John'. He didn't entirely blame her. Too many nights coaching football, too many broken dates, too many beers. God, how he hated the school, his rooms, the staff room bicker.

'How's Lucy?' she asked. Ma liked Lucy.

'Fine, thanks,'

'Dicky.' (God, how he hated that name). 'I'm really worried about Marjorie.'

Briefly his mother explained about his sister. 'She's never really accepted that your father's gone, and now there she is, about to start on a really good job, away on this wild goose chase, raking up old memories, upsetting herself.'

And everyone else, by the sound of it, Richard thought. 'Maybe it's just something she has to do, Ma,' he said patiently.

'I wish you'd have a word with her.'

Ma was always wanting him to have a word with either Jane or Marjorie. No doubt, he thought ironically, she asked them to have a word with him.

'She'll be okay, Ma. Stop worrying so much. It's not as if she's going to find Pa, is it?'

Then there would be really something to worry about, he thought. Why could they not just let him rest in peace? He no longer wondered why his father had killed himself. The longer he lived in this God-damned world, the more sense he could see in what his father had done. What was the point of it all? It would be better all round if he were out of it too.

'Are you still there, Dicky?'

'Yes, Ma, I'm still here,' he said wearily. Where did she think he had gone?

'I do worry about her...I worry about you all.'

'I know you do. Maybe you have to stop worrying about us and get on with your own life. Pa's not going to turn up just because Margie wants him to.' He's got more sense he thought bitterly.

'How's the job going?'

'Fine,' he said evenly. That was not a path he intended to follow, not tonight.

'Will I see you on Sunday?'

'Probably.' Sunday lunch had become a fixture but she always asked.

After a few more questions the conversation petered unsatisfactorily to an end.

When she had gone he sat for a while staring at the phone. Conversations with Ma always left him more depressed than before they began. He reckoned Pa still dominated her life and thoughts just as they did with Margie, but whereas his sister was annoyingly positive, quite mad, Ma was different. No doubt she still controlled her classroom but at home she was too involved in the lives of her children, eternally anxious for them. Poor Ma. Guiltily he wished he could be more patient, more affectionate with her, but truthfully, the responsibility, Pa's responsibility, was often a burden too heavy.

Without thinking about it he opened the fridge and took out another beer.

133

Although days passed when Ro did not actively think of Francis, since Marjorie had rung the previous evening she had not been able to get him out of her mind. Over the years, fifteen of them, a strange thing had happened; she had fallen in love with her husband all over again. She no longer remembered her irritation and anger. They had been replaced by guilt. If only she had been kinder, more understanding, less complaining, if only we had our time over again, how different she would have been.

She remembered with renewed anguish the times when he had woken her in the night haunted by dreams. Instead of soothing him as he thrashed and moaned she had complained. 'For God's sake, Francis, shut up, how can I cope with a class tomorrow if don't get my sleep?' or huffing and grumbling, she had swept out of their bedroom and gone into the spare room to snatch some peace. If she had bothered to listen to him, stopped to comfort him or insisted he see the GP, how different it might have been. Regret dominated her life. It was not as if she hadn't had opportunities to move on, even to fall in love again but it had been impossible. Recently, regret had given way to acute anxiety. Whenever the children were out of her sight she worried.

And now this…

The memory was always the same. She was twenty-one again and he twenty-five and a minor canon at the Cathedral. The C of E school in Chesston was gathered in the hall for morning assembly. The teachers stood at the end of their rows of classes, she had the Primary Threes at that time. Francis, in clerical collar, young, with those incredible dark lashed green eyes had come in late by the back entrance to the hall instead of the platform end where the head teacher was leading the school in singing *All things bright and beautiful* while Sylvia thumped the accompaniment on the upright piano. He had nearly collided with Ro and they had done that stupid dance to the right and to the left and back again. He had grinned and muttered 'so sorry' and their eyes had met. Falling in love had been as easy and as simple as that.

Had it really been love, she wondered yet again, as her mind fell into the usual guilty groove. Granted, a strong sexual attraction was the first step on the road to love but had either of them ever taken that second step? Perhaps he had, but had she? Where had been the comfort, honour, care in sickness and in health required of love?

Completely lacking in her, perhaps in them both, or he would never have done what he did.

There was nothing so sick as a loveless marriage, she thought, and I could have healed it. I could have mended our relationship and now it has broken us all.

She sighed, forcibly put aside her tired guilt and turned to her preparation for tomorrow's lessons.

PART FOUR

Chapter One

St Magnus Isle: Monday June 2 1972

Morning
Aidan stared at the last three names on the brass obituary plaque in the chapel.
Magnus Montgomery Melvick Born August 10 1922 Died April 20 1944
Alastair Arthur Melvick born January 3 1926 Drowned at Sea. May 1946
Aidan Francis Melvick born June 24 1931 Lost at Sea. May 1946
'In death they were not divided.'

Three brothers dead. My brothers, Magnus, Ali, me. I have been lost for - the calculation came slowly and painfully – twenty-six years. That is, if the newspaper he had read in the back of the lorry, had got yesterday's date right. Where had he been? A lunatic asylum perhaps for surely he must be raving mad. Or was this resurrection? Resurrection of the body and the life everlasting. Was this it?

Ali dead? Ali dead! Ali is dead. He sat down heavily in one of the chairs at the back of the chapel and held his head in his hands. Think. Remember the last time they had been together. How had it been? They were in the boat, he and Ali. Bright water all round them, sunshine in his eyes. Ali at the helm, capable, in an expansive mood, talking to him, but what had he said? He could see him now in *Good Shepherd*. He was telling him something important. Something that he had not wanted to hear. He had turned his head away. Ali had shouted 'gybing'. Or wait, was it he, Aidan, who had shouted? Then nothing. Only the thick grey fog that clogged the part of his brain that stored his memory and the stink of fish. Twenty-six years lost.

He dropped his head in his hands, feeling the unaccustomed roughness of his skin. He had not shaved since…when had he last shaved? By the feel of it, he had grown quite a beard. Carefully, he went over the events that he could remember. The old woman, Agatha she had called herself, had not come back so he had borrowed some of her money, twenty pounds to be exact. It had not

136

been nearly enough. The bus to Glasgow had been shockingly expensive. If it had not been for that gentleman-of-the-road in the bus shelter café he would never have got here at all. In exchange for a pint the tramp had shown him where to hitch a ride on a lorry. He was a friendly sort of bloke the driver, a Yorkshire tyke who called him mate, talked the whole time about his girl, dropped him at a squat - that's what he had called it - an empty garage outside Thurso. He had saved just enough to cross on the ferry but not enough to take the bus to the Castle Island. He had precisely one shilling and a few coppers left. A fish van had stopped on the road to offer him a lift to the north barrier. Told him the old Major was still alive as far as he knew - some tragedy in his family - but the Castle was not on his rounds.

As it dawned on him just how long he had been away, he had decided to come to the chapel first. He was not sure how shocked and bewildered his father would be at his reappearance. How would he explain himself, Ali? Something terrible must have happened to have made him lose his memory. The fog in his head lifted a fraction and again he saw his brother outlined against the sun, his lips moving, but all he could hear in his head was the flapping sail and the splash of the waves against the bow. Perhaps it was not his memory he had lost but his mind. If so, would he be welcome after all these years? If it had been a shock to find his name on the plaque, how much more of a shock would it be to his father to find him not dead. If one were to return from the dead... What then? Perhaps he was a ghost. A ghost in a donkey jacket and baggy brown corduroy trousers secured with a black tie. It seemed improbable. Turning instinctively to the God he had not forgotten he prayed aloud. 'Grant me courage. Grant him the grace of forgiveness. Restore me to myself.'

He stood up, paced the half dozen steps of the little nave back and forth, savaging the darkness in his mind. It was as if he was caught up in a great live spider's web and could not disentangle himself, could not see beyond, below or above, only at the great gaping chasm that yawned blackly behind him and beyond that, on the other side, the bright innocence of his boyhood here. The more he tore at the web, the deeper he became enmeshed, the darker the cavern. It was no good. However hard he struggled in his mind, he had no memory of the time between the boat trip and coming to himself, bloody and broke, with a throbbing head in the old

137

woman's hen yard. In desperation he threw himself down at the wooden communion rail. 'God help me.'

More words from Scripture occurred to him. *I will arise and go to my Father and say to him Father I have sinned against heaven and against you and am no more worthy to be called your son.* But there was something wrong there. He could no longer see Ali but he could hear his voice. Can that be right? he asked himself in wonderment or was it another of Ali's sick jokes. His brother was fond of teasing him. There had been other instances. Once when he had been a small child he had believed those outrageous lies. 'Go on, eat it. Don't you know anything? It's full of Vitamins A, B,C and D?' he had said, holding out a grey slug on one of the best dinner plates. And then when he put it in his mouth and made himself sick, Ali had sneered. 'What a silly little boy it is. Can't it take a joke?' Had this been another joke?

Rising from his knees, he automatically genuflected and crossed himself. Gazing once more at the plaque, he hesitated. Would he open the Castle front door and go in as he used to do, or should he first pull the iron handle that tweaked a bell on the kitchen wall? Would Kristin still be there? Would she know him again? Would she associate the clumsy fourteen year-old schoolboy he had been with the unshaven, unkempt, middle-aged tramp he had become? His father must be, what, seventy-five? Would he have a heart attack?

He remembered the door which led from the chapel straight into the long corridor into the Castle. It never used to be locked nor was it today. Turning the handle, he entered the little vestry which had a disused air about it. The safe was locked but the vestment cupboard stood a little ajar. He fingered the green chasuble. It felt damp and had a musty smell. Another door, also unlocked, led into the long corridor which in turn opened into the gunroom where the dogs had been kept. No Thor and Odin to bark excitedly, jump up on him and beseech him to take them out, otherwise nothing had changed. He looked briefly at the faded sepia photographs on the wall taken at shooting parties, most of them before the Great War. Proud young men, his father and grandfather among them, in knickerbockers and deerstalkers lined up behind an obscene number of grouse, long-gone keepers and beaters. Others showed women in large hats shadowing their eyes against the sun as they presided behind wicker picnic baskets on the moors. The gun cabinet was, as

138

it had always been, firmly locked. He remembered the last time he had handled a gun, gone out to shoot pigeons with Magnus and Ali and his father not long before Magnus had died. Magnus had not wanted to be there, had deliberately missed and angered their father. Torn between Magnus' ideals and his father's pleasure, his ten-year old self had not enjoyed the experience, nor, he suspected, had Ali although he had winged a brace to his father's satisfaction.

He opened the gunroom door and stood in the spacious old hall with the loud ticking grandfather clock, the dozen Daniel Orkney prints and the round oak table where the Sporting Times and Punch still shared space with the Orkney Herald and a pile of Scots Magazines. As the old remembered smell, part musty, part Mansion polish, assaulted him, he was overwhelmed with such a love for his home that the tears started to his eyes. Was this perhaps heaven after all? He shook his head. What had he ever done to deserve heaven?

He crossed the hall and started to climb the stairs. He noticed that the carpet had become threadbare. He yearned to see his old room, lie in his old bed before it was too late, before he woke up again, this time perhaps in hell.

'Mamma mia! What the devil? Stop right where you are.'

He turned on the stairs The dark little man with silver hair and angry black eyes who brandished a walking stick - his father's silver mounted crook - was instantly recognisable.

'Luigi? Don't you know me?' As he turned to come back downstairs Luigi lifted his arm threateningly. 'That's my father's stick,' he added, holding out his hand.

Without lowering his arm he peered at the intruder. 'I not know you. What are you doing here?'

'Luigi, I'm Aidan. Remember Aidan?'

The stick fell with a clatter on the oak floor. The little man was shaking. 'Do not say such a thing. You are a bad man. You come to steal. I get polis.'

He took another step closer. 'Please Luigi,' he interrupted quietly. He did not want to frighten his father, not until he had Kristy at his side. 'Let's just go to the kitchen and tell Kristy I've come home.'

Afternoon

Was that the time already? Kristin glanced up at the kitchen clock on the wall and added ten minutes which made it twenty to three.

139

That gave her nearly two hours before the Major's teatime. There were things she needed in Stromness and if the Major was not wanting the car, which was unlikely, Luigi would get them. She might even go with him, but she had half promised to pop in and see Marie Flett whose arthritis kept her confined to a chair. Jimmy too, with the same complaint, was waiting for a hip operation. He had passed the farm management over to Sweyn, when would it have been? - five years since. Although Sweyn and Jeannie ran the farm well enough, it was not the same without Marie and Jimmy at the Mains. Nothing was the same these days, she thought with a sigh. At least Marie had grand-weans to keep her cheery. Never stopped talking about them either, though they were grown men now driving big cars, working at the oil, making good money. But where were the Castle weans? The Major should have had grand-bairns to keep them all cheery.

Three o'clock. Where was that dratted man? Eyeties had no sense of time at all. She opened the kitchen door and shouted 'Luigi!'

She turned back to add a scuttle of anthracite to the range. She sensed rather than saw her husband at the door 'Whaur hae ye been. Will thee chuist look at the time!' She turned.

She knew Aidan at once. Afterwards she could never describe that moment, though there were plenty of times she tried, at the farm, to her neighbours, to Aidan himself. It was a mixture of anger, disbelief, self-justification - hadn't she always said he'd be back? - and joy. Mainly joy, though that was not immediately apparent.

'So it's you!' she declared straightening her back and glaring at him. 'Ye ken what they say about bad pennies. And chuist look at thee! Look at the state of ye!' Then her arms were outstretched and around him and the tears were tumbling down her cheeks. 'Ma bairn, ma bairnie.' She held him at arms length. 'Oh Aidie, my own bairn, whaur was ye?'

He felt fragile somehow, this man all of forty years old and there were grey hairs on his head and in his beard. Her heart trembled with pity and love for him and her embrace tightened.

'Kristy, Kristy,' he was saying over and over again, but he never answered her question. His familiar green eyes were full of tears.

She made him sit at the table. She offered him food, she kept touching him and on and off she wondered if she were dreaming for she had often dreamed this dream, but in her dream Aidie had been

140

the lad he used to be, a clumsy floppy-haired schoolboy. That was how she knew he was real. She could not have dreamed up this slight greying middle-aged man with a beard, not in a million years.

She could not stop talking. She could hear herself questioning him without giving him time to answer, telling him about the Major, about old Mrs Grant, the Major's cousin who had passed away, about Miss Evie her daughter who lived at the Dower now, about Erlend and Inge and his loon who had flown the nest, oh and Old Billock long gone and the Shearers and the Lighthouse which was now automatic. At last, when she was all talked out she dared to ask. 'Is it really thoo then?' but she knew it was because she could see the scar on his neck, fainter now than she remembered but clearly visible under that filthy shirt collar.

When at last she was silent, with nothing more to say, but shaking still, he reached out and took her two hands turning them over, looking at them and then lifting them to his lips. Holding them close within his own two hands, he calmed her. 'It's all right. Kristy. Everything will be all right.'

Then she wept. All the sorrows and upsets and responsibilities that had built up over the years dissolved in a flood of grief. Luigi stood at her back murmuring his astonishment in Italian while Aidan still held her hands in a warm strong grip as her tears fell.

'Has it been so bad?' Aidan asked Luigi over her bowed head.

'Very bad.' He nodded vigorously. 'But you home now. You go see your father now.'

Still with her hands in his, Aidan leaned forward and kissed her brow. 'I will, presently.'

'No', she said tightening her grip on his hands. 'Not yet. Wait a peedie while. Drink thoor tea.'

She was afraid that if she let him go he would be gone again, that this was some strange dream, that Aidan was not real.

He must have known what she was thinking for he smiled a little. 'I'm back for good, Kristy. The bad penny as you said.'

It was his smile that did it. Anger like a hot flush spread throughout her body. 'How could ye do it?' she shouted, pulling her hands from his. 'Was it because ye didna want to go to thon school? Ye chuist decided to walk out? What's wrang wi the three o' ye? Peedie Magnus - 'she still could not bring herself to say the words - 'thoo disappearing and what about Alastair? Whitever happened to him?'

141

'I don't know, Kristy,' he said sadly, 'and that's God's truth. We were in the boat Ali and I, and he shouted a warning at me, or was it I who shouted at him? I don't remember anything. I think it must have been the boom that caught me on the head and knocked the sense out of me. That's all I remember.'

'So where you been all this time?' Luigi asked, taking the words from her mouth

He shook his head.

'And whitna steer thoo'rt in. Whaur did ye pick up they rags?' she added yanking his jacket sleeve After a moment he shook his head again. She had a sudden image of him wandering the roads for a quarter of a century, begging like a tramp, living in one of those night shelters that were sometimes shown on the telly. Unless maybe he had been in the jail... perish the thought. Maybe it was best not to ask too much. Maybe he didn't want to say. That was it, she thought. It was not that he couldn't tell her, but that he wouldn't. If she poked and pried too much maybe he'd go away again.

'Leave him alane,' she said sharply to Luigi.

At the same time he stood up. 'I'm so sorry Kristy. I'd quite understand if you never wanted to see me again.'

'Wheesht yer mooth,' she said. 'What thoo've done or no' done's no concern o' mine. Thoo'rt back where ye belong and high time too. Ah'd best go through and tell yer father thoo're back. If ye go through dressed like that, the shock'll likely kill him.'

She stood up and faced him. Och, Aidie, she thought as she moved towards him. His arms were round her and hers around him. All she felt now was love.

The Major opened his eyes. What was the stupid woman saying? Damn and blast her, surely she knew better than to mention the boys when his gout was playing up. Why gout, for God's sake? He liked a glass of wine and the odd nightcap, always had done, but surely not enough to get gout. The quack had told him to stop eating sardines and turkey. Turkey for God's sake! When did he ever eat turkey? Once a year at most. Hell take it, it was bloody painful... What was there left to say about them anyhow? Dead and gone. Dead and gone. His fault, as Ingrid had repeatedly scolded him, and although he would not admit it to her or anyone else for that matter, he knew she was right. Why had he consented to them sailing? He

142

could have stopped it. He should have stopped it. He sighed impatiently. If blame, regret and agonising self-recrimination could have brought them back, they would have been home by now.

'What in hell's name are you blabbering about, woman?' he roared at Kristin.

'Aidan,' she shouted back at him. He wasn't that deaf. Suddenly he knew what she was trying to tell him. They must have found the boy's body, but after all those years how could they be sure it was him? He must have misheard.

'What?' he shouted back.' Get on with it. Spit it out, woman.'

'Aidan,' she repeated. He could see she was nervous, her hands twisting in and out of her apron. 'He's come home.'

'Good God, woman, what are you trying to say? They've found the boy's body? Is that it?'

'In a manner of speaking,' she began cautiously, 'he's turned up.'

For a moment hope leapt up in him and as quickly died. 'I suppose it was bound to happen one day, but how do they know it's him…after all this time?'

'Because I've come home.'

A man had come into the room. A quietly-spoken stranger who looked like a tinker. For a moment he wanted to laugh at the sheer preposterous notion that this could be Aidan. Aidan!

'I don't know who the devil you think you are, but my sons are dead,' he said dismissively.

'I know,' the fellow said.

'What do you know?' he asked roughly. 'What do you know about anything?' But he knew. Hope was rising like a bubble in his heart.

'I know that you're the only father I can remember.'

The bubble burst. Incredulity turned into joy coursing through every artery in his body. He no longer felt the pain in his foot as he threw off the rug and struggled to his feet.

'Aidan?' he could hear the pleading tremor in his voice. 'Is that you?'

'You know it is. I've come home.'

He wanted to embrace his son, but it was not in his nature. He had not embraced a human being since Davina had died, and even then not that often. The only creatures he ever embraced were the dogs simply to fondle their ruffs. There had been no dogs at the

143

Castle for over a decade at least. His legs were trembling, the pain in his left toe was excruciating.

Kristin came to his aid, but Aidan got there first. Holding him firmly, he lowered him gently back into his chair.

'What happened?' he said querulously. 'I don't understand. What's happening?'

She was quick to go over to him, and, bending over him, touched his hand, reassuring and in control. 'Aidan was no' drooned, Major. He lost his memory when the boom in the boatie hit him.' She looked up at Aidan for confirmation. 'He doesn't know where he's been.'

'What?' he asked. 'Why not? Where has he been?'

'I'm so sorry,' the stranger said too quietly for him to catch but he heard Kristin all right when she told him to speak up, the Major was getting deaf.

'I damn well heard you,' he said mildly, but nothing could spoil the moment.

'Ah'll get thoor tea then,' she said and she was smiling.

It occurred to him that it had been a while since he had seen the woman smile. Bloody good teeth she still had, he thought incongruously.

Aidan pulled up a chair and brought it close to his father. The old man had changed but not unrecognisably. The same great bushy sandy eyebrows bristled over the same deep set sky-blue eyes, but his handsome face was as grooved as a bulldog into heavy lines, his pale hair had thinned and faded, his liver-spotted hands were more bone than flesh, his body was so shrunk that his clothes - still the same knickerbockers and tweed jacket, viyella shirt and regimental tie - hung loosely on his frame. Papa, father, our Father in heaven, my father. I have known many fathers…The thought came to him out of nowhere. It was true, however, that the old man in the adjustable chair with a tartan rug on his knees and yesterday's *Times* spread out in a pool around his chair was the only father he could remember.

'Where have you been then?' he asked querulously.

'I can't answer you that. When I came to myself, I was lying in a hen yard, covered in filth and bleeding, near a town called St Ninians.' He touched the scab on his temple that had almost healed. His father had better know the worst. Over the past three days he had thought of nothing else. 'I may have been in a lunatic asylum. I may have escaped from prison. I don't know. I can't remember anything since I was knocked out on *Good Shepherd* and I would understand if you didn't want me back.'

The old man was quiet for a moment. Then he said, 'Quack's coming to see me tomorrow. Better have a word.'

He agreed. 'And the police.' He was, he supposed, technically a missing person.

'Hmm,' said the old man. 'I'll have a word with the Chief Constable. Nice fellah. Keep it discreet. Don't want the press wallahs poking their noses in.' Without pausing and on the same breath, he said in the same tone, 'We searched, y'know. Too late of course. Didn't know you were missing for several days. Not till the bloody boat was found half submerged off the Skerries.'

'Was Alastair with it?' he asked.

'No.' His father did not look at him. 'He was found on the shore near Durness a few weeks later...' he paused. 'What happened to Alastair?'

Once again he forced his mind back to that boat trip. 'I don't know. He was fine the last I remember.'

He could still see his brother silhouetted against sun and rolling sea. 'You need to know,' Ali was saying. He said it twice, 'It's only fair to tell you.'

'Tell me what? Go on, Ali, what?' he had urged his brother, but he didn't really want to know and now he didn't want to remember. Alastair had told him all the same and now he must tell this man who was the only father he could remember.

'Papa,' he said, though the name sounded odd. 'Pa,' he repeated. It sounded more familiar somehow. He paused then he tried again. 'Father,' he said, 'don't think I'm not grateful, because I am and always will be, but I need to know. Who was my real -' no, that was not right because the old man in front of him was real. 'Who was my birth father?'

The old man looked up and Aidan caught his fleeting impression of guilt. All he said was, 'Who told you?'

He was remembering now. That mocking voice. ...'Alastair mentioned something.'

The Major put both hands on the arms of his chair, struggled to rise, and sat down again heavily. 'How the hell did he bloody know? Nobody knew except - '

145

On the contrary, Aidan thought, everyone knew except for me or so Ali said. 'Everyone on the Island knows,' he had told him. 'It's only fair to tell you.'

'It's true then,' Aidan said aloud. 'I was adopted?' But he had always known that, hadn't he?

The old man shook his head. 'You were never adopted. You've seen your birth certificate, haven't you?'

Not that he remembered. What reason could he have had, a lad of fourteen, to examine his own birth certificate? He had known who he was, or thought he was. He remembered his shock when Ali told him, then had come the gybe, a double whammy, and after that nothing more...except the stench of tar and fish. 'I would like to know the truth.'

Eventually he made sense of his father's garbled explanation. He had been born in Yorkshire. His mother, his birth mother, had been only a child herself. Fourteen years old, a schoolgirl. Davina had left Orkney to look after her for the final month of her pregnancy and the Major's old Nanny - 'You remember Nanny?' - had gone down to help with the birth. The baby had been brought back by Nanny and the gentle woman who, right from his birth, had become his mother. Her name and the Major's were on the birth certificate. 'I suppose we should have done it by the book, but there seemed to be no need at the time. Easier this way all round.' He paused for a moment. 'Nanny must have told Alastair,' the old man sounded astonished. 'That surprises me,' he added. 'No way of knowing of course. She died not long after you were both lost.'

So Nanny had known! Dear Nan. Eventually when he had made some sort of sense of the garbled retelling of his birth, he was able to ask,

'Who were my parents then? My mother? Is she still alive?'

'Very much so,' he said and his voice softened. 'You'll find Evie at the Dower.'

'Evie?' he managed to whisper.

'Evie Grant. You remember Cousin Ingrid's daughter? Come to think of it, I don't believe you've ever met her.' Suddenly he realised the foolishness of that remark. 'Except, of course - '

'The Dower?'

'She took it over when Ingrid, her mother, died. More or less runs the Island for me these days. Does her best. Hard worker. Uphill struggle. Have to show you the ropes sometime. I don't suppose

146

you've any money? No? Ah well. You're back, that's all that matters. Evie will be pleased. Doesn't know you know about her, of course. Better tell her you're back before the word gets out.'

But how? How do you go up to a cousin you've never set eyes on and tell her she's your mother, as if she didn't know. The thought was terrifying.

'And my father?'

The old man looked evasive. 'Only your mother can tell you that.'

But Aidan knew already, or thought he knew, as he rose to help Kristin with the tea trolley. Why else would this old man have bothered to raise him? Why else would he now be so pleased to have him home?

Evening

The phone was ringing. Evie threw her pen down. 'Yes?' she answered curtly. She had been trying to get to the accounts all day and someone had always interrupted. This time it was Kristin. 'Sorry for bothering, Miss Evie, but there's something ah think it best ye know.'

'Well?' she replied a little impatiently. What was it this time? Kristin had a knack of passing on bad news as if it were something she ought to know; a tenant's quarrel or rats in the scullery. Cousin Magnus was getting very frail. She knew that one of these days it would be bad news, but, please heaven, not tonight. The tax forms had been lying about since April and Evie was someone who liked to be ahead of herself. She could not bear to get up a moment after 7.00. Twenty minutes for yoga. Ten minutes to dress. Oatcakes and honey at 7.30 with strong coffee, Then she fed the hens, milked the goats and was in the dairy by nine. Jeannie's girl, Heidi, helped with the cheese and yogurt-making but she made the thrice weekly trips to Stromness and Kirkwall to deliver the produce herself. It was a living of sorts but nowhere near enough to run the Island. Cousin Magnus had a little income including his pension but needed every penny to pay Kristin and Luigi. Her own naval pension from twelve years service in the WRNS was barely enough to keep the Dower wind and watertight. Cash flow was a continual problem. Things were a bit easier now that Jeannie and Sweyn had bought the Mains. The cash had paid for some necessary repairs to the estate cottages but the Castle itself was still badly in need of a major renovation. The Dower dilapidations, including the re-wiring, she had done

147

herself with the professional assistance of a widowed semi-retired electrical engineer, now renting one of the estate cottages and who had generously accepted in exchange for his labour and expertise some valuable bottles of old Highland Park from the Castle cellar. She knew he was after more from her but she was quite sure she had nothing in the way of a relationship to offer.

'Thoo'lt be getting a visitor,' Kristin said cautiously. 'Ah'm no' sure when he'll be over because he's only just got here.' She paused.

'Get on with it, Kristin.' She had no time for guessing games. 'Who is it?'

'Aidan,' she said baldly. 'He's back.'

'Who?' For a moment she had no idea who Kristin meant but she could tell that she was choosing her words with care.

'The Major's laddie, but he's no' a laddie now.'

Aidan? Aidan. Oh God. Although she had not consciously thought of Aidan for a long time he was always there, a shameful bundle of shawl curled up somewhere deep inside her soul. That was all she had ever seen of him, a tiny scrap of black hair sticking out of a white bundle of Shetland shawl. It was not that her mother or Davina had deliberately taken him away from her. It would not have been fair to blame them for what had been always her own decision. She had wanted none of him. If she could have got rid of him before he was born, she would have done so, told no one and got on with her life, but in those days abortion was not possible or if it had been, how would she have known how to arrange it? She had not even known she was pregnant.

It was discovered by the doctor at her Hampshire boarding school after she had twisted her ankle skating on the outdoor swimming pool which had been frozen for most of that January and February in 1931. He had asked her so many questions, some very embarrassing to do with the curse. Then there had been that excruciating internal examination in the San with Sister Macgregor standing grimly by. What had that to do with her ankle, she had thought indignantly and asked timidly, but neither of them had said anything to her. Their disapproval was palpable and she had been sent home immediately. She had not been allowed to contact any of her friends, not even given time to pick up her clothes from the dormitory. Her parents who were living in Army Quarters not far from Aldershot drove over to fetch her. Her father had been on

148

embarkation leave for India and he looked particularly grim. Neither would catch her eye. At home she was sent straight to her room. She had thrown herself on the bed and wept. Then her mother had come in, shut the door and what followed had been perhaps the most unhappy, uncomfortable, unforgettable fifteen minutes of her life.

The only words she remembered were shame, disgrace, disgusting, unforgivable. But why, what had she done? Eventually she learned that she was five months pregnant. That was how ignorant and innocent she had been.

Everything had been arranged without consultation, nor had it occurred to her to query her mother's decisions. She had been too ashamed. The only other girl who had ever got herself 'into trouble' (as it was called) at school years before was still talked about in awed whispers. It was just about the lowest thing you could do. The other girl at least had been grown up, all of eighteen, but Evie was only fourteen. Fourteen and pregnant. How could she! Strangely enough, no one asked her who the father was. They thought they knew.

She had been sent to a remote cottage in Yorkshire and Nanny had come down from Orkney to take care of her. Her father, a full colonel, was posted to India and her menopausal mother, in her mid-fifties and unable to cope with her pregnant daughter, had gone with him. Cousin Davina from Orkney had turned up a few weeks before the birth. She had liked Cousin Davina They had played rummy together and endless games of Cheat and one night she had told her that she would be happy to take the baby and bring it up with Peedie Magnus and Alastair as her own child. 'No one need ever know about you,' she reassured Evie, 'not even the baby. You can join your parents in India and no one will be any the wiser. You can get on with your life. It would probably be the best thing all round for everyone, don't you think?' Evie had been quick to agree and fervently thanked her cousin. It had never occurred to her that she had any right to an opinion. And even if she had, what better solution than this? Nanny and the local doctor had been marvellous. 'Everyone seems to have been quite marvellous' was how her mother put it in her birthday letter - she had become fifteen a week after the baby's birth - except Evie of course. Evie had been far from marvellous, Evie had let the side down, had broken her father's heart, and, by implication if not actual words, her mother's too.

149

Davina and Nanny had gone back to Orkney when the little boy was barely a week old and she had been sent to another boarding school in Cornwall and there she had 'got on with her life', just as Davina had advised. A few weeks after the birth, Davina had written to tell her they had called the baby Aidan Francis for no particular reason but that she liked the names and hoped Evie would too, and that he was thriving in the Orkney air; which was more than poor Davina. Her cancer was diagnosed a few months later and four years later she was dead. At about the same time Evie's father died untimely of malaria and her widowed mother Ingrid had returned to Orkney and taken over the Dower as was her right. She wrote regularly and dutifully but Evie was never invited to stay and Aidan seldom mentioned.

Orkney had always been her favourite place in the world but she had not returned there until Aidan had been long gone and her mother dead. She had been too ashamed. She was still ashamed, but not perhaps for the same reasons. Did Aidan know? Did Kristy know? Had Nanny not been able to hold her tongue? Shame rippled over her because this stranger called Aidan meant nothing to her. Double shame because she had so lightly and so thankfully given him away. How could she ever face him if he knew?

'What happened? Where has he been all these years?' she managed to ask Kristy keeping her voice steady.

'He doesn't remember. The Major thinks he should see Doctor Stout the morn's morn.'

'Why? Is he not well?'

'He's been away for over a quarter of a century, Miss Evie, and he's nothing to show for it and nothing to say aboot it. Would ye no' think something's far the matter? Besides he gey thin and peelly-wally and, aye, old. That wee laddie! Ah'm worried sick if ye want to know.'

Evie knew she was crying, that she had to do something, show interest, concern.

'Are you sure it's him, Kristin?' Perhaps a mistake had been made. She was surprised at her feelings. Desperately now she wanted it to be him. Her son.

'Aye, it's him,' she replied indignantly. 'He's got those scars on his neck to prove it.'

150

'Give me an hour,' she found herself saying for now she could not wait. Shame had yielded to curiosity, anxiety, and, much to her own surprise, concern.

'Thanks, Miss Evie.' She could hear the relief in Kristin's voice.

'Ye can no' get to sleep in the Tower. That room's been shut up all these years. The mattress 'll be wringing wet.' Kristin said tartly as Aidan returned the tea tray to the kitchen and told her he was going upstairs. 'Luigi's away up getting the bed made up in Peedie Magnus's room. No argie bargie now. Just thee do whit thoo're telt.'

He held up his hands in submission, an action that caused her heart to contract. She remembered it so well.

'Oh and ye'll be wanting a bit of a wash and change of breeks. Whitna steer thoo'rt in. Ah'm thinking a pair of the Major's gabardines might do thee a turn. Leave they shoon and Luigi'll gie them a wipe.'

'I suppose there's nothing left?'

She knew that he was talking about his personal possessions and shook her head. 'They all went to the Sally Ann a while ago.' She remembered having to do it herself, and the tears that had fallen as she had sorted the shirts and socks and trousers into two piles, one which Luigi had taken into Kirkwall, the other fit only for dusters and cleaning rags. There were other things too, the little treasures of three lives cut short, battered dinky toys, a Hornby train lovingly cherished by Alastair and still in its original box, a battered teddy which Peedie Magnus had disembowelled to find the squeak, collections of birds' eggs, cigarette cards, lead soldiers, fossils... Those too she had had to sort out. 'Ah put the toys oot but there's still a few books and things.' He would find out soon enough. 'Ah'm heart sorry,' she said, 'but how wis we to ken?'

He turned from the sink where he had started to rinse the tea-cups. That was a change! The old Aidie would never have thought to wash up. Suddenly the incredibility of him alive and here in her kitchen, a grown man, overwhelmed her and she burst into tears. Immediately his arms were around her. She felt his thinness, his frailty and clutched him to her, shaking with sobs. He and his brothers were all the bairns she had ever had, all she had ever wanted. She and Luigi? It simply hadn't happened though not for

151

lack of trying. He was still trying, bless him, though she was well past it. But her lad was back, her Aidie, home where he belonged. A small internal smile slowly began to spread through her body. As she relaxed, the sobs subsided. 'All will be well, Kristy. All will be well,' he was insisting over and over again as if he had still himself to convince.

At last she released him and stood back holding him out at arms length so that she could look at him properly.. 'What happened to thee, son? What happened efter ye lost the boatie?'

'It's no good, Kristy. It's all there hidden in a big cloud at the back of my mind. Sometimes I get flashes... and I dream. I think I know everything in my dreams, but I can never remember them when I wake.'

She hugged him again. 'Ah'm thinking it'll all come back to ye soon enough. Chuist give thoorsel the time. Meanwhile thoo'rt back and about to have a visitor.' Best to warn him about Miss Evie's visit. 'I phoned Miss Evie.'

He stiffened in her arms. Did he know then? If so, how? 'Ah hope ah did right?' she asked anxiously. 'She's family.'

'I know,' he said evenly, but what did that mean? He released himself from her arms. 'I'll go and change then.'

'Ah've put the breeks oot for ye in Peedie Magnus' room, and there's plenty hot water. Oh and niver forget to take off them shoon. The Major's got plenty ye can wear meantime.'

When he had gone she sat down at the table. Her plump reddened hands were shaking and she was breathing fast. 'It's the shock,' she told Luigi when he came into the kitchen seconds later. 'Hid's chuist hit me.' He picked up the scuffed black shoes and took them into the boot room down the passage. 'I do later,' he said. Everything was always later with Luigi but this time she did not argue.

'It all very strange,' he said going over the fridge and pouring himself a mug of home brew from the jug kept cool. Erlend's beer had long ago replaced wine in Luigi's order of importance. 'You want some?'

Automatically she shook her head. She had always disliked the taste, but then changed her mind. 'Aye, but just a peedie drop, mind.'

He filled a tumbler and put it in front of her. 'There be changes I think.'

She took a sip of the strong foul-tasting - in her opinion - brew and then another and gradually felt calmer. 'Aye,' she said. 'I phoned Miss Evie.'

'Her nose flattened, I think.'

She did not laugh. It was a pity Luigi hated Miss Evie so much but she could understand why. He had overheard her calling him a lazy beggar which everyone knew he was, but, as Jennet Flett would say 'lovely with it'.

'That's no' whit Ah'm bothered aboot,' she said with a sigh. 'Och weel, life goes on. Ah'll need to git started on the dinner. Would you ask the Major if he wants his usual tray in the library or are you to set the dining room table.'

'As I am telling you - change, all changes,' he grumbled as he left the kitchen.

Ignoring Kristy's instruction to get changed in his brother's room, Aidan went straight up to his old room in the Tower. He could see that the door had probably not been opened for years for it had warped on its hinge. Inside it smelled mouldy and airless. All four narrow windows were smeared with the salty residue of rain and sealed with cobwebs. He went from one to another to open them and let in the cool sweet air, but the sashes were almost impossible to lift. In the end he managed to inch up the one facing west, leaned on the narrow sill and breathed in the strong air. The wind was rising. How beautiful the Mains fields looked as the cattle browsed in emerald fields dusted with buttercups. The lively sea ruffled and rippled beyond the cliffs. He could hear skylarks calling high above the old walled garden, now sadly an overgrown wilderness apart from a small vegetable patch where he could make out the tips of a crop of early potatoes. Dear God, this was a beautiful place. God, he thought, I have not forgotten God. The knowledge calmed him.

The evening sun suddenly came out and for a few seconds blinded and disorientated him. He turned away from the window to get his bearings. The horsehair mattress had been turned back on the iron sprung frame. The thread-bare carpet had lost all trace of colour and pattern and was now dingy grey. The bedside cabinet was bare. He pulled open the drawer. His bible and prayer book, both printed so minutely on thin Indian paper as to be almost illegible and inscribed with good wishes from Ingrid Grant on his Confirmation, were all that remained of the clutter that he used to keep there. He

153

picked up the prayer book and rifled through the pages. The sense of familiarity was for the moment overwhelming and he was filled with hope. Holding it comforted him.

The cabinet below still contained the cracked chamber pot with pansies round the rim. He had always hated it being there but Nanny had insisted when he first moved out of the nursery because .the bathroom was on the floor below. He might well be needing it again he thought, inwardly amused, for he would sleep here whatever Kristy said.

He turned his attention to the bookcase. His John Buchan's in the small red bound Nelson edition were still there. He pulled *Prester John*, always his favourite, out of the row and opened its damp-spotted pages; *Witchwood. The Thirty-nine Steps*, all firm favourites to be read and reread. There too was his *Princess and Curdie* and *At the Back of the North Wind*, childhood treasures, and his blue leather Collins edition of the Orange and Blue Fairy Tales (Ali had the Red and Yellow, Magnus the Green and Violet), his *Boys Own Annuals, Observer's Book of Birds* never the same since he had left it outside one night and it had rained.

A bit of air and warmth and his books would recover, this dead room would become alive again. And himself? Had he too been dead? He thought not. There was too much busy-ness in the depths of the grey cloud that befogged him unless, of course, death was just another busy life. Do we remember this life when we die? Had his lost life been busy, happy? Perhaps, maybe, but did he really need to know? He was home, wasn't he? What else mattered. If this was all he had, then so be it. Certainly this was all he could remember and if he were to be honest, all he wished to remember.

With these thoughts in mind, he crossed to the south facing window, yanked at the sash again and this time it shot right up to its limit. He pulled out the snib for fear it might fall and shatter the glass. Automatically slipping the prayer book into his pocket, he leaned on the sill to breathe in the strong air.

Someone below was approaching on foot, walking briskly up the weedy avenue between the stunted newly green sycamores that had been planted some sixty years ago and were now bent with the prevailing wind. He watched the woman in jeans and tweed jacket approach the gravel sweep in front of the Castle. His mouth opened but not to call out, his hand rose but not to wave. Then she looked up.

For less than an instant, the fog in his mind cleared and he knew her, recognised that red springy hair, the freckled face, those green eyes. For a timeless second he remembered her. But the moment passed as fleetingly as it had come. Of course he knew her. This must be his cousin Evie. This was his mother.

She did not stop nor wave, did not acknowledge him, nor did she look away. But she knew him just as surely he knew her.

Evie was shaking as she opened the aged iron-barred oak door and let herself into the Castle porch. That she had just seen her son she was in no doubt. Aidan. He knows. If he had not known, he would surely have smiled, waved, shouted a greeting. All he had done was stare. How he must hate her. Why not? He had every right. What had she ever done to deserve his respect, let alone affection?

She stood for a few seconds in the porch in the midst of the usual clutter of coats and sticks and wellingtons to calm herself. There had been many other difficult moments in her life, some of them flashed through her memory, that dreadful day when her mother had told her she was pregnant; seeing her father for the last time as he lay delirious and dying of malaria on that trip to India in 1934, getting that letter from Chas, the only man she had ever loved, telling her that he had a wife in Texas. All bad enough moments but none quite like this. She looked at herself in the fly-spotted mirror built into the coat stand and as quickly looked away. She did not like herself. She never had. How could she expect this stranger who once she had carried shamefully as an unwanted foetus to bring himself to understand, let alone forgive her.

Straightening her shoulders she opened the porch door and entered the hall. The silence was profound. No doubt Magnus was dozing over a whisky in the library. He would not have heard her come in. Kristy would be in the kitchen preparing dinner. Oh Lord, would she be expected to stay and eat with them?

The swing door to the kitchen quarters opened and Luigi emerged with a tray.

'Good evening, Luigi,' she managed to say.

He nodded without smiling. 'Miss Evie.' He was so surly these days. She'd obviously done something to upset him. Now he did not even stop on his way to the dining room.

'The Major in the library?' she asked for something to say.

155

He nodded his head in that direction then added significantly, 'Aidan back.'

Did he know too? She supposed all the Islanders must know. That knowledge she could live with as long as Aidan had been away. But now... 'Thank you, Luigi,' she said dismissively.

'You staying?' he asked insolently over his shoulder.

When she chose not to answer, he disappeared into the dining room and she could hear the noisy clatter of cutlery, the opening and shutting of drawers, as he laid the table for dinner. She decided to wait in the hall till Aidan came down and she was still there leafing through a magazine when Luigi had finished. He grinned at her knowingly and disappeared back through the swing door to the kitchen quarters.

When next she looked up, Aidan was there on the stairs watching her. He looked exhausted and unkempt and he was wearing no shoes.

'Aidan?' she said uncertainly searching his face for what? She could not tell. But she saw that his eyes were like hers, his thinning black hair like her mother's, his angular bony body not unlike Cousin Magnus, his black growth of beard streaked with white. This man is my son? she thought incredibly. This is my son, she thought with a strange emotion, not unlike pride, but more like joy.

'Aidan.' She went up to him, and, uncharacteristically, for she was not demonstrative by nature, touched his arm.

'Evie?' he said and leaned forward to kiss her cheek.

And inwardly she relaxed. He had not called her 'mother'. That would have been a step too far. She was relieved, she supposed, so relieved that she found herself saying 'I'm sorry, I'm sorry, I'm so dreadfully sorry.' Her hand was still on his arm.

He half smiled and then incredibly he was teasing her. 'That makes a change. Kristy was rather pleased.'

'That's not what I meant,' she protested, allowing herself to relax a little.

'I know and you have nothing to be sorry about.' His eyes were warm and knowing and hers inexplicably filled with tears.

'It's not too late then?' she asked. 'I'm forgiven?'

'If I am,' he answered quietly.

She touched his hand. He looked frail and, yes, dirty. Was he ill? She was engulfed in an emotion entirely new to her. 'Are you well?'

she asked quickly, 'You look tired.' A maternal streak, she thought with incredulity. Is this what it feels like to be a mother?

He enfolded her hand in his. 'I meant to change. Kristy will scold if she sees me like this. Tell father I'll be down soon.'

'Thank you,' she said and added impulsively, 'I'm so very glad you're home.' And she was, unbelievably, incredibly, glad as she watched him climb the stairs.

Luigi carrying another tray came back into the hall. 'Luigi,' she said in her normal voice, 'Please tell Kristy I'll stay for dinner.'

'So there you are?' Magnus, struggling to rise as Evie came into the library, ignored her insistence that he stay where he was. 'G and T? or will you ruin a good whisky with that ginger fizz?'

'Gin,' she said. 'I'll get it. Shall I fix you another?'

'I'm perfectly capable of pouring us both a drink,' he said testily. 'Are you staying?' His hands shook on the decanter of Highland Park as he poured them both a drink. It was his third, stupid really with his gout so painful. He handed her a tumbler and told her she could add her own tonic.

'How's the gout?' she asked as she watched him settle back into his chair overlooking what had once been a garden. Stupid question. Surely she could see for herself.

'You got the sheep then?' she asked. They both of them looked out on what had once been a lawn but was now no more than an overgrown field. Several ewes with some half-dozen frisky lambs were munching the grass contentedly.

'Erlend brought them over yesterday. Should keep the grass down a bit.' Silence stretched out between them and then they both spoke at once. 'Seen him yet?' he asked as she was saying, 'I met Aidan in the hall.'

He looked at her closely. 'Rum do,' he said. 'Remembers nothing. God alone knows where he's been.'

They were both silent for a while. 'Does he know about me?' she asked but so quietly that he could not hear.

'What? Don't mumble.' He was not deaf. People didn't bother to speak properly these days, or so he told himself.

She repeated the question.

He nodded. 'Seemingly Alastair told him he was adopted. Last thing Aidan remembers on the boat. How the devil did Alastair know? I suppose it must have been Nanny.'

157

She said nothing. He looked at her closely. 'That's all he knows. That's all anyone knows...' He waited for her to comment, but she said nothing. In all the years he had known her, she had refused to talk about Aidan's conception. He knew that Davina had thought him responsible though she had never accused him outright or even blamed him. She blamed herself. Since Alastair's birth, she had not wanted him in bed and he had strayed many times and no doubt about it, he had been attracted to the glorious golden-red-headed teenager she had once been. He still found Evie attractive or had done until this wretched gout had taken over his life.

Sighing impatiently he said roughly, 'He thinks I'm his father, of course.'

'I'm glad of that...'

'You're mumbling again –'

'I said, I'm glad. You've been a good father to him and I'm grateful.'

At that moment the door opened and Aidan came in. Thank God he was looking more respectable in a decent pair of what were obviously his own trousers, a check shirt and his Lovat tweed jacket. Needed a hair-cut though, and the beard should go. He disliked beards. Usually meant a chap had something to hide. Hah.

'A drink to celebrate, what?' This time he made no effort to rise. The pain had eased a little. 'Evie will see to it.'

He watched them together at the drinks tray, mother and son, and marvelled. What was there, barely fifteen years between them, yet he looked, if anything, the older of the two. That damned beard.

'Good to have you back,' he said, raising his glass in a toast when Aidan had brought forward one of the fiddleback Victorian chairs that Davina had brought to their marriage and sat between them, cradling the tumbler of whisky in his thin nervous fingers. They were very alike, mother and son, green-eyed and slight, nothing like his tall broad brothers, God rest their souls... but he should not be looking so old. 'Get rid of that damn beard,' he added.

Aidan raised in glass and smiled. 'Whatever you say, father. Will tomorrow do?'

'I rather like it,' Evie said challengingly. 'You do as you please, Aidan.' She reached over to touch his arm, and, while they all laughed, he thought ...and he will, do as he pleases. So long as that didn't mean leaving the Island. He could stand anything but not that.

'Any plans?' he asked with studied casualness.

'Don't rush him,' Evie interrupted and he could sense her own anxiety. 'He's only just arrived.'

'All I wanted to say was - you're needed here. Evie manages well enough but when I'm gone....'

'I've no plans,' he said simply.

'Thank God for that. No more bloody boat trips.'

Suddenly he found himself weeping. Shame on him and in front of a woman. His empty glass was shaking in his hands, his nose and eyes running. His foot was throbbing. He fumbled in his pocket for his handkerchief.

Aidan was by his side, hands on his arms, calming him while Evie rescued his drink. His hands were surprisingly warm and strong. 'All will be well, Father. I'm here to stay. I'm here for you both.'

At that moment Luigi came in to tell them dinner was ready in the dining room.

While they were finishing Kristin's exceedingly good lentil soup, the telephone started ringing.

Aidan half rose to his feet.

'Drat the bloody thing,' his father was muttering. 'Let them ring back.'

Evie said, 'I'll go,' and left the room.

'The word's out,' she told him and briefly looked at Aidan. 'That was Meg Shearer. She wanted to come round and see Aidan for herself. She's pretty amazing really,' she explained to Aidan. 'Eighty if she's a day.'

'Remember her?' he asked Aidan

'I don't think she approved of me,' he replied half-smiling. 'The last time I saw her I was drunk.'

'You weren't!' Evie exclaimed indulgently, 'How old were you!'

He remembered. The boy had behaved mostly oddly at dinner. Next day, after the boat had gone, Luigi had told him in Kristin's hearing and they had laughed. Kristin had tried to disapprove. That was before the boat had gone missing. 'Erlend's home brew,' he explained to Evie.

'How is Erlend?' Aidan asked.

'Much as he always was, I imagine,' his father answered as the telephone rang again.

It was to ring seven times more that evening. Friends, tenants, acquaintances, the editor of the Orcadian. Congratulations, pleasure, curiosity, questions, more questions, but they could all wait till tomorrow. Tonight was for the only two people in the world he cared a damn about, Evie and now unbelievably Aidan.

Chapter Two

St Magnus Isle: The Next Day

Morning

The busy dreams receded as they always did the moment Aidan opened his eyes. For a nano-second he knew all there was to know, then he was awake, uneasy, back in his old tower room with the sunlight pouring through the east window.

He had had no intention of sleeping in Peedie Magnus' room, so, when Evie had gone and his father settled in his room on the first floor, he had ripped the bedclothes off his brother's bed and trailed them up to the tower. Kristy had been right about the damp mattress, so he had slept on the quilt on the floor with the window wide open to the short June night. He had not thought he would sleep at all, but his father's excellent whisky and exhaustion had finally given him some peace. He had not dreamed.

Now as he lay there, his gratitude and his joy were heavily edged with anxiety. Guilt, worry, uncertainty drove him to his feet. He forced himself to be calm. Familiar words from Julian of Norwich dropped into the uneasy turmoil in his mind. *All will be well and all will be well and all manner of things will be well.* Calmer now, he rose and dressed. He had no idea of the time for he had handed over his watch to the long distance truck driver who had given him a lift from Glasgow and had clearly expected some sort of remuneration. Besides he had been grateful. How else, with only a few pence in his pocket, would he have ever got home?

The Castle was silent as he crept downstairs in his stocking soles carrying his father's heavy brogues that Kristin had put out for him. As he washed he saw that she had also laid out some shaving gear, but he had no time for that. Besides he had no intention of getting rid of his beard. Somehow he was finding it sheltering. The grandfather clock in the hall told him it was not quite six. There was only one place he knew he should be.

The stillness in the chapel calmed him. Picking up a prayer-book from the case below the brass plaque he automatically turned to the Order for Morning Prayer. The words were so familiar to him that he turned the pages automatically muttering the prayers under his breath. One verse in Psalm 17 pulled him back to awareness of what

161

he was doing and gave him peace. *Keep me as the apple of an eye: hide me under the shadow of thy wings.*

He would visit the cave. He would be safe in the cave. As he wound his way round the old grey Castle and through the outbuildings, he was sadly aware of their dilapidation. I'm needed here, he thought, and then another thought; I was needed there. But in this instance he realised that he no longer wanted to know. If he remembered he might have to go back.

Finding his old pace, he took the direct route to the cave through the fields and over the rising moor-land, the same way he had gone that last night in the dusk when he had never wanted to leave. He was back, he was home, he should be elated, happy, relieved, but he was not. This time, he told himself, he did not have to leave. How remarkable was that! The threat of departure had gone, but not, perhaps never, the dis-ease.

A skylark trilled above him, oyster catchers foraged the fields as they had always done, terns wheeled as he strode over the tussocky moor-land spattered white with bog cotton. As he approached the cave, the cacophony of the nesting birds on the cliffs was deafening. He rejoiced in the old familiar noise, even the stench. Later he would find the puffins.

The first thing he looked for was the crude cross carved into the back wall of the cave and there it was, St Magnus Cross. He traced its outline with his fingers. It had not been there the last time he looked, had it? How odd was that.

He sat on the familiar boulder just inside the cave's mouth and looked down at the sea. Memories of his misery last time he had sat on this precise boulder watching the sunset threatened to overwhelm him. This time, in shadow, he made himself a promise. This time I'm going nowhere, please God...ah, but that was the problem. What would please God?

Ewan Stout looked at his new patient. Slightly built, under six foot in height, dark hair thinning, dark beard whitening, face drawn, expression closed, fine eyes wary. He must be about his own age, fortyish, but he looked older. He knew a little of his history; who in Orkney did not? The tragic loss at sea of the two boys only a couple of years after the suicide of their elder brother had taken the islands by storm. The old Major had been a pitiful remote figure of tragedy all his life but it was only since the retirement of his senior partner

162

when he had taken over the old man's medical care that he had come to know him. He visited the Major on a regular basis as he did all his elderly patients, mainly to keep an eye on his blood pressure. For were it not for that troublesome gout and damaged knee he would be remarkably fit for his seventy-five years. He was deeply sorry for the old man. Castle Island had for centuries belonged to the Melvick family and though the Major had a relative living in the Dower, she was unmarried without children.

He was an Orkney man himself. His father, a merchant seaman who at retirement had taken over the local store on one of the northern islands, had sailed with Sweyn Oag who farmed the Mains and they had remained friends. Sweyn had phoned his father with the news last evening and his mother had rung him. 'What a turn-up for the books,' she repeated. 'Where has the poor man been all these years?' With his new patient before him in a corner of the vast and largely unused drawing-room, he hoped to find out. The Major, whom he had just left in the library, had murmured something about total memory loss, but, to his knowledge, total memory loss existed only in the pages of fiction. But first things first.

'Good to meet you. I'm Ewan Stout,' he said holding out his hand.

'Aidan Melvick,' he replied. 'Good of you to see me.'

After some preliminary questions which included his age, health record and the name and address of his previous physician to which he replied 'your predecessor, I think,' for as far as he remembered he had seen no one during the twenty-seven years he had been away, Ewan said, 'I'd better take a look at that cut, hadn't I?' He peered at the inch long scab just above Aidan's temple. 'It seems to be healing nicely. How did it happen?'

'Tripped over, I think... Must have knocked myself out for a bit... Came to my senses in a hen run covered with chicken shit. An elderly woman, - I don't think I ever knew her full name - patched me up,' he replied lightly.

'And made a good job of it too. It's healing nicely.'

He had already noticed the scarring on his neck. 'And these?' he asked gently touching the torn tissue.

'Boyhood accident,' he said dismissively.

As Ewan's fingers continued to probe he found something else, a distinct indentation in the skull just above the hair line close to the recent cut. 'Been in the wars a bit haven't you?'

'Ah, that,' Aidan said. 'That too was a long time ago.' He explained briefly about the sail across the Firth and how the boom had caught him. 'My own fault entirely. I wasn't paying attention.'

'And then?' Ewan asked casually as he brought a chair round so that he could face his patient. 'What happened next?'

Aidan was silent, his expression inscrutable.

'Your father told me that you had some memory loss?' Ewan probed.

'Yes...well perhaps, for a time. Do you tell your father everything?' It was an effort at humour that missed the mark. He turned his head to look out of the window. 'I was picked up by a Norwegian fishing boat. They were good men, brought me back to life. I can't have been in the sea more than ten minutes.'

Ewan waited. 'And?' he insisted.

'And...nothing much,' Aidan turned to him and looked him full in the face. 'Wandered a bit. Here and there. All over. Boring stuff. Ended up in Israel. Worked in an orphanage.'

'Go on, I'm interested,' he said encouragingly.

'It's a long story. Perhaps I'll write a book. Save it for then.'

He could not force his patient's confidence. 'So, no memory loss?'

He did not reply directly as he turned his head away. 'For a while, perhaps. A good night's rest in my own bed and - thank the good Lord - I'm as right as rain.'

'Sleeping all right?'

His patient looked down at his hands. 'I dream.'

So, he thought, not sleeping. 'I could give you something temporarily.'

'Thank you,' he accepted briefly.

'Glad to be home?' he asked, as he scribbled out a prescription.

'Glad to be home,' Aidan repeated firmly.

And that, thought Ewan, was probably the only truthful answer he had given 'Your brother, Alastair, wasn't it? What happened there?'

'Ah,' he answered sadly, 'that I can't tell you. I was unconscious or so they told me when they fished me out.'

'I could refer you to someone who might be able to help with the memory?' Ewan suggested but Aidan politely and firmly refused and changed the subject.

'How do you find my father?'

164

And that was that, at least for the time being. His temperature was normal. His blood pressure a little raised, but still on the right side of high, his reflexes normal and as far as he could tell, his memory more or less recovered.

'I mustn't keep you,' he said politely as he rose to his feet but Ewan could sense his evasiveness, his desire for him to go.

'I'd like to take some blood samples first, if I may?' he asked. He did not want to lose touch with his new patient. He was not at all sure he had been honest, that his recovered memory had been truthful or a convenient lie.

Evie was in the library when the doctor left. She rose spontaneously as Aidan came in, crossed the room, put her hands on his arms and kissed his cheek. 'How did it go with Ewan?'

She marvelled at herself, wondered yet again at her happiness for she'd had not felt like this since - she did not think she had ever felt so full of joy. So this is this how it feels to have a son? Her son. She had gone to bed not quite allowing herself to be happy and awoken terrified that she had dreamed him up. But he was still here, he was still here.

He kissed her in return, a warm genuine kiss. Light casual pecks either in greeting or farewell had never featured highly in her life, so this little act of love was completely pleasing.

'It seems my memory has conveniently returned.'

She closed her eyes briefly. 'What does that mean, 'it seems'?' she asked, her elation collapsing. Would he now leave? Go back to that other life that he must have had, other friends, a wife perhaps, children?

'It means, as far as I am concerned, no tests, no specialists, no psychologists.'

'So your memory's come back. Is that what you're trying to tell us?' his father asked from his chair by the window. 'Thank God for that. Go on, then. What happened?'

He repeated to them what he had told the doctor. 'Any of it true?' the old man asked shrewdly. She wished he had not asked.

'I remember a smell of tar and fish and diesel, someone called Hans. He spoke English.'

'And the rest?' she asked.

He shrugged.

165

'Best leave that can of worms unopened, eh?' Magnus said knowingly. 'No doubt it'll all come back soon enough. Meanwhile you're here. You're well. All that really matters.'

She agreed fervently.

'It occurs to me,' he continued, 'that we might have a few of the locals in for a drink. Satisfy the nosy-parkers. What say you?'

Hideous thought. What was the old man thinking of? He never entertained if he could help it. Watching his aged, grooved face she was aware of his profound pleasure. He wanted to celebrate the return of his son and she understood how he felt. For the first time perhaps she appreciated how great had been his loss.

'Some?' she said with smile. 'Magnus, it must be all or no-one.'

He turned to look at Aidan. 'What about you, m'boy?'

'Whatever you think best,' he said evasively.

So it was agreed. She would speak to Kristin and ring round the Islanders to ask them for drinks in the Castle on Saturday at six.

Luigi opened the door. 'The local Mafia,' he said conspiratorially, 'at the door, wanting-a- 'im'. He looked meaningfully at Aidan.

Magnus nodded. ' I telephoned the C.C. first thing. Just a formality. Show 'em into the drawing room.' When Luigi disappeared Magnus turned to her, 'Best leave this to us, eh, Evie. Suspicious bastards, the police. Don't want them putting two and two together here and making half a dozen, do we?'

She nodded. In any case, she needed to get back to the dairy. 'Come for lunch?' she asked Aidan and he nodded.

As she crossed the sweep of weedy gravel where the police car was parked, an ancient black Morris Minor drew up beside her. She knew Arthur Vass quite well. He had written an article about her goats for the *Orcadian* a couple of years back. It had done wonders for the dairy and they had got on well enough. She knew exactly why he was here today.

'Evie!' he called through the window. 'Can you spare me a minute?'

He was stout and it took him a moment to extricate himself from the small car. 'Too much of your excellent cheese, I fear,' he said ruefully patting his rounded constitution. 'I gather the Major's son and heir has returned from the dead. You must all be well pleased.'

'We are,' she said dutifully smiling.

'Any chance of a word with the prodigal?'

166

'You'll have to wait your turn, I'm afraid. He's busy just now and so am I. I've got to get home.'

'Is that an invitation? I like my coffee sweet and black. Get in and I'll give you a lift.'

Anything to keep him away from Aidan. She got into the passenger seat. It seemed very crowded in the small car, which stank of chips and cigarettes. She inched down the window. He asked her about her business as if he were really interested as he drove the short distance to the Dower.

Heidi was still in the dairy, all smiles. Evie could see the questions in her eyes and knew she was as curious as the rest of the Islanders. 'I'll be there shortly,' she explained. 'Just going to give Mr Vass some coffee.'

He followed her into the kitchen and, as she shifted the kettle to the centre of the Aga hob, he took out his notebook.

'How did you feel when you heard - your cousin is it - had turned up? It must have been quite a shock.'

Maybe if she were open now, he would not notice her reticence when it came to the trickier explanations, so she told him what he expected to hear, of her delight on her own behalf but more especially for Magnus.

'I gather his memory is a bit dicey?'

'He's fine, Arthur. Been abroad travelling.' She told him what little she knew, but realised it would never satisfy him so she found herself pleading, 'Go easy on him, Arthur. There's nothing sinister here, nothing to hide, just a tragic accident. He got picked up by a fishing boat when he was hit by the boom and knocked out. Although he has no memory of the accident, he thinks his brother was probably drowned trying to save his life.' That was an embellishment of her own but it would look good in print and Aidan could not deny it if he could not remember.

'Right,' he said blandly. 'Well thanks. You've been a great help.' She knew he was nowhere near satisfied. 'Can I have a piccy?'

'For heaven's sake, you don't need me. I'm only a distant cousin.'

'Good publicity for the yogurt,' he coaxed.

She allowed herself to relent so far as to ask him to the party. 'You can take your pictures and ask your questions then. It's only two days to wait.' The more co-operative she was now, the easier she hoped he might be on Aidan.

167

He put away his notebook. 'I need to warn you, Evie, this is a big story. I might be willing to wait but the rest of the brethren are going to be all over it like a rash. Best if I see him soonest. Don't worry. It's a feel-good story. It's not as if he's done anything wrong, is it?' He was looking at her shrewdly.

'No, of course not,' she agreed quickly, but inwardly she wondered, how did she know? Aidan was on his own there. She sighed. It was a bit late in the day to start fighting his battles.

She walked him to his car.

The young police constable had been polite, professional and reserved. He would make his report, circulate the other forces, and if all was in order, close the case.

'Ah see ye went back to thoor old room,' Kristy accused him when he went to collect his own shoes. His father's brogues were heavy and clumsy on his feet.

'You were right about the mattress,' he placated her, 'I slept on the floor.'

'Aye, weel,' she relented. 'Luigi's put it into the airing cupboard to get it properly dried off. Thee cannot sleep on a damp bed. Thoo're no so young as ye was,' she added accusingly as she handed him his shoes. 'Thoo've Luigi to thank for they, though ye'll no hae much cause to wear Sunday shoon hereaboots. Thoo'd best get yourself a pair of boots or them trainers they're a' wearing these days.'

As he took his thin polished black shoes from her, the grey clouds shifted uneasily. Sunday shoes…

'Did ye no' hear me?' She repeated what she had said and the clouds once again thickened. When he had reassured her that he was grateful, she looked at him closely.

'Thoo'rt a bit deeskit the morn,' He could hear the concern in her voice. 'Maybe ye need a peedie jobby.' For Kristy work was the answer to everything. 'There's a hundred and one things aye need doing.'

He agreed to chop some kindling from the drift wood stacked up in the woodshed.

There had always been a shortage of wood on the Island. No wonder at that when the only trees were those stubby wind-bent sycamores on the drive. Round in the stable block the shed smelled damp and mouldy while fungi had scribbled patterns on the ancient stone walls. He pulled out a branch of salt-whitened driftwood from the pile and attacked it unsuccessfully with the axe.

'Beuy, thoo've no got a clue,' a voice said scornfully behind him.

A giant of a man loomed in the narrow doorway blocking the light. He knew him at once, though, with his enormous beer belly and coarse ruddy features under the greasy tweed cap, he looked nothing like the Erlend Linklater he remembered.

'Wis it the home-brew that kept thee afloat then?' he asked when they had clapped each other several times on the shoulder in wordless greeting.

The cloud shifted again. No, it had not been the home-brew. It had been the life belt. He had not wanted to wear it in the boat but Ali had told him to put it on and they'd had an argument.

Erlend pushed back his cap and regarded him. 'Jesus Christ, beuy, ye even look like him.'

'Who?' he asked, recoiling at what he took to be an expletive.

'Jesus Christ,' Erlend repeated with a grin on face. 'Must be the beard. Beuy, what ha'e thee been doing? Ye look like a meenister. That's no' an insult, by the bye.' But somehow the way he spoke, it was.

The clouds were racing. Not a minister…a priest. The image of his hands on the chalice flashed and vanished, but not entirely.

'Beuy, ah was jokin', Erlend was saying. 'Here gi'e me thon axe.'

In seconds he had split the post and taken another log of leaden driftwood from the pile.

'How're Inge and Angus?' he asked, forcing himself to concentrate on the sticks as he piled the kindling into a wicker basket.

'I'm a grand-pappy twice over,' Erlend said proudly between the strikes of the axe. 'Angus is wed and gone. Good jobs to be had in the oil. He's in Aberdeen. Wed to a teacher.' He pulled out the whitened stump of a tree. 'And thoorsel? No' tied the knot yet', eh?' He did not wait for a reply. 'Beuy, it's no' too late by a long chalk. Find thoorsel a nice local quine, that's my advice. Plenty to be found even if ye're not looking.' He laughed coarsely.

He did not reply. Inwardly the clouds were racing again. Marriage seemed such a familiar state. Children? An image of Evie's lively red hair as he had first seen her in the castle hall leapt into his mind.

Suddenly he remembered he was supposed to go to the Dower for lunch. Gathering up the sticks, he promised Erlend to call in that evening.

'A pint'll soon will put thee to rights,' he said hitching his jeans which had no hope ever of containing his belly.

Evie was still in the Dower kitchen washing the coffee cups when he tapped on the back door.

'Do you remember this house?' she asked when he had accepted her offer of a goat's cheese sandwich.

He told her that he had often visited Cousin Ingrid. 'We played chess and backgammon and she was a demon at Poker Patience,' he said with a smile.

'My mother played cards?' She was astonished but then she had hardly known her mother; only marginally better, it occurred to her, than she knew her son. 'She left you everything she had. Not much I'm afraid but there are some good pictures. She wanted you to take care of her dogs.' she told him, adding, 'she died herself not long after you were lost, but she never changed her will.'

'She called them her children,' he remembered, taking her proffered sandwich. 'I suppose they're long gone.'

She noticed his hands. Slender, sensitive, a great deal smoother than her own. The hands of a scholar, perhaps? She had vowed she would not nag him with questions but she could not help herself.

'Aidan,' she began. She liked saying his name...Davina had written to her to shortly after taking the baby. Evie had convinced herself that she had not wanted news of him, but, somehow, the words of that letter had burned into her memory. 'I don't intend to burden you with unwanted information,' she had started, 'I know you need to get on with your own life. In future I'll let you do the running. If you want news of the little one you only have to ask. He's a good little mite and Nanny adores him. His brothers already regard him as our own...' She had never asked for news and the longer she left it the more impossible it had been to write. Then Davina had become ill and her father had died and her mother had moved into the Dower and the war had come. She had been posted to Ceylon. That was where she had met Chas. Her mother would occasionally mention Aidan in her letters, casually dropping his name into the general news along with that of the other boys. It was almost as if her mother had forgotten who he was and she had

170

accepted that. She knew she had no right to feel resentful, but whatever her mother had done in those days would have seemed wrong to Evie She had had to remind herself that it had been her decision to have nothing to do with him, not her mother's. Nevertheless she had never forgiven her. She found it easier to send the occasional post card or food parcel and keep her distance than come to visit. Then when she had been told that he had drowned, the regrets began. For twenty-six years there had been that dark stain of anger, regret and resentment - if I had been his mother this would never have happened - of guilt - if I had not given him away - he would be here now...He was here now. She needed him to stay.

'Aidan,' she said sitting opposite him and leaning her elbows on the table. 'Have you thought at all about the future?'

His slender hands trembled on his coffee mug. She longed to reach out and touch them. Well, why shouldn't she? He was her son. 'You will stay, won't you? Money need not be too much of a problem. You still have my mother's inheritance. Besides, I believe that the estate can be made into a viable concern if you take it over. Magnus is beyond it and I can't manage everything on my own. I have my own small business and there's so much to be done.' In spite of herself she reached out to cover his hands with hers. 'Now you're home, you will stay? You won't disappear again?'

He looked at her then and his eyes were wretched. 'I might have no choice.'

'What do you mean?' she asked and then it dawned on her. 'You've remembered something?'

He did not deny it.

She snatched her hands away and put them to her ears, shut her eyes. 'I don't want to know. Don't tell me. You don't have to remember. Now is all that matters. All we have is now. You're safe now,' she pleaded and immediately relented. 'Was it prison?'

He did not answer for a while and then he said quietly, 'In a way.'

Afternoon.

After his rest the Major was in a talkative mood. 'Evie manages most of the business nowadays,' he said between noisy slurps of tea, 'Does a good job up to a point but she has too much on her plate. She needs to build up her own business – goats y'know. Nasty brutes but they bring in a small income. What people see in yogurt, God alone knows. Disgusting stuff... There're grants you can get

171

nowadays. Cottages to do up and let. Thing is, m'boy, the Island need a factor. Better be honest with you, an unpaid factor. What about it?'

He had prevaricated. The idea was tempting, too tempting.

'Let me sleep on it, father,' he had temporised and left his father with yesterday's Times and a cigarette.

Outside it was raining and the wind had risen. There were still gum-boots in the gun room so he exchanged his black shoes for the first pair to fit him, pulled on a burberry jacket and went out. Tonight, he thought with no joy, I will remember my dreams.

It was when Erlend thought him a minister that the cloud had lifted a few more inches. The fishing boat had not taken him to Norway, only to Hull. His clothes had been dried on board for him. His consciousness had, to outward appearances, returned. That he was still suffering from shock, memory loss and concussion had not occurred to the crew when they had called briefly in at a small harbour near Hornsea which cost them no harbour dues, wished him well, and, no doubt believing him capable of finding his own way home, abandoned him. He had never known the name of the village. Nor, had it been necessary, could he have recalled his own name. He had been dazed and penniless, and, with his wallet and term money missing, he had not known who he was, why he was there and least of all where he was going. The following few days he had wandered, sick, dazed, hungry, ill, over endless flat fields until he had been found by Father.

Father, he thought, as relief flooded through him. Father was a priest. No wonder the image made so much sense to him. No wonder he had felt at home in the chapel. Father had nursed him back to health, fed him, cared for him, educated him – teaching him English literature, sending him to a colleague in Selby for Latin and to a retired science teacher for maths. He had given him his name, his son's name, taught him to serve at his altar. 'All will be well,' he had reassured him time and time again after a night of bad dreams. 'Dreams cannot harm a child of God.'

So he had become Francis Freel. Was he still Francis Freel? It had been a good life, hadn't it? Or had it all been a dream? Had the nightmares, forgotten at waking, been the reality? What had Francis Freel done with his life? He would know in his dreams, but did he want to know. 'All will be well,' Father had said and Evie had told him. 'You are safe now.' Amen. So be it. But the dis-ease remained.

He walked on through the rain without direction, struggling with his confusion of memories until he saw that he had reached the Mains. There was the house, a solid grey stone Victorian farmhouse with a walled garden, a front door that was never used and a rash of farm buildings at the back. The silo tower was new, as was the huge ranch-like cattle-shed, and, just beyond the garden, a new white-harled bungalow. The whole place had a cared-for, prosperous look. The surrounding fields were full of sleek, contented, black and red cattle, some lying on the rich spring grass, others standing still, only their jaws in perpetual motion. Each, to a cow, turned its head as he approached. He remembered Kristy telling him that Jimmy had bought the farm from the estate and that Sweyn and Jeannie now lived in the farmhouse. Jimmy and Marie Flett had built the bungalow for their retirement..

He had hoped to pass by unseen for he was in no mood for conversation but the rain had stopped, and, as he approached, Jimmy came out into his garden.

'Man,' he said striding down his short garden path, his hand outstretched, 'it's yourself! I was chuist saying to the wife, Aidie'll be here to see us, you mark my words. Aidie'll not forget us, and here you are!'

As Aidan clasped the leathery work-roughened hand held out to him he was suddenly at peace. His raging memory calmed. The grey cloud seemed less oppressive. All will be well, he told himself. All will be well and all manner of things will be well. Father's mantra had become his.

Pots of bright geraniums lined the walls of the glass porch. Slipping off his boots while Jimmy did the same, he followed his host into the bright modern sitting room. Marie was seated in the wide window on an adjustable chair trying to knit.

'Aidie!' she exclaimed with delight.' I never thought I'd live to see the day! Away you and put the kettle on,' she ordered Jimmy. 'Sit yourself down, and let me take a look at you.'

Apart from the same kind, shrewd eyes, she had changed almost beyond recognition. Her body was twisted and her joints swollen with arthritis. When he asked her about it, she dismissed his concern. 'There's plenty worse than me. What about yourself?'

He told her briefly the little that he had told the others and when Jimmy came in with the tea tray, they both told him all about the grandchildren - 'Heidi's working with Miss Evie at the Dower.'-

173

with photographs, and the local gossip, much of which he had already heard. He felt his whole body relax under the warmth of their affection for each other, their family, the farm, the Island and, incredibly, himself. He did not have to think, not even listen. He could just be. That was all he had ever really wanted, wasn't it? To be himself, whoever that was…Stop there, he ordered his busy brain. Be still.

After an hour he rose to his feet. It was nearing five o'clock.

'You cannot go, not yet,' Marie protested. 'What's the time? Give her five more minutes. She'll not forgive us if we let you go.'

'Who?' he asked.

'They both laughed. 'D'you mind the day you slipped in the midden?' He did, ruefully. He had measured his length in cow shit and no one had been a bit sympathetic, least of all Jennet.

They were still laughing when the door opened and Jennet herself came in. 'Look who's come to see us!' Marie exclaimed happily.

'Aidie? I don't believe it!'

He stared at her short dark curling hair, thin face, navy blue eyes and was seized by a strong sense of deja vue. He knew her, knew every inch of her pretty, neat, capable body but he did not know her as Jennet. Her proper name was on the tip of his memory, but he could not reach it. The image passed almost as soon as it had come. She was Jennet not as he remembered her, a mischievous teasing teenager, but the Jennet he had always been looking for.

He rose to his feet and held out his hand which she ignored. Instead she put her arms round him, hugged him and kissed him hard on both cheeks. Now he was home, truly home. Now he was content to forget.

She told him that she taught infants in Stromness. 'I thought you had the Primary Fives,' he said without thinking.

'Whatever gave you that idea?' she said with a laugh

She walked him to the gate. 'Will I see you at the Castle on Saturday?' he asked. 'My father's having a party.'

'Maybe,' she teased. 'I'll have to consult my diary.'

This time he kissed her briefly, easily, catching the corner of her mouth.

'I'm glad you're home, Aidie.' She said as if she meant it.

Yes, he thought as he tramped back to the castle, I'm home. He too was glad…wasn't he?

PART FIVE

Chapter One

St Magnus Isle: Thursday 28 May 1987

Morning

There it was in black and white in the newspaper archives for May 1972 with a photograph to prove it. Minnie stared for a long time at the grainy picture under the banner headline. *Laird's Lost Son Returns from the Sea.* Not for a moment did she doubt that the bearded, unsmiling face standing outside the redoubtable door of the Island Castle with two other people, one of them an older man, was her father.

She could not read it here. Suppressing her excitement, she asked the librarian if she could have a photocopy. With shaking hands, she folded the sheet of paper carefully and pushed it into her bag which she placed carefully on the passenger seat beside her in her car. She would not look at it yet but every few moment she took her hand off the steering wheel to touch it. She wanted to savour the moment a little longer. Over and over in her head she repeated the refrain, 'My father is alive. I was right, I always knew it'.

Five miles out of Kirkwall, she drew up in a lay-by and switched off the engine. She was shaking so much now that she had become unsafe on the road. The sea sparkled to her left, the distant hills of Hoy blue on the horizon, the fields to her right with their browsing cattle lay drenched in sunshine. The ditches were cushioned in dark pink clover and through the open window she could hear a skylark's song of joy. God, she thought, this is a beautiful place.

Opening her bag, she took out the folded paper, gazed at the photograph for a long time and with greedy eyes devoured the print. *The Castle Islanders celebrated with their laird, Major Magnus Melvick (75) the unexpected return of his son, Aidan Francis Melvick (41), believed drowned with his older brother Alastair when their sloop was found abandoned off the Pentland Skerries in May 1946. Mr Melvick told our reporter that after an accident on board the* **Good Shepherd** *in which he had been knocked senseless, he had been rescued by a Norwegian fishing boat. Suffering from severe memory loss, he has only a hazy recollection of the following*

175

twenty-six years which he believes he spent travelling in Europe working for a short time with blind children in Bethlehem. When a further recent head accident triggered his failed memory, he returned to his childhood home on Tuesday to the rapturous welcome of his family and the Islanders.

The Melvick family has been dogged by disaster. Magnus Melvick Jr (24) died under tragic circumstances in 1944. The body of Alastair Melvick (20) was found washed up on the shore near Durness in 1946 and it was assumed then that Aidan too had been drowned. His return last Tuesday was viewed by one Islander (Mrs Marie Flett) as 'nothing short of a miracle'. We offer our congratulations to Major Melvick on the safe return of his youngest son whose family have contributed so much to Orkney life for the past 400 years.

Scouring the sheet again, she tried to link up her father's recovered memory with the facts of his life that she knew. Had he ever been to the Holy Land? She thought not. She knew however that the congregation had supported a charity for blind children in Bethlehem who printed carol sheets and Christmas cards. Was this then the source of his so-called 'triggered' memory? As for 'travelling in Europe', he had once taken the family on holiday to southern Greece on the proceeds of a small unexpected legacy from a grateful parishioner when she had been about five. Otherwise she could not remember hearing that he had ever travelled abroad. It seemed to her that either his memory had become distorted or that he was lying, which, knowing Pa, seemed unthinkable The awful thought struck her that perhaps this Aidan Melvick was not her father after all, that her hopes and beliefs had clouded her visual judgement.

Uncertain as to what to do next, she clicked her seat belt and started the car. She would go straight to the Castle, brazen it out somehow. The nearer she got, the more fearful she felt. What if he didn't recognise her? What if he rejected her? Worse, what if it wasn't him at all? Why had she put herself in such a position? With these thoughts clamouring in her head, she hardly noticed crossing the Churchill Barrier perched a few feet above the waves on a bed of boulders, with a wreck sunk fast into the sand to her left and the sea black and deep blue on her right. She felt sick. Butterflies - she remembered that old family description of them as 'musical evening pains' - fluttered in her stomach. What if Ma was right and that her obstinate insistence on coming here had been a headstrong stupid thing to do? What if Sam were right when he hinted that perhaps her father did not want to be found.

All too soon she reached the tree-lined avenue. The bright green canopy of wind-bent sycamores caught her attention immediately. These were the only trees she had come across since leaving Kirkwall. The drive had been recently tarred and laid over with a pale grey gravel. A tasteful sign post announced that this was the *Castle Island Hotel. Visitors Welcome,* and under it, quite simply, three stars, which told their own story. But would she be welcome?

She must have sat there for half an hour trying to make up her mind as to how to approach. In the end she parked the Mini on the side of the road and decided to walk up the drive. Automatically her eyes sought out the innumerable haunts and roosts of the woodland birds for there were few havens on Orkney quite like this. She stopped to listen to a thrush which was singing its distinctive mimetic song while her trained eye quickly discovered its pale brown spotted breast as it perched on one of the higher branches of one of these wind-bent trees, singing its heart out. It sounded like a paean of welcome and she took heart.

The gravel spread in front of the Castle was weedless, bordered with beds recently planted with annuals, some already beginning to flower. Beyond, the knife-neat lawn was marked out with croquet hoops. Behind and to one side, the ivied wall obviously concealed a garden and to her right she recognised the distinctive outline of a private chapel, obviously a Victorian addition for the ornate architecture differed in style from the sixteenth century Z-shaped fortalice which climbed to four storeys in the tower. The ancient place looked trim and cared-for with newly pointed walls and its deep-set sparkling slits of window, complacent in the bright June sunshine. Could Pa really live here?

Although the front door stood open and welcoming, she was too shy to approach directly. Keeping to the edge of the gravel sweep in the hopes of not being seen, she walked round the croquet lawn. Behind the Castle among the rash of outhouses, she recognised stables, and beyond these a paddock where she counted three ponies. Ponies! There were ponies here… By now, however, she had been seen.

A girl in jodhpurs carrying a saddle came out of the tack room attached to the stable. She looked about ten years old, though it was difficult to be sure. Beneath her hard hat, long yellow hair straggled across her shoulders and down her back.

'Hullo,' she called out. 'Are you looking for my mother?'

Minnie was mesmerised. Who could this self-assured child, who owned not just one pony but three, belong to? 'Actually,' she said, clearing her dry throat 'I was looking for your…'(go on just say it, she urged herself.) 'I was looking for your father.'

'I'm sorry,' she called out, 'he won't be back until tomorrow afternoon. But Mum's there. Just go in. She's in the kitchen doing menus.' She indicated the back door with her head and raising her free hand gave a little wave and hurried off, her yellow hair streaming down her back.

As if in a trance, Minnie made herself walk the few dozen yards to where the back door stood open to the sunshine. She could hear voices and laughter as she found her way down a stone passage and tapped on what she took to be the kitchen door.

'Come in', someone called out brightly and she opened the door. The big homely kitchen that would normally have been rather dark and gloomy gleamed with neon lighting and expensive equipment dominated by a huge solid fuel range. There were five people present seated round the table, three women and two men, one of whom wore a short white jacket and looked like a chef. Of the three women, one was old and stout, another wore a flowery overall, while the third, about thirty, was pretty in designer jeans and a blue cashmere sweater with streaked blonde hair caught back in two tortoiseshell combs. She stood up and came towards Minnie with her hand outstretched. 'Hullo, I'm Miranda Hope-Sinclair. Can we help you?' She sounded and looked exactly like her daughter.

Minnie cleared her voice but even so she did not sound like herself as she asked, 'I'm looking for someone called Aidan Melvick?'

'Ah,' said the younger woman, turning to the older, 'Over to you, Kristin, I think.'

The old woman was staring at her intently. 'Who is it that is wanting to know?' she answered cautiously in a strong Orkney dialect.

She said the first thing that came into her head. 'I was told he knows a lot about puffins.' Her voice sounded barely recognisable to herself.

'And thoo art?' the old woman asked still watching her intently.

178

'Majorie Freel.' She was shaking.

The younger woman was about to say something but Kristin talked her down. 'Thoo'd best speak wi' Miss Grant at the Dower,' she said firmly. 'Thoo'lt find her back down the drive and on a bitty. Thoo cannot miss it.'

'I don't think –' the younger woman began, but Kristin again talked her down. 'Ah'll show the young lady whaur tae gae,' she said firmly.

As soon as the kitchen door had opened interrupting Madam's staff meeting, Kristin had recognised the stranger. Miss Evie all over again; same abundant red hair, same green eyes. Then when she had asked for Aidie she felt the hairs rise on her neck. Was it possible that this could be good news? The Lord alone knew how much that was needed.

It was not that she disliked the incomers. Madam was nice enough, found her a peedie jobbie to keep her from wearying all alone in Nanny's cottage which Aidie had gifted her for life when the Island was sold. 'The Castle will always be your home, Kristin,' Madam had said rightly and put her in charge of the staff tea breaks which she could still just about manage without having to climb the stairs.

Madam had instructed the staff to call her Miranda but none of them did. Archie the chef called her Lady M to her face, and Lady Muck behind her back, but that was not right. She did not approve of that. Madam was no heap o' rookel. No one, not even the Queen of England herself, would have pleased the Islanders after the Melvicks.

But there were no more Melvicks at the Castle. The thought was always there at the back of her mind that soon there would be no more Melvicks on the Island, unless …

Outside the back door they both watched the child mounted on one of the ponies cantering round the field. 'All I ever wanted when I was that age was a pony,' the stranger said as they watched her.

'That's Lucy,' Kristin told her. 'Her fither owns the Island now, Sir John, a big man in London. Flies back chuist for the weekend. Fancy that!' She paused and turned to look at the girl whose looks were so familiar. 'Whit were ye wanting with Mr Melvick?'

The girl looked at her full in the face with those glaikit green eyes that she knew so well...'I'm not sure,' was all she said, but Kristin was sure. Sure enough.

'There's been Melvicks here at the Castle for four hundred years,' she said. 'It's his - ' she hesitated, then continued, - 'it's his cousin Evie thoo should be speirin'. Miss Evie bides at the Dower. Yonder.'

'Thank you. I'll find it,' she said and turned to go. Kristin was aware of her suppressed excitement.

'Dinna get thoor hopes up too high,' she warned under her breath as the girl turned to wave.

Kristin stood there for a while and watched her walk away, her hair like a small reflection of the sun. You're too late, she thought as the easy tears of old age filled her eyes. What kept you so long? If you had come sooner it might all have been different. Change, change, everything was changed. The Major had been dead a good ten years now and she had buried Luigi in the Italian section of the kirkyard not long afterwards. Aidie had seen to it all. Aidie had taken care of her. They had all thought the Island safe in Aidie's hands. Aidie would marry Jennet and there would be Melvicks forever at the Castle, but none of it happened. Aidie had changed. Nothing like the boy she remembered. Gone all into himself. Lived like a hermit in old Beelock's bothy. Evie had offered him a home at the Dower, but he preferred the bothy.

The next she heard was that the Castle and the estate were up for sale The tenants had the chance to buy their crofts and cottages, and some like herself got theirs in a gift, so no one could complain, but she had never really understood what had happened. Something to do with death duties, it was said. Right enough, there was no money, but what was new in that? There had never been any money. They could have managed fine without it. Aidie and Jennet could have managed together.

She was not going to say that Sir John was a bad landlord. Quite the reverse. The Island had never been so prosperous and as for the Castle, they even had pop stars getting wed in the chapel and fishing the loch and shooting the grouse. Madam had been more than good to her, told her she added an 'extra dimension to the whole Castle experience', but, at seventy-five, arthritic and going a bit deaf, her days at the Castle were numbered. It was maybe time to move on. Heidi at the Dower had helped put her name down for a sheltered

180

home in Stromness and she had been thinking the time was right, but now with this lass on the scene, maybe she would wait a peedie bit longer. Something like hope sprang a shoot in her heart. There was always hope.

When the girl turned up on her doorstep asking for Aidan, Evie too was shocked into recognition. Her own hair was fading now, but eyes don't change.

'I was told at the Castle to ask you how to find Aidan Melvick,' the girl was saying.

'Why?' Evie cleared her throat. Even to her own ears her voice sounded short and cold.

'I'm an ornithologist,' the girl explained. Evie could see how nervous she was. 'I believe Mr Melvick knows the best place to see puffins?'

He may well do, Evie thought, but who had told her? 'You'd better come in then.'

The Dower sitting room faced south and was full of sun. The girl went straight to the window which looked out over fertile farm land sprinkled with buttercups and cattle to the sea. Evie who had been eating her lunch from a tray offered her coffee and a sandwich which shyly she accepted. 'Thank you,' she said and drank the coffee thirstily but ate very little.

'You've come to look at birds. Is that right?' Evie prompted her eventually. 'A walk round the Island at this time of year especially is very rewarding. The best place to find puffins is to the north-west. You can't miss them. The cliffs there rise to over 1100 feet.'

'Thank you,' she answered politely but without much enthusiasm and then added in a low voice, 'I was rather hoping to meet Mr Melvick.' Her pale freckled skin flushed as she spoke. How well Evie remembered herself blushing with an embarrassment that would turn her body scarlet all over. She leaned forward. 'Marjorie? You did say Marjorie was your name, didn't you?' The girl nodded. 'Who are you really looking for?' The time for small talk was over.

The girl looked her full in the face. Her eyes were intense, wretched, expectant all at once, but the glance was fleeting. 'My father,' she said quickly and immediately looked down at her hands twisting on her lap.

For a moment Evie said nothing. If this were true, if only it were true and Aidan was her father, this girl who called herself Marjorie was her grandchild.

'What makes you think that Aidan might be your father?' she asked carefully. She could not let herself become too hopeful, not yet.

'I'm not sure,' she said looking up again. This time her eyes were pleading. 'That's why I hoped to see him. Is he here?'

Ignoring her question, Evie repeated firmly, 'Hadn't you better tell me why you think Aidan is your father?'

So she did, from the beginning; though the tale was garbled and interrupted by Evie's questions from time to time, she understood the gist. Fifteen years ago Aidan had walked out of his life as a parish parson in south-west Scotland leaving his wife and children to think he had drowned himself. The police, too, on the evidence available, had believed him dead, and, because of that, maybe their inquiries had not been as thorough as they might have been. She, Marjorie, however, had never thought him dead so as soon as she had finished her studies and had some free time she had decided to go and have another look for him. Her inquiries had led her to Orkney which was a co-incidence really because she had always wanted to look at the birds, especially the puffins in the Northern Isles. 'It was my father who first told me about birds. He showed me where to look and how to listen. I remember him making me laugh with his description of puffins and I never forgot it.'

'I still don't see why you should connect Aidan Melvick to your father, this Reverend Francis Freel?' she insisted. still not daring to hope. A clergyman indeed! If that were so, much of what he had done, how he was, began to make sense.

The girl picked up her bag and took out the newspaper photocopy and held it out to her. 'I think this is him, though he never used to have a beard,' she said 'I'll know when I see him. My father had - has - scars on his neck.'

Evie nodded. The scars of course. Those nasty jagged reminders of an accident he never spoke of. 'Then I'd better take you to him,' she said simply. She longed to reach out and touch her, to tell her that she was her grandmother, to talk about her son, how he was, how he might be with her, but she restrained herself. It was too soon and there was always the possibility that the girl was mistaken. Time enough to talk later.

182

'I don't want to trouble you,' she was saying firmly. 'If you could just tell me where to find him I would be so grateful.'

Evie nodded. 'Of course. Beelock's bothy is about four miles from here. There's only one way to get there if you're driving. Come, I'll show you.'

Outside she explained that when Aidan had been forced to sell the Island for death duties, he had kept the cottage for himself 'and of course the Dower for me'. There had been other gifts too, but having come to know her son a little over the past fifteen years, nothing that Aidan did surprised her.

'Thank you,' she said sincerely but Evie could see she was longing to leave.

'Wait a moment.' She touched the girl's arm impulsively. 'He might be out in his boat. He makes a living of sorts from lobster fishing.' Or used to, she added to herself. How was she to explain? How to prepare her? 'If he is your father, you may find him greatly changed.' Tears sprang suddenly to her eyes. 'He might not remember you.'

'I don't expect him to,' she said simply.

Evie shook away the tears. 'You will come back and see me won't you? Whatever happens? After all you are my – ' She had been about to say 'my granddaughter,' but changed her mind.

'Your cousin? Is that right?' the girl completed her sentence. 'They told me at the Castle. Of course I'll come back.'

Evie watched her walk towards her car. When she had opened the door she turned and waved. 'My father used to call me Minnie,' she said with a brilliant smile.

Oh Jesus, God, she thought as she watched her turn and drive the four miles across the island towards the track that led to the cottage, I already love this girl. Inside the hall, with hands that shook, she reached for the telephone.

Afternoon

Minnie too was trembling. She too had recognised in the elderly woman the same green eyes, the same strong springing red hair as her own, though the older woman's had faded with the years. Now she had little doubt that Aidan Melvick was her father, that this man whom she was soon to meet was truly Pa. She realised that up till now, although she had always professed to believe him alive, it had

183

been little more than a fantasy. The reality was terrifying. She stopped the car and dropped her head in her hands.

Of course he won't know me, she told herself. How would he? If he were capable of recognising her then surely he would have come back a long time ago. Would he want to know her? What would she say to him? Would it not be better to go now and never come back? But that was unthinkable.

Leaving the car at the end of the metalled road, she decided to walk the single track scored with tyre marks that followed the small burn downhill towards the cottage that stood above the curved bay that lay snugly between two rising barriers of cliffs. Her hands were shaking so badly that she could not insert the car key into the lock, so she left it unlocked, and, on trembling legs, took to the track. She hardly saw the grass of Parnassus, the water-avens, the marsh cinquefoil that gardened the banks of the little burn, or heard the distinctive wail of a curlew or noticed the incurious oyster-catchers intent on foraging the field to her right.

As the track descended she began to hear the faint chatter of nesting birds. The further she walked, the louder it became, until she could see the curving cliffs that were white with birds, their precarious nests interspersed with clumps of yellow crows-foot trefoil and pink sea thrift. The noise was like an orchestra that had its own system of tuning. For a moment she forgot where she was, why she was here and just listened. A few steps on and she saw the sandy bay with the short wooden pier. Redshanks and dunlins were foraging the tide line and for a moment she wished she had not left her field glasses in the car. The track dropped again and there before her stood a very small cottage some twenty yards above the high tide line. A rusty somewhat battered Ford truck, its open back stacked with empty lobster creels, stood outside the back door and a small boat with an outboard engine was tied to a bollard on the jetty He was in then.

She stopped to catch her breath and to gaze; at that moment this seemed to her to be the most beautiful place on earth. Then the sun, which had been playing hide and seek all morning behind fat clouds suddenly came out again and the dazzle of white sand and glittering sea took her breath away. No wonder Pa lived here. Pa…

Now she was hurrying, running down the track, impatient to know and to be known.

There was no garden. Instead some hens foraged in a wire netting enclosure to the left of the door which included an ancient dilapidated hen house. To the right of the door an enormous rosemary bush threatened to obscure the small sashed window. The door itself stood wide open.

She tapped on it, waited a few seconds then knocked more loudly. No one came. She could hear only, above the beat of her own heart, the occasional complaint of a hen and the cacophony of the nesting birds. 'Mr Melvick?' she called out and then tentatively for it sounded so strange, 'Pa?'

When she was convinced that no-one was in, she stepped over the threshold. The door to the room on her left was closed but the other, which led into the living room, stood open so she went in. Three of Daniel's Orkney prints adorned the walls, a bookcase contained several rows of well-thumbed classics; the local paper lay crumpled on the seat of a shabby upholstered chair and an oil lamp with a blackened chimney and what looked like a Scottish Prayer Book sat on a round central mahogany table with barley sugar legs which had seen better days.. The fireplace had not been properly cleared of a fine grey ash. A creel of peats stood to one side of it and there were two half burnt candles in saucers on the mantelpiece. Groping in her jacket pocket she found what she was looking for.

They looked good on the mantelpiece propped up against the candles. The photos were all familiar and recent, one of Ma and Jenny with her two children taken last Christmas; one of Dicky skiing in the Alps, laughing and happy as he so rarely was these days. The third was of herself in cap and gown, a formal picture taken at her graduation.

She was still holding it in her hands when she heard footsteps in the lobby.

She opened her mouth to call out his name but when the sitting room door was pushed wide and the huge elderly man in flat cap dressed in dungarees and sea boots with a navy gansey stretched over his protruding belly entered, she thought wildly - surely he can't have changed this much.

He was as surprised as she was. 'Whit might thee be doing here?' His voice sounded exactly the same as the old woman she had spoken to at the Castle. This was not her father then. Disappointment and relief flooded through her as she answered. 'I'm so sorry. I thought Mr Melvick lived here.'

185

'And whitnawey is it to dae wi' thoo?' His voice was guarded.

'I was told he could show me where to find puffins,' she explained defensively.

'Weel, ye willna be finding them here,' he told her firmly. 'Follow the trackie up to yonder heidland. Thoo canna miss them.'

'Thank you,' she said in a small voice.

He took a step closer. 'Whit's thon ye've got there?' he asked curiously.

Mutely she held out the photograph. He took it, looked hard at it and then again at her. 'Did thoo bring that here?'

She shook her head vaguely and indicated the mantelpiece. He noticed the pictures of Jenny and Richard. 'Whaur did they come frae? Ah've niver seen them afore' he asked angrily. 'Didst thee put them there?'

'I just found them,' she lied nervously.

'Who are they?' he asked curiously and turned to look at her. 'Who are ye all?'

'Is it any business of yours?' she asked more boldly than she felt.

He looked at her calculatingly. 'It chuist might be. Thoo'rt trespassing. I could get the polis on to ye.'

'What about you? What are you doing here?' She retorted defiantly. She refused to be bullied by this stranger.

He nodded. 'Fair enough. Ah'm Erlend, Aidan's partner at the lobster fishing. Ah've ivery right to be here.'

'And so have I,' She decided to tell him the truth. 'My name is Marjorie Freel and that's Richard, my brother, and my sister Jane with her children. The man you call Aidan is our father.' Her voice trembled as she spoke his name.

He stared at her in astonishment. 'Well Ah'll be jiggered!' he said after a moment, pushing his cap back from his thick unkempt white hair. ''Is that so?' he said with wonder. 'Is that really so?' Then he laughed. 'Aidie's a sly de'il, right enough. Fancy keeping thee lot quiet. Wait till Ah get at him!'

Her eyes filled with tears. 'I have to see him,' she said

Aware of her distress, he put his great calloused hands on her shoulders, drew her towards him and looked at her closely. 'Aye, quinie, of course ye do…Ah didna mean to fleg ye. So it was thee put up the pictures?'

She nodded. 'I thought perhaps if he saw them it would help him to remember us.'

'Ah'll find him,' he said. 'Don't thee fret. He'll no' have dildered far.'

'No,' she insisted. 'Let me go.'

'Aye weel, maybe that would be best. My hip's giving me gip. Try the heidland yonder.' He pointed out the direction from the cottage window. 'Like thee, he's an awful yin for the birds - then added at an attempt to be humorous - 'the feathered kind, thoo ken.'

She was able to smile, just.

'I'll chuist take the weight off my legs while ye're awa'. Niver walk while ye can stand and niver stand when ye can sit, that's me motto.' He bundled up the newspaper to remove it from the chair. A letter in an official looking envelope fell to the ground. Without looking at it, she bent down to pick it up and handed it to him.

'Thanks, quinie. Thee and me'll get along chuist fine. Ah've grandbairns meself all grown like you. Go find thee da.'

He was looking down at the letter as she made her escape.

Aidan had to reach the Cave. He was not sure why. Something to do with Evie's phone call. But had there been a phone-call? It was all mixed up with his dreams. Just lately he had no way of distinguishing truth from reality in his short-term memory. It was all right when he was with Erlend or Evie or indeed any of the Islanders. It was only when he was alone that he could not trust his memory. Had Evie's phone call been part of his dreams; was her talk of a visitor who wanted him to show her the puffins all part of the nightmare? Someone who knew him? She had not sounded her strong, confident self. Was that too part of the dream?

He had a great desire to sleep. He slept a great deal of the time these days and when he first awoke he could feel the dreams slip and slide dizzily away, just out of the grasp of his consciousness. Ewan had been helpful, he supposed. What Ewan had told him, was that all part of the dream? What exactly had Ewan told him? But it was written down, wasn't it? Somewhere safe. He had to write things down these days for he was finding it increasingly hard to distinguish reality from his dreams.

He reached the Gloup. Peedie Magnus stormed into his mind. Magnus was at his elbow now telling him something. 'I can't sleep,' he was saying. 'Night after night I lie awake. I need to sleep. Not

187

sleeping is driving me mad'. 'I sleep too easily,' he answered aloud. 'Night after night my sleep is driving me mad.'

The Gloup had been recently re-fenced. Three strands of new steel wire had been strung between sturdy posts and topped with barbed wire. Not that sort of sleep, he thought. That sort of sleep would come soon enough without any help from him. That sort of sleep might trap him forever in the nightmare. He turned abruptly away.

Someone who knew him wanted to see the puffins. So be it. It had been a while since he had visited them. He would check and see if they were still there. A strong offshore wind hastened his approach to the cliff edge, but the puffin ledge, he realised, would be sheltered. It was, and they were there.

At this point the cliff sloped downwards less steeply for just over a metre in stepped shelves of rock before descending in a perpendicular drop to great rounded boulders hundreds of feet below. Negotiating the crumbling tussocky surface, pot-holed with the puffins' nesting burrows and threaded with eyebright, he climbed carefully down some half a metre to the first of the great protruding shelves and sat down safely between two great clumps of wild thyme. No wind here and the fitful sun was for the moment hot on his face. A metre below him on a narrow ledge he counted ten puffins, solemn little clowns with their grotesquely large painted bills and smart dinner jackets all facing outwards waiting to take turns at diving for their dinner. He watched them for a moment then he closed his eyes...

'She calls herself Marjorie Freel,' Evie was saying. 'Does that mean anything to you?'

Of course it did. Red hair aflame, dark green eyes, skip-hopping through the garden. 'I'm a pony, Pa. Call me Polly.'

He had never much liked the name Marjorie, but Ro's mother who had recently died had been called Marjorie, so out of respect he had not argued with Ro. He had always called her Minnie. Minnie Mouse... Jenny Wren... Dicky Bird and Ro. Shadows from his dreams. They haunted him. Every time he had looked at Jennet, those shadows had crowded in, watchful, accusing, sorrowful, demanding his attention. So Jennet had gone, left her school, left the farm, found work in Aberdeen. She had come back twice briefly, first to bury Marie and then her father. Seeing her again had hurt. Not seeing her, hurt. But it hurt more when she was here, available, needy, full of that love he was not able to return. 'You need a drink,

188

beuy,' Erlend had said. That had always been Erlend's solution. It had been Ali's answer too. He had been drinking that day when the motor bike had spun out of control, throwing his twelve year old brother into the barbed-wire fence, ripping his neck open in a long jagged cut. He was drinking on *Good Shepherd*... But home-brew had not helped Aidie. The shadows took on more substance when he drank, fluttered around him like demons. No, drink had never helped.

What helped? To begin with, the Island had been his salvation. When his father had died, it had become his Island for a while, a very short while. He still thought of it as his Island. The debts had been huge His father had been living for years on overdraft. There was no way he and Evie could have kept the Castle. The newcomers, 'ferry-loupers' the Islanders called them, were nice enough folk, rescued the Castle, put it on the celebrity map, kept the chapel fresh with flowers, (so Evie told him) and advertised it with photographs as available for weddings. He had only once been back to the Chapel since his father's funeral. Its smart emptiness appalled him. It seemed no longer validated by prayer, and he could no longer pray there. His father had gone, his brothers were gone, the Castle had to go, that had been expected but now it seemed that God had gone too. Mea culpa, mea culpa, mea maxima culpa.

He awoke. Opening his eyes he watched the little birds about their business. Never idle, they growled at each other, twisted their clownish heads as if in conversation, scuttled up and down the ledge, flew off to become lost in the throng of other seabirds taking time off their nests to fish in the crested waves far below. A couple of black-backed gulls wheeled ominously, always on the look out for a careless flight or a neglected nest. The sun was a blessing on his skin, the birds dived and chattered, the scent of thyme and sea and bird-shit filled his senses. He supposed he had better go. Go where?

He sensed rather than saw the girl on the turf above him. Shading his eyes against the dazzle of the sun he looked up. 'Can I join you?' she called down. 'I've come to see the puffins.'

'Take care!' he warned her. 'The turf is riddled with nesting holes.'

As he moved along the flat shelf of rock to make room for her, the puffins all took flight, their squat little bodies taking on a new and graceful dimension in the air.

189

She scrambled down the slope to join him on the ledge. 'Don't worry. They'll soon come back,' he reassured her. So Evie's phone call had not been a dream. He did not wonder particularly at her presence for the Island welcomed bird-watchers, especially at this time of the year.

In a low voice he began to talk about the puffins. 'Extraordinary birds' he explained. 'Do you know that they spend most of the year at sea? They rest on the waves, they swim under the waves using the water with their wings as if it were air. They can fly over fifty miles an hour. They nest in those burrows just above your head.'

She said nothing, so he turned for the first time to look at her, such a pretty girl… familiar somehow. Evie had said she knew him.

'Hullo Pa,' she said so softly that he was not sure if he had heard her properly. He thought he must be asleep again, yet she was not like the child of his dreams.

'Do I know you?' he asked tentatively, but he did. For years now he had known her in his dreams.

'Have I changed that much?' she challenged him.

'You came here to see the puffins,' he said diffidently. The clouds in his head were swirling, storm-driven.

'I wanted to see you more,' she said, adding on a small puff of anger, 'Oh, Pa, why did you ever leave us?'

He had no answer to offer. No excuses to make. No reasons. He could not speak.

'We thought you were dead. What happened?' She was still angry. He could feel it emanating from her like the heat of another sun.

He shook his head. Her voice was a gnat buzzing in his head. He could not get rid of it. He could not wake up from this dream. He put his hands over his head to shut her out.

'I was on my way to the Cave,' he said. 'I must get to the Cave.'

Her anger dropped from her like a garment. 'Why?'

He groped in the swirling mists of his mind for an answer but could find none.

'Can I come too?' she asked in a small voice and this time he knew her. 'Can I come too, Pa?' He heard the child she was, saw the child she had been cantering after him down the Rectory path.

'You wanted a pony!' He said turning to her in instant recognition. The mist in his head lifted for a moment and he knew her. 'Oh Minnie, Minnie Mouse, what happened to us?'

She was crying now. He found it easy to put his arm around her and this time, there were no accusing shadows to condemn him. His head was clear.

'I've missed you so much,' she told him.

He held her tighter, half-listening to all she had to tell him about her life. 'Missed' was not the word, he thought. He had lost his life three times. He had lived three lives. Yet none of those lives had been whole. Evie's unwanted infant had become Aidan Melvick, the child by adoption had become Francis Freel, the priest by adoption had become Aidan Melvick again, the crazy Islander. Three chances and he had ruined them all. Oh yes, he thought, no wonder they all think I'm crazy.

'I'm afraid I'm a bit crazy.'

'I forgive you,' she said lovingly. 'So will Ma and the others.'

Not that he would stay 'Aidie the mad Islander' forever. There would be another death, of that there was no doubt. Would there be another resurrection? If so, would there be another forgetting? Please God, no.

'Why did you do it, Pa?' she was asking.

'Do what?' he asked appalled. How could she know?

'Leave us. Walk out of our lives. Let us think you were dead.'

He was silent for a while, groping for reasons, searching for truth, finding no answers. In the end all he could do was agree. 'It was unforgivable.'

Clouds had covered the sun and the wind had changed. It was growing chilly. He felt her shiver.

'We should go,' he said. 'It's going to rain.'

'Will you show me your Cave?' she asked as she rose easily to her feet.

But now, strangely enough, he was in no hurry to visit the Cave. 'All in good time,' he said, beginning to rise. The Cave could wait...

She turned to scramble ahead of him up the two sloping feet to the cliff edge.

Perhaps he had been sitting too long. Perhaps he was just getting old. It took all of his strength to rise. The mists that had lifted momentarily, suddenly descended in a great occluding cloud. He was engulfed in dizziness and took a step backwards to save himself from falling... and fell.

This time he had not needed to go to the Cave.

191

Erlend heard the cry. A thin high wail that lifted every seabird from its roost and flegged them skrecking high into the rain.

For a timeless period after he had read the letter he had sat with it clutched between his two hands, pole-axed by shock. He had thought there was something badly amiss with Aidie, but he had always known there had been something wrong with him from that moment in the woodshed where he had found him with the axe fifteen years ago. The Islanders all knew something was wrong. The crack was that maybe he had been in the jail and done time. ' Twenty-six years awey! Must have been murder, beuy,' but Inge would have none of it. 'Aidie widna harm a fly!' She was shocked that they should think it of him. 'Look what he's done for us,' she would protest. 'And why wouldn't he?' he had grouched. The truth was no-one knew what had turned Aidie from the inquisitive, mischievous, friendly loon who was always getting himself into bother into the silent, unsmiling recluse he had become. Erlend didn't believe a word of the so-called 'travels in Europe', still less the 'orphanage in Bethlehem' that the newspapers had got hold of… (orphanage in Bethlehem, where had he got that daft notion?) And now here was this peedie quine, calling herself his lass. He didn't doubt it. Her origin was unmistakeable. The Islanders bred redheads. This child was Evie all over. Evie as he had first known her. Given him quite a turn when he found her in Beelock's bothy, like the past overtaking the present.

Maybe he should not have sent the quine out after him. Maybe Aidie had gone to the Gloup like Peedie Magnus. What had he, Erlend, been thinking of to let her go out on to the cliffs alone with Aidie the way he was?

Crushing the letter between his hands and stuffing it into one of his copious pockets, he got stiffly to his feet and hastened out of the cottage towards the cliff track, but he could not go fast enough. He was carrying too much flesh, as Inge was never tired of telling him, and his knees were bad. He was near his three score years and ten, too old for capering. He cursed the boots that hampered his progress.

It had begun to rain and the wind, never idle for long, had risen. Above him a monstrous head of purple-grey cloud was eating up the remnants of blue and the sun had vanished He stopped for a moment to catch his breath. Every part of his creaking, overburdened body protested as he tried to hurry, but it was like running in a nightmare. He could make only slow progress up the steepening track.

He was near the top when he heard the scream, but it had not come from the Gloup. He saw the wheeling whitemaas soaring high above the cliff top and suspected the worst.

He saw her on the cliff edge and called out but she did not hear him, or appeared not to hear him. His breath sawed his lungs and every part of him protested but still he hurried on over the cropped cliff-top grass. He shouted again and this time she turned her head.

'He's down there,' she cried near to hysteria, turning towards him. 'I killed him,' she said. 'I killed him.'

Puffing and wheezing, he had no words. He put his massive arm around her shoulders and led her away from the cliff edge. 'No!' she protested, resisting him strongly, 'You're not listening to me. He's down there. You have to find him.'

'Aye, we'll find him,' he said to comfort her but he knew there could be no real comfort. If he had fallen a thousand feet on to those great barnacled boulders pounded by the sea, there could be no chance of him being alive. He hoped with the nearest he ever got to prayer that he was not alive.

With his arm around her shoulder, he walked with her back towards the track while the rain stung their faces. 'It was my fault,' she gasped between her sobs, 'it was the shock. I killed him,' she repeated over and over as the wind snatched the words from her mouth. He let her ramble on while his mind raced ahead of his slower steps.

Back in the cottage with the lass at his elbow he rang the police and explained meticulously where the accident had happened. Then he turned to the girl. 'Ah'm away out in the boatie.'

'I'm coming with you,' she insisted.

He nodded. No point in wasting time in argument. Instead he opened a cupboard opposite the front door and handed her Aidan's life jacket then put on his own. Down at the slip-way he pulled in the boat, lowered himself down, threw out the empty creels, instructed her to cast off, then held out his hand for her.

The engine started at the third pull. It was a rough ride for the wind had strengthened and the waves slapped and snarled and spat at them. There was no chance of words between them for she was kept busy bailing the foamy water that slapped over the sides, while

193

he needed all his wits about him to steer a safe course. What am I doing here? he wondered. I'm a shepherd, not a blinking sailor, it was always Aidie that steered the boat. All he ever did was to drop or lift the creels, but now there could be no turning back.

It was not far, but it took long enough, for there was no approaching the jagged shore line where the waves trod hard on the seaweed-clad rocks. This was the daftest thing he had ever done in a lifetime full of daft mistakes. Here was another of them clinging on to the edges of the boatie with tears indistinguishable from the rain and sea-water on her face.

She was the first to spot him. 'There!' she shouted and attempted to stand up. He was lying spread-eagled on a boulder a foot or so above the high tide line. The boat lurched dangerously. 'I can see him!'

'Sit doon!' he commanded her while he tried to steady the boat.

'I'm going to try for it!' She shouted back.

'Thoor'rt not to get aff till I let ye.' he ordered. 'I may not be your da but I'm yer grandfither and thee'lt do as thoo're tellt.'

There, he had said it and he had not intended to say anything. He had kept quiet about Aidie for well over fifty years for Inge told him it was not his secret to tell. He could have bitten his tongue out, but maybe she had not heard him for she paid him no attention. Heedless of her own safety, she was over the side. At the same time a wave carried her forward towards the great slippery boulders. Soaked through, she clutched at a frill of bladderweed and clung on until the next wave thrust her on and she was able to haul herself up to comparative safety.

Some yards on there was the break in the rocky coast line that he had been looking for, enough for a small spit of shingle between two jagged protrusions of rock that was wide enough if the tide was high to beach the boat in comparative safety. He switched off the engine and let her glide ashore.

From the box by the engine, he took out a flare and looked up at the grey rainy sky. He could hear above the seabird's chatter the distinctive sound of the coastguard's helicopter.

Then with a heavy heart he went to find the body of his son and comfort his distraught grand-daughter.

Chapter Two

St Magnus Isle: Thursday June 4 1982

Afternoon

Closure, Ro thought, as she sat in the little chapel, waiting for the funeral to start. This is what they call closure. Finally freedom. Why then did she not feel lighter, happier, relieved? For fifteen years she had woken each morning with a sense of heaviness, that all was not right with the world. Though there were hours on end when she did not think of Francis, sometimes with fury, sometimes with agonising love, there were few days and no nights at all when he did not storm into her memory. Anxiety had been her constant companion, worry over her children, often with good reason, dread of her classes, fear for the future. This was what Francis had made her, a tentative, anxious, mistrustful, middle-aged woman. For fifteen years she had been unable to grieve, or forgive, far less forget him and get on with her life.

Now she supposed she could. She looked at the coffin bearing the single posy of rosemary with its little blue flowers picked by Jane's children from outside the bothy last night when they had all visited his home. The bothy had reminded her of the Francis she knew, impersonal, modest, minimalist to the point of Spartan. There had been nothing of himself here and yet that in itself was somehow pure Francis. Leaving the little girls with Inge, they had also visited the funeral parlour in Stromness and she had been able to see for herself the body that had once been so familiar to her, if not the person. He looked, as he had never looked in life, at peace. The tears she had been unable to shed for fifteen years flowed freely then and she was filled with a new emotion, pity; but this was not the old self-pity that had been her constant companion for so many years. This was clean and pure and it flooded through her like balm and brought tears to her eyes.

The little chapel was filling rapidly with people who meant nothing to her. Soon every inch of space was occupied, and, she learned later, outside they had gathered in their dozens. The whole Island and a great deal of the rest of Orkney had come, some to pay their respects, others out of curiosity, and a few, more than a few,

195

for love. The undertaker kept coming up with more flowers, which he arranged in banks around the simple coffin that stood on trestles in the tiny chancel.

Jane, beside her, with the two little girls awed into silence, whispered, 'I can't believe this is happening'.

'No,' she said. What else was there to say? Richard, on her other side was silent. She reached out to touch his hand. His fingers closed over hers protectively. Marjorie was sitting at the end of the pew with Evie, the woman who had rung the previous week to tell her what had happened.

'There's no easy way of putting this,' Evie had said. 'Minnie's father is dead.'

'I know,' she had replied calmly enough. 'He died fifteen years ago.'

'No,' the woman had told her crisply. 'He died this afternoon. Marjorie was with him.'

'What happened?' she could hardly get the words out.

So Evie had told her. Francis, who for some reason or other was now calling himself Aidan, had been showing Marjorie a puffin roost. He had fallen over the cliff to be broken on the rocks a thousand feet below. 'It was a dreadful accident and the poor child is naturally terribly upset.' Evie's voice held out to the last, but Ro knew she was close to tears.

'May I ask who you are?' she had asked sharply, for she was unable to believe that this was not all some elaborate hoax.

'I'm sorry. I thought I said. I'm Evie Grant.' She had paused and then added in a stronger voice. 'I'm Minnie's grandmother.'

Minnie's grandmother? How could this be? Was she trying to tell her she was Francis' mother? 'I don't understand. Is Marjorie there?'

The woman called Evie had tried to explain. 'I know it must be hard for you. It's hard for us all. I'm Aidan's mother...' Her voice broke and Ro knew that she was finding it difficult to speak. Then she said, 'Minnie will ring you herself when she gets back. She's with her grandfather.'

At least, that was what Ro thought she had said for her voice had sunk to a whisper and the conversation had come to an abrupt end, leaving Ro with a mind full of questions. How could this man whom Evie Grant called her son, be Francis, her husband? It was almost impossible to comprehend. She waited for Minnie's call, not daring to let the telephone out of her sight.

An hour later she had rung. She tried to explain what had happened but she was so deeply upset that the doctor had been sent for. 'It was my fault, Ma. If only I had let things alone...' she had repeated over and over again. Ro had then rung Richard and Jane and all of them eventually managed some sleep.

Gradually over the next few days Minnie had grown calmer and Ro, through conversations with her and with Evie, had learned more of what had happened and who Francis had been.

They were busy, troubled days for them all. She had never for a moment considered not going to the funeral, for Marjorie's sake if not for Francis'. She had contacted her school, rung the airport, spoken again to Jane and Richard who had both finally chosen to go with her, and, as soon as flights could be arranged, which was five days later, they had all travelled to Inverness and from thence caught a flight to Kirkwall the day before the funeral. They had been met in a minibus by a sympathetic young woman whom she subsequently learned was the wife of the owner of the Island Castle Hotel - somebody Hope-Sinclair - who had also offered them all accommodation at the Castle   That had been yesterday. She was still in a daze, her head still full of unanswered questions, still could not quite believe what had happened. Nor could she believe it when Marjorie told her that Sam had offered to take the funeral.

'Evie doesn't mind. I hope that's okay with you, Ma?' she had said in that still flat voice a few days after the accident. 'He loved Pa too.'

'Of course it is,' she had agreed 'Are you feeling stronger, darling?'

'Not really...It was my fault you know. Whatever they may say, I just know it was my fault.'

Ro had become angry. When Francis had 'died' the first time she had thought it her fault. Now he had died all over again and Marjorie was blaming herself. What more could the wretched man do to hurt his family?

When she heard the result of the post mortem her anger subsided and she thought about the early years of her marriage. In those days the broken nights, the dream terrors had been infrequent and she had held him and comforted him until exhausted he had fallen asleep again. As the years passed, so the nightmares gradually increased.

197

She remembered endless nights of broken sleep, as his restlessness and distress had woken her time after time. Latterly in exasperation she had begun to huff her way out of the bed they shared into the spare room for a few hours of peace. Her friends would complain of their husbands' snoring but Francis never snored. He never slept long enough to snore.

'Did you ever love him, Ma?' Jane had asked her last night after the little girls had been settled for the night.

'Of course I did,' she had answered automatically, but now the question haunted her. I did, Francis, she whispered to him in her heart, I did love you, only not enough.

Sam in surplice and white stole entered from the vestry door and announced the first hymn. '*Jerusalem the Golden.*' She remembered it had been a favourite of Francis.

Would he and Inge sit with Evie and the family? Although it was never spoken about, there was barely a soul in the kirk who didn't know that he, Erlend Linklater, was Aidie's birth father, including this new family, who were now his family too, he thought with pride.

At the door of the peedie kirk Inge had urged him,'Go on up to the front. You've every right,' She had always known that he had fathered Evie's bairn and she had long ago forgiven him because she had believed rightly that he had loved her, Inge. 'Everyone's allowed one mistake in life,' she had told him. Right enough, he had thought wryly. She could afford to be forgiving for she had conceived a bairnie he had not fathered before they met. Angus was not his son. 'That Evie must have been a right one for the laddies,' she would say, not with disapproval, more a hint of respect, but it had not been like that. They had just been two bairns at the time having a bit of a raffle after the harvest supper at the Mains and they'd both taken a skinful...Evie had never clyped on him, but everyone on the Island had guessed when yon poor Mistress Melvick had gone off one day and come back a few weeks later with a bairn nine months after the harvest.

No room for them both in the pew alongside the family but the folk in the row behind moved up to let them in. Inge leaned forward and laid her hand on Minnie's shoulder. She turned her teary eyes to look at her with gratitude. Inge had loved Aidie too and she had already learned to take this poor quinie into her heart. Evie's

198

shoulders were stiff and straight. He was right sorry for her, sorry for them all including the tall broad-shouldered laddie the one they called Richard, whom, secretly and proudly, he thought resembled himself, and the tired-looking lassie with the two peedie quinies. He knew Inge was itching to get her arms around them both. His flesh and blood. That took some getting used to.

Aye, but he didn't half miss Aidie. Though he had never called him father he had always treated him with respect. He was not even sure that Aidie had known he was his father. They had never spoken of it. Now it was too late. He'd fair miss the lad. ...Jesus what couldn't he do with a dram? He hoped there would be plenty of whisky at the wake.

The quinie still thought it was her blame. After the hospital he had taken her to Inge who had engulfed her in her warm arms and he had shown them both the letter addressed to Aidie that had been lying already opened under the newspaper in the bothy. It had come from Doctor Ewan.

...Further to our conversation I can confirm with much regret that the brain tumour in the visual cortex tumour of your brain is inoperable. We can discuss the available therapies when I see you on Friday. I understand and respect your wish for no further medical interference but you need to know and think about what is available. I must emphasise again that you should no longer drive nor should you take the boat out alone but this you already know. I only write as you requested because of the way your short-term memory is affected and to remind you of my forthcoming visit on Friday afternoon.

'What does it mean?' she had asked through her tears and Inge had explained 'It was the tumour that killed him, not you, my lovie, not you.' and so the post mortem had proved it to be the case, but she had still been distraught. 'You don't know that for certain. How can you tell?'

She had wanted to go back to the bothy. 'Someone's got to feed Pa's hens,' she had argued stonily, and it was only after he had promised to see to them himself that she had consented to stay with her grandmother at the Dower.

The English minister was asking them to stand for a lot of Bible stuff. *'Blessed are they that mourn: for they shall be comforted.'* Aye, he thought as the shoulders of the peedie quines' ma, the one

199

they called Jane, began to shake. Fair enough, he thought, but how? Can you tell us how?

Jane supposed she should feel something. This was Pa's coffin barely six feet in front of her. If she reached out she could touch it. She shivered, suddenly chilled, though the little chapel was not cold. Pa was in there. Pa was dead. She had seen him dead but as far as she was concerned, Pa had died fifteen years ago and if it had not been for Minnie he would have remained dead. He had chosen to leave them, preferred his old home to the Rectory, his first family to his own children. That had been his choice so what was she doing here? She had not wanted to come. It was all so false, Ma pretending to be the grieving widow all over again. Done that, been there…and Dicky with his long face, not to mention Sam. What on earth did he make of it all?

But she supposed there were some pluses. She liked the doctor, Ewan someone or other. He had been really helpful last night when Amy's ears were still hurting from the flight. He had stayed long enough to sit down with them all in a corner of the Castle lounge and tell them about the tumour, why it was inoperable and how he believed it had affected him. 'Is that what caused him to forget about all of us?' she had asked with a hint of resentment. He had tried to answer her honestly, told them that he thought that the sailing accident which caused his brother's death had affected him not only physically but also mentally. 'Knowing your father for fifteen years, I don't believe he chose to leave you. He couldn't help himself.' 'Are you sure?' she had persisted and he had told her calmly that this was what he believed. That had been a help.

Then the little girls liked the beach and Lucy's ponies and they had somehow acquired a great-grandmother. She was not sure how she felt about that. Evie was a decidedly scary old dame. Awesome. Had a baby when she was only fourteen! No pill in those days. How hard was that! She had not yet spoken properly to her grandfather, the rather cuddly old bear of a guy sitting behind them. All a bit of a secret, Minnie had told her, not the sort of thing you could ask about outright but she bet everyone on the Island knew. Come to think of it, she might ask that old woman, Kristin, who helped out in the Castle kitchen. She had known Pa when he was young. 'He was a lovely laddie, your da, chuist. Ah mind the time ..' and off she went on one of her reminiscences in that strong strange dialect that Jane only half understood. She could not connect the lively mischievous boy of Kristin's memory to the unsmiling man in the dog collar who always seemed so disapproving.

Strange, she thought, how differently Minnie remembered him. Janus, she thought. He was the God with two heads, was he not? To Minnie he was a smiling God. To her, he had an altogether different aspect. Yet she had loved him, how she had loved him, tried to please him, though he never seemed to notice. Always so busy. 'Be quiet, Jane, Pa's in his study,' or 'Don't pester your father, Jane. Can't you see he's busy.' The only way she could hold his attention was by tears and tantrums when she was small, defiance and impertinence when she was older. How had Ma put up with them all?

And Dicky…. How did he remember Pa? Maybe Janus had three heads, a sort of trinity. The smiling head for Minnie, the disapproving one for herself and - what for Dicky? She did not know. And Ma and Kristin and Evie and Sam? To each he had turned a different face. Who was he then, this father whose genes she carried, whose features her children bore?

Sam was announcing another hymn. *'The Lord's my Shepherd, I'll not want'*. The Islanders knew this tune, as they had not known the last, and their voices filled the little church. She could not join in. There was an ache in her throat, the sort of ache that prefaced tears. We all want something, she thought. I want ….I want… she thought of her life, her lovers, her children and as her tears spilled over she knew exactly what she had wanted for fifteen years, still wanted. I want my father but my father never wanted me. She groped for and found her mother's hand. She clasped it and let the tears fall. And suddenly the Janus face with the disapproving sneer turned away, its head to be replaced by another image of her father, one that she had forgotten. Her birthday party; lots of prissy little girls; ten candles and a voice that smiled and bid her, 'Happy life, Jenny Wren'.

Sam asked the congregation to sit while the laird rose to read the first lesson. Sir John Hope-Sinclair had offered, Richard had been told, out of respect for the old laird. *Now is Christ risen from the dead and become the first fruits…* Richard tried to listen but with his mother's thin bony fingers cold in his hand he felt surprisingly buoyant, better than he had felt for years, as if some heavy yoke had been lifted from his shoulders. From the moment the plane had touched down in the airport and he had seen the sky he felt at home. The huge expanse of mottled grey canopy delighted him. This is what has been missing in my life, he thought, alighting in the crisp windy air, space to breathe. I have come home.

For the first time in his life he was able to think of his father with interest rather than an embarrassed sort of pity. The life he had led as a parson seemed so unutterably boring and fraught, no wonder he had been driven to throw it away, or so he had believed at the time. He, along with his mother and Jane, had been convinced that he had drowned himself, and it had not really surprised him when he thought about it. His own life had not turned out that much better. There had been times when the dreariness of city life, or relationships that never quite worked and the pettiness of staff room politics had driven him to the edge. He had enjoyed his rugby, of course. That had kept him sane. Physical exhaustion, the company of like-minded mates, a pint or two of ale, had made life bearable, but now after a couple of knee operations and a tricky back, his rugby days were numbered.

The Island had come as an unexpected legacy from the father he had secretly despised, for, it seemed to him, he had taken the coward's way out. Good for Marge for finding out the truth, for finding him a father he could perhaps begin to respect, for giving him roots, however belatedly, in this amazing place. The old guy sitting in the pew behind them, unbelievably his grandfather, had already promised to take him out lobster fishing. 'Beuy' he had said in that quaint way of speaking. 'Ah'll tak thee out the morn's morneen. Then thoo'll tak a pint o' home brew. Beuy, ye hevna lived till ye've tasted me home brew.'

How strange to think that the Castle where he had slept last night might well have become his property. A bit of a relief not to have that responsibility, he supposed, but more of a disappointment. The woman who called herself his grandmother had explained about the debts and the death duties, that the sale had been inevitable, but he would have liked to live here. He would have changed his name to Melvick. Richard Melvick of Castle Island. Sounded good. He could still change his name.

Early days of course, but he was already thinking of handing in his notice and taking a sabbatical, finding employment on the Island, if not teaching PE then whatever came to hand. For the first time in fifteen years he realised that he had a future that he could look forward to. He might even find a decent girl up here...

But he must come down to earth. It was his turn to read. At a nod from Sam and with a new confidence evident in his posture, he rose and squeezing past Evie and Marjorie moved up to the lectern. *'Jesus said...'* he began.

Kristin found it hard to hear. Everyone mumbled these days. Fortunately she could still see, and what she saw was an amazement to her, Aidie's son, a pew full of Melvicks and a kirk full of Islanders all come to pay their respects as well they might. There was not a man, woman or child in the Kirk today who had not good reason to be grateful to Aidie. He may not have been the laird on paper but he was still the laird in their hearts. See, Aidie, she said to him in her heart. Did I not tell you? They're here for you, just as you were there for them.

In her mind she ticked off all those who had benefited from his benevolence, starting with herself and Nanny's cottage. Instead of selling it along with the estate, he had had it rewired and repainted and given it to herself and Luigi unencumbered, whatever that meant, for the rest of their lives. Erlend and Inge too had been gifted their cottage outright with enough acres for a handful of sheep sufficient to keep Erlend out of mischief. The Dower had gone to Evie of course, as was right. Evie had wanted her to work and live there, but Luigi had not hit it off with Miss Evie so Aidie had come to the rescue. When the Castle had been sold and the debts repaid, there was enough left for a peedie pension for her too.

The old days...the good old days? Maybe; maybe not so good. Aye, well, the brothers were united now for better or worse. She sighed. Would Ali welcome Aidie to the other side of the pearly gates? Peedie Magnus now, that was a different kettle of fish. Peedie Magnus and Aidie were soul brothers in spite of the difference in years. Poor Peedie Magnus. Too good for this world. It was the war that finished him, in the head that was. Couldna stomach the army. Maybe he should have been born a lassie. Just like his mam in nature, he had been, gentle and clever. That pencil o' his could make a body come alive on paper. She still had all his scribbles as he had called them, stashed away safely. Maybe she would give them to the loon up there reading the good book. He'd no' chuck them oot wi' the stour, surely. Aye, aye, she sighed in her heart, poor Peedie Magnus would be waiting for Aidie at the pearly gates right enough.

Not Ali, though. She sighed. Ali wouldna give him the time of day. Jealousy, she reckoned. He'd been his Mammy's babby till Miss Davina had turned up with a new bairn, whom everyone kent was not her own. She had soon got it out of Nanny who his real mam had been. No' the pa, though. Miss Evie never told a soul, not even Miss Ingrid. Nothing was ever said but they all kent fine who he had been. Did Peedie Magnus know? Ali knew, or thought he knew. The only bairn who never knew was Aidie.

Poor Aidie. Always turning up with a scraped knee, a bruised arm, a bloody nose. 'Accident prone,' the Major said. 'He's a careless clumsy lad.' But she knew fine that clumsiness had been nothing to do with it. Nor had it been carelessness that had caused the accident that ripped his neck open on barbed wire. Thought he was done for, they all had. 'That'll teach him a lesson to be more careful,' the Major had said, 'he should never have taken Alastair's bike.' She sighed. Well maybe up in heaven Ali and Aidie would sort themselves out, or the Big Man would sort them out for good.

She sighed again. The truth was she had never cared for Ali. Why, she wondered, had she disliked the laddie so much? Was it just because he had it in for his peedie brother? Was it just because he took a dram too much with or without Erlend's assistance? Was it just because he was aye sneaking to whoever would listen behind his brother's back. 'Aidan took the last biscuit,' 'Aidan's left his muddy boots on the carpet.' 'Aidan's spilt the milk on the table.' Never stopped clyping. 'Why did Aidan have to come and spoil everything?' he would whine. Then one day, 'Aidan made my Mummy sick.' He even blamed him for his mother's death. No doubt if he had survived the *Good Shepherd* he would have blamed Aidie for the wreck. Recently she had tried to ask Aidie about it but he had not remembered, conveniently not remembered, she reckoned, for Aidan was no clype.

She wondered about this new family. Jane, dark like her da with those two peedie quines, Aidie's grandweans. Would you credit that! Minnie was the spitting image of her nan and now this tall broad-shouldered young man they called Richard who was as tall if not as broad as his granda. How had they fared all these years without their da? The wife must have been a bonnie soul once but she was too thin, no meat on her, and as lined as a wrinkled apple.

Little wonder at that. The crack was that Aidie had walked out on her and his bairns. She'd not believe it. Aidie would never do such a thing on purpose. Not the Aidie she knew.

The strange minister thanked the loon and took his place at the pulpit. She hoped he would not mumble.

Sam had not thought twice when Minnie had rung him to tell him about Francis. 'Would you like me to take the funeral?' He had been as swift to offer as she had been to accept, after consulting with her grandmother. He had also felt not a little shame that he had been so quick to believe Francis dead and that he had not given her more support. As he listened to her quiet, sad voice explaining everything that had happened, he was appalled.

'The doctor said it was a brain tumour,' she told him, 'but, Sam, I just don't know what to believe. One moment he had recognised me and the next –' But she could not finish her sentence.

She had met him herself at the airport yesterday and arranged for him to stay at the Dower with the somewhat daunting Miss Grant who turned out to be Francis' mother and gradually the whole strange story unfolded. Ro and the rest of the family had come by an earlier plane and they had all had dinner together at the Castle. Mostly the conversation had been catching up over what each one was now doing, with the occasional query about old friends at St Ambrose. Francis was not mentioned. It seemed surreal to be all together here because of Francis, and yet now it appeared that there had been no such person. He realised that the family was still in a state of profound shock. Perhaps the talking would come later.

That night after they had eaten, Minnie told him she had to feed and shut up the hens at Francis' cottage. When he suggested he might go with her, she had agreed. What he found on that still light, late June evening moved him profoundly...

But now it was time to put into words what had been much in his heart and mind since Minnie's phone call.

'In the name of the Father and of the Son and of the Holy Spirit ...' he prayed, then with an arrow prayer upwards for help, he began. 'I want to tell you about a man called Francis Freel. I never knew Aidan Melvick. That's all right because most of you did and you don't need me to tell you about him. For many generations, he and his family before him have been your landlord, benefactor, companion, friend, adviser, employer, and, on this farming Island, the shepherd of your lives. Francis Freel was mine. He was my employer, my friend and the shepherd of my soul.'

His searching eye caught a glimpse of two other clerical collars in the congregation and he remembered that Miss Grant had told him that the local Episcopal priest visited the chapel once a month. His colleague might be the parish Presbyterian minister who looked after a handful of islands. He made a quick mental note to invite them both to say a prayer at the graveside.

'I first met Francis at Chesston Cathedral. He was what was called a minor canon, a journeyman priest, and I was a brash teenager who had got into trouble with the police for a series of silly pranks. I was a very stupid kid who thought spray-painting cars, joy-riding and generally taking the mick, funny. Francis was in court and spoke up for me, bullied someone in the congregation to get me into the under-sixteens rugby club, and generally kept an eye on me, and some years later encouraged my vocation to the priesthood. Ten years later after I had got into a spot of bother in my first curacy in an English diocese, he rescued me again and invited me to come north to assist him in his Scottish parish.'

No need to go into detail about the whole of that appalling situation when he was nearly driven suicidal by blackmail. He reckoned that his love for Francis was triggered by that priestly care.

'Who exactly was this Francis who was not only my employer but who became my friend? I'll tell you all I know. Away back in 1946, Francis as a lad of barely fifteen was found by a elderly vicar in his churchyard in the Yorkshire Dales. He was sick, hungry, disorientated and hurt in his head. Out of his right mind. Father George Freel took him in, nursed him back to health and discovered that he had lost his memory. After extensive inquiries, he was thought to have been one of two brothers from Liverpool called Francis and Aloysius who had spent a few months as evacuees in the village during the early years of the war. After the rest of his family had been killed by enemy bombers, it was thought that Francis had somehow found his way back to the village. Deeply unhappy, the priest who had lost his son to the war and his wife to cancer, saw this poor sick lad as a gift from God and in due course adopted him and gave him his name. Francis in turn learned to love and respect the old man, so much so, indeed, that he himself became ordained.

'But Francis' amnesia caused him many problems. He suffered intermittently from appalling nightmares and blinding migraines. Fifteen years ago, somehow or other, we shall probably never know quite how it happened, he became Aidan Melvick again and it was as if Francis Freel had never existed, or if he did, buried deep in his subconscious mind.

'Today Francis Freel and Aidan Melvick are reconciled the one to the other. Both are mercifully at peace. Nor were they so very different from each other in life. Let me tell you how I know that.'

How much would he tell? There flashed through his mind a memory of Francis/Aidan's bedroom in the bothy. It had contained nothing except for a narrow bed. The wooden floorboards were bare, the mattress made of horsehair, the bedstead black iron. Minnie had told him it had been his boyhood bed in the Castle. Beside the bed, the simple cabinet, also from the Castle, was empty except for a Bible, a box of matches and a notebook. A chest of drawers held his few belongings and there was a crucifix on the wall.   The room resembled nothing so much as a monk's cell. Somehow he could not speak of this. Instead he continued:

'Last night I visited his home. I was shown something that I want to share with you. When Francis was a priest he had a notebook, his proper prayer book, he called it. In it he kept the names of his parishioners, his friends and acquaintances and his family. Beside their names he listed their needs and their hopes. Last night, beside his chair I found Aidan Melvick's prayer book.   All of you are mentioned, your families and your concerns. You were all always in his thoughts and prayers.

' I know that today he and his family, both families, will be in yours... And now to God the Father...'

Minnie watched Sam as he returned to the lectern and announced the next hymn. Automatically she looked up the number and saw that it was another of Pa's favourites or so Sam told the congregation. *'Dear Lord and Father of mankind'*. One of the Islanders belted out the first line on a keyboard because no one could play the old harmonium that still stood at the back of the church. 'It hasn't been touched since the days of your great grandmother,' Evie had told her. But which great-grandmother?

Although at the time she had not fully taken in what Erlend had called himself in the boat, afterwards she remembered, or thought

207

she remembered. 'I'm your grandfather,' he had shouted at her, 'and you'll do what I tell you.' Maybe she had misheard.

The day after the accident she had insisted to Evie that she wanted to stay in Pa's cottage but Inge had not allowed it to happen. She had climbed into their old landrover and bumped her way down to the bothy where she had found Minnie slumped in her father's chair unable even to feed the hens. 'I chuist tellt Erlend ah was bringing ye straight back home and to put the kettle on,' she told her as she bustled around making and feeding the hens. Minnie had tried to protest but she never stood a chance. 'You canna stay here alone, my girl, and that's that; your grandpa could do your company. Aidie's death has knocked him for six.'

'My grandpa?' she had said, roused momentarily from her grief. Of course...her grandfather.

'Aye, girl. Erlend's your grandpa and it's time you knew the truth.'

'Did my father know?' she asked.

'Of course he knew,' she said contemptuously. 'They all knew.'

'Then why did Evie - my grandmother - not say?'

'Just her way. She told no one, not even her own ma. Let folk think what they liked. She'll no' admit it even now. Fair enough. No one wanted it blabbed all over the Island, but I'm no' one for secrets myself and Erlend was that proud of Aidie He was a son to the both of us and it's high time your family knew the truth.'

So she had gone back to their cottage and Erlend had just held his arms out and engulfed in a beery bear-like hug and without another word on the subject she became his grand-daughter and Inge a second grandmother.

Evie had listened to her in silence when she had somewhat diffidently brought the subject up. 'I told no one,' she said tersely, 'yet everyone knows, or thinks they know my business,' she added grimly.

'But they 're right, aren't they?'

'You want the truth?' Evie said bitterly. 'The truth is I don't know. I don't remember. I was fourteen years old and drunk at the time.'

She had been silent for a while, deeply aware of her grandmother's shame. 'There are tests,' she began tentatively.

Evie held up a hand. 'No tests,' she said firmly. 'If Erlend claims that Aidan was his, then so be it. What does it matter now?' she added in a deeply sardonic voice, 'he's gone and this time he won't be coming back.'

'Grandmother,' she began tentatively, the name sounding odd to her ears. Yet she could not bring herself to use a diminutive.

'Evie will do,' the older woman had said with a touch of humour.

'Grandmother,' Minnie had repeated more forcefully, 'I need to tell the family.'

'Oh, do what you like, do what you want,' she said wearily. 'I'm too old to argue.'

It was permission of a sort, so she had told them all last night.

As for the rest, she was still not sure.

But it would have to be faced. Whatever her decision, she would have to take the consequences.

Evie watched the undertakers, led by Sam, wheel the coffin on trestles down the narrow aisle to the door. There the pall-bearers took over, for it was not far to the small scatter of family graves that lay walled off to the far side of the chapel. Minnie slipped her hand under her arm and held it there. What a comfort the child was.

The mourners gathered round the church door while Richard, Dr Ewan, Erlend, Rory Forbes-Sinclair with Sweyn and Jeannie's lad, directed by the undertaker, hoisted the coffin on to their shoulders. Led by Sam reciting the funeral sentences they followed him to the prepared grave. This was where all her family through the generations had been buried. She too would lie here. Unknown to the others, she had arranged for two layers to be prepared, so that when the time came she could be buried with her son. They might only have had fifteen years of life together but there was always eternity; not that she necessarily believed in eternity but she liked the thought of being close to him, one way or another. Over those fifteen years she had learned to love him more than she could have believed possible.

She had known about the tumour for almost as long as Aidan. She had done her best to encourage him to try the chemo-therapy that had been offered, but the prognosis was so uncertain that he told her that he preferred to let nature take its course. 'I'll probably outlive you all,' he had said. trying to make a joke of it. 'Seemingly I've had it for long enough.'

What he had not told her was that the nightmares, the headaches, the memory confusion, retrograde and now also anterograde, were worsening; that he was finding it hard to distinguish reality from fantasy and that the medication prescribed made him physically dizzy. She knew all this from Ewan who visited the bothy regularly and monitored his progress. To her direct question, he had replied reluctantly, ' I don't know. Three months perhaps. A year at most. I suppose it could happen at any time.'

She had wanted him to move into the Dower, but he would not hear of it. 'Don't make me regret telling you, Evie,' he scolded her. 'Just let me be.' He had never called her mother and she had not expected it of him.

So she had nodded, refusing to let the tears flow in his presence. Their relationship thrived on not being too close. They saw each other most days, but she got anxious if he missed a day, imagining the worst had already happened. How ironically tragic that the day his child turned up was the day the tumour killed him.

'We commend into thy hands, most merciful Father, the soul of this our brother Aidan ...' Sam had reached the committal. The two other ministers had both had their say and the coffin was gently lowered into the prepared grave. As the awed little girls reached forward, impatient to drop their posies of rosemary on to the coffin, Sam was saying *'we commit his body to the grave, earth to earth, dust to dust ...'* When she had taken the token handful of the undertaker's proffered earth and dropped it into the grave, Ro stepped forward to be followed by all her family. Finally Erlend, to no one's surprise, cast the final handful.

Then Sam was saying a final prayer. *Grant, we beseech thee, merciful Lord, to thy faithful people, pardon and peace that they may be cleansed from all their sins....* Ending with the Grace the service was done and Sam was shaking her hand and the Islanders were all around, embracing her, exclaiming over the little girls, euphoric with relief that it was over, satisfyingly over.

With Minnie's hand under her arm, she turned and led the way back to the Dower, where the Castle staff had laid on sandwiches, tea and plenty of whisky. She noticed wryly that Erlend was first to find his way to the bottle. He had Richard with him. She could not help noticing how alike they were, identical figures although Richard had not yet run to stoutness, identical smiles. Proof, then, that he was his grandfather? She supposed it must have been so. The truth was that the harvest supper, held during the half-term break in the Castle with her parents, had vanished into nothingness.

Either she had been too drunk to remember or too ashamed. She had no memory of what had happened that night. Now watching their shared grandchildren and great grandchildren she could not doubt it.

The wake wore on. Nothing formal was said, but by the end of the evening Barbie, the younger of the two little girls, who was getting tired and cross, protested in a sleepy voice that she wanted her Grampa to read her a story. He gathered her up in his arms and took her up stairs closely followed by her older sister to Minnie's bedroom in the Dower.

After midnight Richard, who was still sober, energised, different, drove Erlend and Inge back to their cottage where he had another dram and stayed the night. When Jane went up to look in on the little girls, Ro and Evie found themselves alone.

'Shall I make us some cocoa' Ro asked tentatively. Evie nodded, too tired and emotionally drained to care.

She brought back two steaming mugs. They talked for a moment about the service, the good behaviour of the children, the flowers that had been gifted, the people who had been present, then fell into an uneasy silence. Evie could think of nothing to say to this thin, tense anxious-looking woman who she supposed was her daughter-in-law.

Then they both said the same thing at the same time. 'You must be tired.' They looked at each other properly for the first time and laughed. I like this woman, Evie thought. Aidan chose well. The conversation became more relaxed when Ro said, 'I think you might be seeing quite a lot of us all from now on. Will that be all right with you?'

'Of course,' she said warmly. 'The Dower will be yours eventually. I want you all to see it as your home.'

'I did love him you know,' Ro whispered so quietly that Evie could only guess at what she had said. 'In spite of how it might seem.'

'And so did I,' Evie held out her hand. 'In spite of what I did.'

Friday Dawn
It does not get dark in Orkney at midsummer. After the wake, Minnie left the children asleep in her room at the Dower intending to walk down to the bothy but once outside in the light dusk she decided that she would try to find her father's cave. He had spoken of it in that last unforgettable conversation and all week she had

211

intended going. Erlend had told her how to get there, offered to take her, but somehow it had never happened. There had been too much going on, too many things to do, people to see, arrangements to make. Her job at the Bird Sanctuary in Kent for a start; that was due to start on Monday. If she were still to take it, she would have to leave by tomorrow's ferry.

Evie had told her she was willing for her to stay at the Dower for as long as she liked. Perhaps she should stay on for a while if only to take care of her grandmother. Part of her wanted to stay here forever and never leave the Island but another part of her realised that perhaps the time had come to take up the first proper job she had ever been offered, move on with her life. This beautiful place would, after all, always be close, if not in reality then rooted in her heart. A few hours on her own might help her make up her mind.

The sky was enormous, the clouds streaked dark red and gold with an occasional star in the pale patches between. As she crossed from field to field, the grass beneath her feet was grey in the half-light and scattered with quiet sheep and sleeping lambs or dozing cattle. The half-closed globes of buttercups gleamed white. A barn owl, annoyed by her presence, hissed, snorted and barked at her, giving her the fright of her life and a nesting lapwing sprang up almost under her feet pweeting loudly.

Eventually she reached the links. The tussocky turf was scented with thyme, sprinkled with tormentil and eyebright. Her footsteps were like whispers in the hushed pre-dawn morning. Erlend's directions had been detailed and accurate so she found the cave with no difficulty, climbing down the sloping sides of the raised beach headland between clumps of thrift and trefoil, half-listening to the subdued chatter of the drowsy seabirds Almost at the same moment as she reached the cave, the wind rose and the sun lifted the rim of its head above the horizon. The whole world came alight, painting the dank lichened walls of the interior with a pink light so that the first thing she saw was the carved cross. Erlend had not told her about this. Had Pa seen it? Of course he had; perhaps this was why he had come here.

She sat on a boulder just inside the entrance, sheltered from the chilly dawn wind. Now, she thought. It has to be now. Reluctantly she reached into the back pocket of her jeans and took out the folded sheets of paper.

212

It was quite by chance that she had found them. She had not been able to spend much time in her father's bedroom. Its sparseness, its shabby neatness, had filled her with an unbearable tenderness beyond the healing power of tears. There had been a Bible in the drawer of the bedside cabinet, one of those floppy leather books with tiny print on Indian paper. She had taken it out, looked at the flyleaf and seen that it had been given to Aidan Francis Melvick for his baptism in August 1931 by Ingrid Grant, Evie's mother, whom she supposed had been her own great grandmother. Rifling through the pages, two sheets of paper torn from a notebook had fallen out. She had glanced at them briefly and then as quickly refolded them and guiltily slid them back inside the Bible. Then she had changed her mind, taken them out, folded them and slipped them into the back pocket of her jeans. They had been there for three days.

Now she smoothed the sheets out and forced herself to look down at the closely written first sentence that still seemed too private, too personal for human eyes.

I, Aidan Francis Melvick, while in my right mind confess to God Almighty, Father, Son and Holy Ghost that I have sinned by my fault, my own fault, my own most grievous fault.

Again she hesitated. Perhaps she should give the papers to Sam or destroy them unread. Yet she had been the one who had heard that voice in the other cave; she was the one who had believed her father alive and found him again. He would surely not have written, let alone preserved, these words if he had not intended them to be read, if he had not wanted someone to know, perhaps even someone to forgive. The responsibility was hers. So she tried again, forcing herself to decipher the small closely written letters.

I have remembered my dream. I remember the boat, The Good Shepherd *that it might have been had I allowed it to be. I see the boy I was, the clumsy, blundering, intrusive, irritating, boastful, insensitive boy who had two older brothers whose lives I picked at like a horse fly. I thought I loved my brothers, now I know I only wanted their time and their attention, above all, their friendship. I saw little enough of them. During the school holidays and their short leaves from the war, I would stalk them, interrupt them, haunt their goings-out and comings-in. I would hang over Peedie Magnus while he hung over his drawing pad but I was no more important to Magnus than a burr stuck to a stocking. He lived an interior life which he expressed from time to time in his drawings. What*

213

happened to those unforgettable war sketches of death and horror that I glimpsed once when he left his pad unguarded? The only time Magnus escaped my clinging attention was the day Luigi found him in the Gloup. If I had kept up my vigilance would he have survived? I once thought so, and blamed myself. Magnus was always kind to me especially when I was a young lad, but he was kind to everyone except himself.

She had seen the plaque in the church and Inge had told her about Peedie Magnus. 'A lovely loon,' she had called him with sadness in her voice. 'Too good for this world,' she had said shaking her head sadly 'After the war, they never understood him at the castle. All he ever wanted to do was paint but he was the laird's son. Things were expected. Post-traumatic something they call it these days. If his mam had not died, maybe he would have recovered. He was away at that school down in England when she passed away, and he never got over it, God rest their souls.' Inge had shown her a couple of pencil drawings he had sketched of Erlend shearing his sheep. They were good. She turned back to the letter.

Ali now. That was a different matter. I irritated Ali beyond endurance. I know that now and can only regret my crass behaviour. Worse, because he was six years older than I was, he was blamed for our fights and disagreements and I let it happen. Then he too went to the war and when he came home he had changed. I still nagged at him, followed him, pestered him for attention, which he chose not to give. He seldom spoke to me but he smiled a lot, though the smile never quite reached his eyes. I knew he did not like me, but that made me worse. I was the one who took his motorbike and crashed it and slashed my neck on that barbed wire fence. He was the one who found me and got help but because he had had a drink in him at the time he was considered responsible. All I ever wanted was for him to love me.

Thus it was a complete surprise to me when he agreed to let me sail with him to the mainland. The journey started well enough. He was agreeable, so agreeable that I thought at last he cared, until I realised that he was drinking. He did not even attempt to hide the bottle. I see him now sitting with his hand on the tiller, the strong breeze blowing through his hair, the sun lighting the smile on his face, that smile that I had come to recognise, the smile that said 'I am trying, but you would test the patience of a saint'.

Then he told me, 'for my own good' he said, that I was not his brother, that his mother was not my mother, that I was a bastard and that my very existence had so upset his mother that it had killed her. Killed her? She had died of cancer when I was four years old. That was when I lost it. I stood up, moved forwards and lurched at him. The boat rocked and heaved. Caught unawares, he fell overboard. Clinging to the mast I watched him, unable to move, as he struggled. By the time I had come to my senses,he had gone. He did not even shout. I had drowned him.

Oh my God, she thought, my poor father. With her breath coming in short gasps of shock she read on.

The rest is forgotten. Did I try to rescue my brother? I like to think I did. Or did the boom hit me before I could help him? Did I even want to help him? Was I rescued by a Norwegian fisherman called Hans? I've told the story so often that I have come almost to believe it, but I wonder. Did I perhaps sail ashore, ditch the boat, catch a train south? Did I try unsuccessfully to drown myself? I can't remember. All I know is this. I killed my brother. I have always known deep down in my soul that I killed my brother. He would never have forgiven me. How then can I forgive myself? Mea culpa, mea culpa, mea maxima culpa.

For these and all my other sins which I cannot now remember I humbly ask pardon and remission, time for true repentance, amendment of life and the grace and comfort of the Holy Spirit.

Too shocked to weep, she read and re-read her father's words. It seemed to her that his whole life had been lived in expiation for that moment of murderous rage. The tumour, the nightmares, the half-forgotten, half-remembered dreams had surely been punishment enough. Can hell last forever? No more, she thought crushing the pieces of paper between her fingers. You are forgiven, Pa. Of course you are forgiven.

Her first thought was to tell her mother but then she thought again. How could she lay this burden on her mother, how could she tell any of her family? The last fifteen years of not knowing what had happened to him had been burden enough. This final knowledge was too much. She did not want them to think of Pa as a – she could not bring herself to think the word. She wanted them to remember him with love. She could tell Sam. As a priest, Sam could forgive him, release him from having broken a commandment of God. Yes, she would tell Sam. She smoothed the sheets out and folded them.

215

Suddenly she was aware of the world around her, the bright choppy water, the tugging wind and the shouting, diving, wheeling, circling, wideawake birds. All of nature seemed to demand her attention, to protest at her decision, as they screamed at her, 'why?'

'Why?' she asked aloud.

The answer came at once. 'Coward!' Each one of them screamed at her again and again, 'Coward! Coward!'

It was true. She was a coward, unwilling to bear the burden of this knowledge alone. Why should she cast it on Sam who had loved him too? This was her responsibility, her punishment for her interference, her curiosity. Whatever they might say, she believed that she had been responsible for his death, as surely as he had caused his brother to drown. What, she wondered with awe, had he awoken to this time?

Her fingers moved of their own accord. Deliberately, carefully, decisively, she tore the pages in half, into four and then into tiny pieces. Moving out of the cave she scattered them over the cliff. Instantly they were seized by the wind and gone. Then she heard the voice, that same voice she had heard in that other cave fifteen years ago. 'All is well,' it said, or she thought it said. Once again she knew it was true.

Postscript

Tuesday June 24 1997

Computers had their uses, Ewan thought, as he sifted through a thick pile of old buff-coloured files, sorting them out into three bundles, those of current patients which needed to be given to his secretary to be saved on line, those to be kept pending a future decision and those that could safely be shredded. He opened the one labelled Aidan Francis Melvick/Francis Freel. 24:6:31 - 11.6.87 and noticed that today would have been his 66th birthday. He wondered if any of his family would remember.

He did not need to glance through the pages of notes, letters, and X-ray reports to recall this patient. Courteous, remote, private, Aidan had interested him from that first visit a quarter of a century ago. While never less than polite, he had also been stubborn, steely in his resistance to treatment, and, he suspected, not altogether truthful. His had been an absorbing case, if not entirely convincing.

216

The causes of amnesia may be organic or functional. Organic in that they are caused by physical damage sustained to the brain; functional causes are psychological. Aidan Melvick had certainly suffered several injuries to his head over the years, but there was undoubtedly psychological trauma there too which he had hoped unsuccessfully to be allowed to probe. It was only when the headaches had reached unbearable proportions that his patient had consented to be further investigated. Just how long the tumour had been there it had been impossible to say, but Ewan suspected it could have been dormant since boyhood. However he had never been fully convinced that his memory loss had been as severe as he had been led to believe. He suspected that there was something he had not wanted to remember.

It was difficult to separate his memories of Aidan Melvick from what he had subsequently learned of Francis Freel. Difficult sometimes to differentiate between the reclusive man who, had he lived, would have become his father-in-law and the busy parish priest who had walked out on his family.

She was very like him, or so her mother told him and indeed he could see for himself; delicately built, dark haired, pale-skinned with those remarkable green eyes that she shared with her grandmother and her red-headed younger sister; Jane, Jenny Wren, his Janey.

They had been married now for seven years. Amy and Barbie were teenagers attending Kirkwall Grammar School, and their two boys, Frank, a lively six year old and Peedie Erlend who had inherited the red-headed gene was coming up for four. His mother-in-law, after she had retired from teaching, had moved into the Dower to look after Evie, now eighty, who, apart from blood pressure problems, was admirably fit and still as sharp as a needle.

Richard, his brother-in-law, also lived locally. He had married Sweyn's and Jeannie's daughter, Heidi, and there was second baby on the way. After a somewhat precarious start, encouraged by Erlend, he had taken up lobster fishing and farmed part-time at the Mains where they now lived in Jimmy and Marie's bungalow. Erlend had died of a stroke some years ago and Inge was getting frail. Their son, Angus, now retired, and his wife had moved into the old cottage to look after her.

Come to think of it, the only member of the family who had not ended up in Orkney was Marjorie, strange little Minnie, who had found her father again and had been with him at the end. Minnie had never returned to the Island. About a year after the funeral. she had moved to Australia to stay with her Aunt Anna and there she had remained, married a zoologist and together they ran guided nature trails. She had agreed to come home for a holiday this year to see them all, but she had promised many times before. It had never happened.

He had last seen Minnie on the day after the funeral. He had been going to Edinburgh for a conference and they had met on the ferry. He had found her leaning on the rails, gazing into the folds of dark water and had gone up to speak to her.

Conversation had not been easy; he had asked some non-intrusive questions, made some conventional remarks but he had not had her full attention. Then he had added 'I hope you are not still blaming yourself for what happened.' She had turned to him and looking him fully in the face, replied quietly, 'Of course I do. I always will, just as he blamed himself – ' and then she stopped.

'Blamed himself?' he prompted.

She turned on him then and answered with passion. 'It's none of your business. It's no one's business now. For God's sake let him rest in peace.'

He suspected that she knew more about her father than anyone else, certainly more than she was willing to share. He had nodded, respecting her grief, and changed the subject. He also knew that she would be thinking of him today, his birthday, and that she probably still thought about him every day of her life.

He sighed, closed the file and marked it for the shredder.